Date: 9/8/21

GRA TANIGAWA
Tanigawa, Nagaru,
The intuition of Haruhi
Suzumlya /

THE
OF HARUHI SUZUMIYA
INTUITION

NAGARU TANIGAWA

YEN ON
NEW YORK

The Intuition of Haruhi Suzumiya
Nagaru Tanigawa

Translation by Andrew Cunningham
Cover art by Noizi Ito

Suzumiya Haruhi no Chokkan
©Nagaru Tanigawa, Noizi Ito 2020
First published in Japan in 2020 by KADOKAWA CORPORATION, Tokyo.
English translation rights arranged with KADOKAWA CORPORATION, Tokyo through TUTTLE-MORI AGENCY, INC., Tokyo.

English translation © 2020 by Yen Press, LLC

Yen On
150 West 30th Street, 19th Floor
New York, NY 10001

Visit us at yenpress.com
facebook.com/yenpress
twitter.com/yenpress
yenpress.tumblr.com
instagram.com/yenpress

First Print Edition: June 2021
Previously published as an ebook by Yen On in November 2020.

Yen On is an imprint of Yen Press, LLC.
The Yen On name and logo are trademarks of Yen Press, LLC.

Library of Congress Cataloging-in-Publication Data
Names: Tanigawa, Nagaru, author. | Ito, Noizi, illustrator. | Cunningham, Andrew, translator.
Title: The intuition of Haruhi Suzumiya / Nagaru Tanigawa ; illustration by Noizi Ito ; translation by Andrew Cunningham.
Other titles: Suzumiya Haruhi no chokkan. English
Description: First print edition. | New York, NY : Yen On, 2021.
Identifiers: LCCN 2021012083 | ISBN 9781975322564 (trade paperback)
Subjects: CYAC: Supernatural—Fiction. | Clubs—Fiction. | Japan—Fiction.
Classification: LCC PZ7.T16139 Inw 2021 | DDC [Fic]—dc23
LC record available at https://lccn.loc.gov/2021012083

ISBNs: 978-1-9753-2256-4 (paperback)
978-1-9753-2255-7 (hardcover)

1 3 5 7 9 10 2 4 6 8

LSC-C

Printed in the United States of America

775.249

THE
OF HARUHI SUZUMIYA
INTUITION

N A G A R U   T A N I G A W A

First released in Japan in 2003, *The Melancholy of Haruhi Suzumiya* quickly established itself as a publishing phenomenon, drawing much of its inspiration from Japanese pop culture and Japanese comics in particular. With this foundation, the original publication of each book in the Haruhi series included several black-and-white spot illustrations as well as a color insert—all of which are faithfully reproduced here to preserve the authenticity of the first-ever English edition.

CONTENTS

RANDOM NUMBERS

"Seven hundred seventy-five thousand two hundred forty-nine."

With a puff of white breath, those words flitted past my ear but were soon swept up in the freezing wind, vanishing into the upper atmosphere.

The weather was so clear and bright, it almost hurt to look at the brilliant blue sky, but cold was still cold. It had only been three days since the start of the year, and there was still quite some time before the northern hemisphere would begin doing warm-up exercises to prepare for spring.

I walked on in silence for a bit, but I could tell my strolling partner was waiting for my reaction, so I mustered my scant reserves of courtesy and said, "What are you counting, Koizumi? How much mochi you've eaten thus far in life?"

"Hardly," the self-professed esper boy said, a touch of self-deprecation in his smile. "There's no real meaning to that number. It simply popped into my mind as I arrived—or perhaps I just remembered it. A random string of numbers of no significance to you, humanity at large, or indeed anyone besides myself."

But the fact that those whispered numbers reached my ears completely invalidated this "talking to myself" argument.

Monologues meant to be overheard were like junk mail blown in on the wind—whoever wound up with them would generally be annoyed.

"I beg your pardon."

If that's how you really feel, then spare me the apologies and just answer the question. What the hell's seven hundred seventy-whatever? Even what happened last August never reached such insanely high numbers.

"If I said it was the total sum of cash gifts I received from relatives over the holidays, how would you respond?"

Is that even a question? I'd just turn you into the SOS Brigade's walking wallet. And part of that responsibility would include always arriving after me whenever we meet up.

"That would be difficult. I don't mind treating everyone, but arriving later than you is nigh impossible."

How so? Even I'm capable of planning things well enough to arrive ten seconds before you if we've made arrangements in advance.

Koizumi shrugged. He was wearing a bulky jacket and didn't look cold at all.

"I have tried to arrive last any number of times, deliberately lingering behind. But each and every time, you arrived after me without fail. No matter how many adjustments I made. I find it hard to believe this is a coincidence. I have to assume this is one of Suzumiya's unconscious desires."

"What a specific and obnoxious desire to unconsciously have."

Now I was the one breathing out clouds of white.

"Anyway, given what day it is, you'd better stuff somewhere around the average café tab into that offering box. You know, buy yourself some peace of mind."

I looked ahead at a sturdy stone torii gate, and the larger red-painted gate that yawned open in the frigid air beyond.

January 3, just past noon, in front of the local shrine.

Haruhi had announced the plans for today during our winter retreat, and this was the result—not some cryptic manifestation of her unconscious thoughts but a clear, deliberate decision.

We were doing our New Year's shrine visit together.

By *we*, of course, I mean the five members of the SOS Brigade and not a bleak two-guy party with just Koizumi and me. Yet at the same time, we were both a bit reluctant to stand too close to the three girls in our party, which left us trailing a few steps behind.

It was at this point that the one responsible for all this spun around and proclaimed, "We'll start with this shrine! We've gotta hit up every shrine and temple in town, so let's kick it into high gear and go!"

I'm fairly certain my body doesn't have a gearbox or a clutch. Maybe she had both, like in her stomach somewhere? If anything, she probably has a turbocharger.

"We couldn't make it on New Year's Day, so I'm sure the resident god here has been breathlessly awaiting our arrival. We've gotta pray hard to make up for the delay!"

Haruhi was decked out in the kind of fancy kimono you saw on the very top row of a *Hinamatsuri* display. She was flanked by Nagato and Asahina, each clad in equally elegant fashion.

She thrust a finger toward the heavens and said, "Set plans for the year within three days of New Year's!" conveniently riffing off an old proverb.

"We've gotta make all our wishes today!" she added, almost certainly jinxing us. Her beaming smile gave off so much heat, she seemed like the physical embodiment of a warm anticyclone.

When I came strolling up to our usual station meeting spot, everyone else was already there, waiting. This happened every time. I would always be the last one to show up, even when I purposefully came before our agreed-upon meeting time. This normally prompted a strange sense of guilt that tormented me—but not today. Koizumi wasn't a major concern, but for once, I was legitimately relieved to have arrived after the brigade's female trio.

Haruhi, Nagato, and Asahina had assembled at the Tsuruya manor before coming here, so we'd decided to meet up later to account for that. Haruhi had arranged the schedule the previous day, and Tsuruya had backed her play. Naturally, no consideration was spared for the needs or convenience of any other parties involved. Still, I surprisingly had no objections.

Why had the three girls taken a detour to Tsuruya's? See for yourself.

"Well? Aren't these outfits fabulous?" Haruhi said, puffing up her chest with entirely unnecessary levels of arrogance, beaming with a smile even brighter than the colors of her garb. "Yuki and Mikuru, too!"

She grabbed their shoulders, pulling the two reticent girls closer. For once, Haruhi wasn't exaggerating. *Fabulous* was absolutely the right word.

They were nailing that classical Japanese vibe so well that it would've been an understatement to say they were drawing the eyes of everyone around us. It was like the three stars in Orion's belt glittering in the winter sky. Asahina in particular wore hers so well that she looked like the cover model of a pamphlet produced by a kimono company trying to court rich clients with the tagline *A must for your lovely daughter's graduation ceremony.* Totally a case of a top-notch outfit being elevated by the person wearing it. And she was neither demanding as much attention as Haruhi, nor stifling it the way Nagato was—she struck that sublime balance on the scales of beauty that marked her as truly a goddess among men. You can always count on Asahina to

4

deliver. I'm not sure exactly what that might be in this situation, but deliver she did.

"You all look splendid."

Like me, Koizumi was wearing his usual clothes. He offered up this verbal applause and then glanced my way. There was a trace of a smile on his lips that could only be described as reproachful, but Haruhi failed to notice. It was a bit disconcerting that I seemed to be the only one able to discern the subtleties of Koizumi's expressions. If I could do the same with Asahina, I'd be thrilled. Less so with this dude.

But he only kept this loaded smile on me for a second before turning back to Haruhi.

"Did Tsuruya choose all the outfits?" he asked.

The fact that she had a selection broad enough to flawlessly match three very different girls was itself impressive but also weirdly expected. The place she lived in screamed *old money* so hard that if you dug a hole in the garden, you'd probably find money from the Genroku era before you hit well water. Tsuruya was the kind of girl whose family owned a villa near a ski resort. We'd actually just returned from an all-expenses paid trip to that villa the day before. It had been an exhausting trip, all told, but on the train home, Haruhi had been going on and on about the first shrine visit of the year and what they should wear. That's when Tsuruya had readily agreed to outfit them all.

"Feel free to borrow any that strike your fancy!" she'd said, like she was renting out disposable hand warmers. "No, seriously, they're not doing anything but rotting in a drawer somewhere. Dad would love to dress me up in them, but I can't stand wearing clothes you can't run in."

"Same here," Haruhi said, clearly meaning it. "But it's a shame to leave them stashed away like that! We'll be happy to wear them for you—before they start holding a grudge for being neglected and come back to haunt you like a poltergeist!"

With that, she and Tsuruya exchanged high fives. "Whoo!" "Heyo!" The meaning of this act was unclear to anyone but themselves. All I could do was assume this was the sort of high-energy shit only comprehensible to people whose default state of mind was positive and outgoing.

Asahina was listening to their conversation, uttering a series of yelps and perplexed noises ("Huh?" "Er…" "Polterwhat?") and clearly not following a word of it.

"………"

Meanwhile, Nagato was sitting perfectly still, only her bangs swaying with the rocking of the train, her eyes never once leaving the unnaturally thick book in her hands. My sister and the crated cat, Shamisen, were both sound asleep.

Incidentally, Tsuruya herself had to board an early flight for Europe and consequently wouldn't have time to be with the girls, so she told them to just go on in and take whatever they pleased. She'd promised to inform her household, but the idea of just strolling in like that still seemed daunting to me—though not to Haruhi. And what did Tsuruya want as payment?

"Just snap of pic of everyone in those kimonos! That'll suit me just fine."

"You got it!"

Haruhi had shot her a thumbs-up, and without prophecy or prior planning, Koizumi and I both hung our heads.

As my flashback ended, Koizumi said, "I remember. It was just *yesterday.*"

He emphasized that last word, a note of gloom in his voice.

"But that is not where *your* memories of yesterday end, is it? Although, that was all I witnessed—and all Suzumiya saw."

Despite her kimono, Haruhi was taking great strides forward, leading us through the shrine grounds. It was still the third day of the year, so the place was packed. Fortunately, Haruhi's pace was as conspicuous as a wild rabbit's. Plus, she wasn't alone—Nagato was shuffling along on one side, and Asahina was valiantly trotting after her on the other, so keeping them in sight wasn't an issue. That said, there was an overwhelming number of stalls on both sides of the path, and the crowds were so dense that it made me wonder where all these people had even come from, barely leaving us any room to breathe—which was exactly the sort of stimulation Haruhi lived for. She was living her best life, you might say. All the tantalizing scents were really doing it for me, too. I hadn't had takoyaki in a while.

Still, either Haruhi or one of Tsuruya's servants had a real eye for dressing people, and the costume change had apparently gone rather smoothly. My fears of standing in the frozen winds rolling down from the mountain peaks, just me and Koizumi stuck waiting forever—a chilling idea on multiple levels—had been thankfully averted. For once, arriving last was a good thing.

I was deliberately and actively pretending I hadn't heard what Koizumi said, but he clearly saw through my ruse and let out a sigh that materialized as an extra-large cloud.

"You, Nagato, and Asahina weren't yet done with the winter trip. The three of you enjoyed extra innings together, correct? It was quite impossible to not feel left out after learning what had happened. I *am* the SOS Brigade's deputy chief, after all."

Aha, that explained the faint whiff of despondency I thought I noticed in his elusive smiles.

After we'd split up at the station post-trip, Nagato and Asahina had pulled off a feat I'm not sure can be described in Japanese in a way that makes any sense; it was essentially *Let's go to December 18 of last year and come back sixty-two seconds after we left*. Naturally, it didn't leave us tired at all. In fact, I felt great. I didn't ask, but I think Nagato felt the same. Asahina had been thoroughly confused the entire time, so everything Nagato and I did must have been extremely weird. Then again, if you thought about it, nobody who could be found in Haruhi Suzumiya's wake was ever *not* weird, so I wasn't too worried...

But apparently, this dude was pissed we hadn't invited him along on our time-crossing jaunt.

"It certainly feels like you were deliberately excluding me and Suzumiya."

Oh, come on. We couldn't invite Haruhi! That would've created a mess way beyond a simple time paradox.

"Couldn't you have managed something if it was just me?"

No use asking now. You weren't there at the time. Complain to the me who made the second time leap. If that me had seen you or even heard your voice, you'd have been a part of the chaos whether you liked it or not. That much I can guarantee.

Koizumi still had a faint and possibly reproachful smile on his lips, so I said, "You've already got your hands full with the closed space. Becoming the boy who leaped through time is just working way too hard. Show some restraint."

"If it comes up again, please *do* ask. At least retain the notion in a corner of your mind..."

I certainly hoped no such opportunities arose. And save your wishes for the god of this shrine, not me. If you drop an offering between each wish, you might feel better. Then again, I guess your Agency doesn't worship the many gods of Shinto, but Haruhi herself.

Haruhi was lined up with Nagato and Asahina, plodding along in front of us. Everything they had on was borrowed from Tsuruya, not just the kimono, but the traditional zori, *tabi* socks, obi, obi fasteners, and hair decorations, too. With my low-income mentality, I couldn't even begin to guess how much it all cost, but I was pretty sure if we took it to a pawnshop, we'd get a pretty penny. Maybe not the most productive line of thought.

By this point, we'd reached the designated hand-washing spot. Haruhi was super slapdash about most things but extremely meticulous when she chose to be, and she made sure we all picked up the ladle, cleaned our hands, and rinsed out our mouths.

"Like this? Wah, that's cold!" Asahina squeaked, blinking furiously and trying to copy Haruhi's movements. She looked like she was getting ready for an early coming-of-age ceremony.

"………"

Meanwhile, Nagato was standing perfectly still, holding the ladle, like a folktale ghost that had shown up at the *Shichi-Go-San* festival.

Either way, they soon moved on, coins ready for the offerings, only to discover that the crowd by the front of the shrine building open to the public was even more packed. I was worried Haruhi's typical impatience would result in her charging into the slightest gap in the crowd like a unit of heavy cavalry spotting a weak point in the enemy formation, but apparently even our brave chief hesitated to resort to violence in the presence of a god.

"Obviously!" she said with a full duck face. "I know how to pick the time and place. I mean, if prayers were first come, first served, I might not have a choice, but…" Then she pulled Asahina closer. "Oh, Mikuru! What do you say we try that outfit next?"

Haruhi was pointing at the part-timer selling wishing plaques and fortunes at the office window. She was wearing a *miko* uniform, and the white top and red *hakama* were certainly easy on the eye.

"A proper *miko*! A shrine maiden in the flesh! We should definitely get you a *miko* outfit. We'll have to buy a fortune later and ask if they sell those outfits somewhere."

We didn't "have to," and they probably didn't sell them, but fine. I'd like to see Asahina in a *miko* outfit, too. This habit of forcing Asahina into different costumes was one of the few Haruhi impulses I was always up for.

Even Asahina didn't seem to object this time.

"Is that a genuine *miko*? Wow, real clergy!" she said, eyes glittering. Maybe they no longer existed in her time.

For a while after that, we were swallowed by the crowd. Progress slowed to a crawl as we simply went with the flow of traffic. It was hard to stay in a group, but we didn't seem to be in danger of being overwhelmed by the press of bodies.

Special occasions tended to get our chief worked up. No matter how dense the crowd, she stood out like a mole popping out of a snowfield. Asahina was sticking to her like they were sisters, and that only made them even easier to spot.

Nagato was right behind them, her eyes at least three degrees frostier than normal, observing, like a navigator hunting for reefs, a stall selling masks for the festival.

Koizumi and I wound up walking side by side, and I finally remembered to ask, "So what was that number all about?"

"Seven hundred seventy-five thousand two hundred forty-nine."

Writing it out like that was confusing. It's 775,249, right?

"A prime number?" I said, guessing.

"Close, but not quite," Koizumi said, like his heart wasn't in it. "It's the result of multiplying three prime numbers together. Since prime numbers are integers greater than one that are divisible only by one and themselves, your answer is incorrect."

Man, he was really nursing that grudge about not inviting him to come time traveling with us. Wasn't like him to be this depressed. Being the boy who leaped through time really wasn't all it was cracked up to be. Maybe being the girl was a different story...

"So what meaning do those six digits have?"

"None," Koizumi said firmly. "I simply multiplied some prime numbers I happened to know together. The resulting number doesn't even mean that much to me. But, well..."

Here, he smiled his best client-facing smile.

"Can you guess what the three primes were?"

Was this a quiz now?

"I'll give you a hint—there's two two-digit numbers, and one three-digit number. Simple, right? Trial and error will get you there soon enough."

What a pain.

"Suzumiya would likely solve it instantly. She'd just say a random prime number, and it would almost certainly be one of the three. I promise you when she visits that fortune booth, she'll draw the best one possible."

We all know she defies probability, but I'm not her.

"Also, asking Nagato would be cheating. Let's say you have until we leave this shrine."

Is there a prize for getting it right?

"I'll consider it. What would you like?"

"Lemme see…"

But ultimately, I was never forced to pit my antimath brain against this problem. Or rather, we never got the chance.

"Kyon! Koizumi! What are you doing? Keep up!"

Haruhi had reached the front of the shine and was beckoning us with both hands.

For the next several minutes, Haruhi let her love for festivals run wild like a puppy on the savanna, dragging all of us along in her wake. I started to seriously consider adding more synonyms for *geez* to my vocabulary.

Let me quickly run through what happened next.

After dropping my change from the vending machine in the offering box (look, that counts as splurging for me), I rang the giant bell (what is that bell for anyway, some sort of ancient intercom?), bowed twice, clapped twice, bowed once more—the standard routine for shrines—then made some sort of prayer while looking all serious (I prayed Haruhi wouldn't pray for anything that would piss off the resident god), drew fortunes, and had a good time checking one another's results (everyone drew basically what you'd expect them to draw), then browsed the still densely packed stalls (worried Haruhi would eat something and stain her kimono), kept an eye on Nagato, who kept trying to wander off and read the signs on the grounds (they explained the origins of the shrine and the god worshipped here), watched over Asahina, who was delightful in all things (the way she was acting was much like the way I would act if I was suddenly flung back in time to the Kofun era), so basically, all the stuff you'd expect to happen at the first shrine visit of the year.

I don't really remember how it happened, but at some point, Haruhi and I got separated from the others. Not sure if it was good or bad that it happened in that brief interval.

In any case, that was when the strap on Haruhi's sandal broke.

"Well, that's rotten luck," I muttered.

Haruhi was crouched down, struggling with the strap, and she looked up at me like she was demonstrating how to furrow a brow.

"Very! I want my offering back. Is the god here taking a nap?"

Slightly relieved her anger wasn't directed at me, I said, "Crouching here is just gonna block the path. C'mon, I'll lend you a hand."

We were right in the middle of the main shrine thruway. One stream of people on their way to say a prayer, and the other on the way back out. If we stopped moving, both of us would be in everyone's way.

"Nah, this is nothing."

She snatched the broken zori off her right foot and tried to hopscotch away on her left alone. This might have been doable in street clothes, but with those long, dangly sleeves, she quickly lost her balance.

I caught her before she fell.

"Let's just hurry and move to the side."

With her leaning on my shoulder, we beat a hasty retreat over to a nearby lantern. Definitely getting some uncomfortable looks here.

"There won't be any fixing this, huh?" Haruhi said, inspecting the strap. She sighed.

This was unlike her. Was being stuck to me like a morning glory on a fence post putting her in a strange mood?

"It's not about *you*," she said, applying a bit more pressure to my shoulder. "If I hop the rest of the way back, I'll end up ruining *this* zori, too. I don't believe in returning things I've borrowed in worse condition."

You're more the type to borrow things and then claim they're yours now, yeah.

"Say that again."

I dodged her glare and pulled out my phone. Probably best to regroup with the others sooner than later. Koizumi would most likely love having Haruhi cling to him like this.

He picked up, but his answer surprised me.

First, he was with Asahina and Nagato.

Second, they were already by the shrine's main gate.

Third, in a crowd this big, even covering that short distance was a lot of work, especially if they were just going to end up going back the way they came. I conceded this point.

Fourth, even if they did come back, the only thing that would accomplish is making somebody else help Haruhi walk, so I might as well be the one to do it.

Fifth, we'd already done everything we'd planned to do at this shrine. Time constraints dictated we should get out of here as soon as possible, and retracing our steps back to the entrance

was the optimal choice. Deliberately picking a new route seemed entirely unnecessary.

For these reasons, it was simple, clear, and objective logic that decreed Haruhi and I should go to them, rather than any or all of them come back to us.

In summary:

"It won't be that hard." Even through the phone, I could tell Koizumi was enjoying this. "All you have to do is give Suzumiya a piggyback ride to our present location. You could carry her in your arms like a princess, if you prefer. I leave that decision in your capable hands."

He really had to add a ridiculous suggestion, dammit. Then the asshole hung up.

Haruhi had been watching my expression become more haggard as the phone call went on, frowning all the while, but when I informed her of Koizumi's terrifying suggestion, a look of horror appeared on her face. Her gaze flitted across the passing crowd.

"There's no other option?" she rasped, sounding like a front-line officer who knew the war was lost and had just been ordered to retreat even if it meant abandoning allies on the field.

I wasn't exactly pleased about this, either, but carrying her sounded less awful than running a three-legged race through these crowds. Mostly because it would be faster. Needless to say, the princess carry was absolutely, 100 percent out of the question. Do you even realize how many people would stare?

Haruhi was dangling the zori with the broken strap in front of her, glaring at it balefully.

"It is what it is…," I said, kneeling down in front of her. She hopped on board readily enough.

Feeling her weight on my back, I tried to secure her legs with my hands, but…

"Hey! Watch where you grab me!"

…not being familiar with the proper piggyback procedures, I

had imagined, based on the concept of fulcrums, that securing her thighs under my arms would be best for balance. Better than grabbing her butt, clearly. Just grin and bear it.

I made sure I had a grim look on my face before peering over my shoulder. When I did, I saw the edges of her brows were drooping like weeping willows.

"The hem," she said, refusing to meet my eyes.

"Oh," I said, catching her drift.

That made sense. Being a guy, I had no experience with long-sleeved kimono, and I had neglected to account for this garment's construction. But if I just considered it like a fancier *yukata*, then it made sense that hopping on someone's back while wearing one would cause the hems to part, revealing a lot of leg. Maybe at night, that wouldn't be too bad, but this was broad daylight. We stood out like two jewel beetles in a swarm of drab drone beetles. The attention alone might not be so bad, but a witness from North High might well leap to alarming assumptions. I could say I was using Haruhi as a weight for some hill work like I'm a racehorse, but nobody would believe me. Not that they should or anything.

"Try to get a little higher," I said, squatting like a prematch sumo wrestler. If I couldn't support her weight with my hands, then all the work would fall squarely on my neck and back. And I couldn't exactly crawl around like a doggy. This was the only option.

"If you can just lean against me like you're on your stomach, that should be good enough."

"Undignified, but better than doing it face-to-face. And this should stop the kimono from riding up too far."

Well, good. But it was definitely more ungainly than the usual piggyback posture and left the rider's arms one short slip away from strangling the courier. The slightest tightening of her arms and... Well, it was tough to feel safe.

"Don't mess around back there," I said.

Basically, everything from my waist up was parallel with the ground, and Haruhi was thrashing her arms, yelling, "Just go! Get it over with!"

I was all in favor of spending as little time causing a scene in full view of the public. Sadly, the sneakers I was wearing did not have golden wings on the sides, and the crowd was too dense for running to be a real option.

"It was shaping up to be a good New Year, too," she muttered in my ear. "Yesterday and the day before were nothing but fun. I guess my luck ran out today."

Her hands were dangling on either side of my neck, one holding the zori, the other her *kinchaku* pouch.

"If I'd known..." She trailed off.

"What?"

"Never mind. Just keep moving. Move!"

Maybe this was divine punishment. Was this shrine dedicated to a goddess by any chance? Koizumi says you basically are one yourself, so maybe you unwittingly rankled her. *How dare you be such a wild and impulsive deity!* or something like that.

"By the way, you're heavier than I expected," I said. "How much mochi did you gobble up?"

She hit me with the *kinchaku*.

"Kimono weigh a lot! Say another word, and I'll bite your ear off!"

Don't scream in my ear, please. My back ain't a car service with a kindhearted taxi driver behind the wheel.

I once saw a knickknack that had a frog carrying a smaller frog on its back.

Feeling like that frog, I wasn't sure if the time it took to carry my grumbling passenger through the red gates was more accurately measured in minutes or seconds. Internal clocks were really unreliable at times like these—and either way, it was a minor detail of no concern to anyone else.

The group members waiting for us each reacted differently.

Koizumi had his arms folded, grinning. Asahina had both hands covering her mouth, gasping, "Oh my!" For some reason, Nagato was facing sideways and crouching, but she soon stood up and fixed her unwavering gaze upon me.

It had been a short journey that felt improbably long, but I knew we just had to get through that torii and go our separate ways, so I was starting to feel better about the whole endeavor. Haruhi had quickly scrambled down from my back, leaving me unburdened in more ways than one. But how would we manage the final leg of our journey? Was there someone out there who could deliver us a replacement shoe?

"I know of no such service," Koizumi said. "But I think we can do some emergency repairs. We spoke a moment ago, and Nagato professed to have some skills in that area."

Much later on, I'd wonder why she wasn't dispatched to our location to perform those emergency repairs. (I mean, sure, it wasn't an actual emergency, but still.) Why did it take so long for this thought to cross my mind?

Because it was at this moment that Haruhi said, "When you think about it, it's not fair that *we're* all dressed up, but Kyon and Koizumi are both just *normal*."

It was like a light bulb had lit up over her head. The gloom that had been hanging around her mere moments ago was nowhere to be seen, leaving only her *I've got a great idea!* grin.

"Make like some proper Japanese gentlemen celebrating the New Year and come back in *hakama* with your family crest on them! You've got ten seconds!"

Don't be ridiculous. My family doesn't even *have* a crest.

"In that case," Koizumi said, doing his thing again, "an

acquaintance of mine runs a clothing rental shop in the area. I'll see if he can set us up."

At least feign reluctance, Koizumi. Are all your acquaintances this absurdly generous? I mean, come on. The New Year was only days ago, but every person in the Agency is standing by, around the clock, to satisfy Haruhi's every whim? There isn't even a chance to catch your breath, sheesh.

I dunno if she read my mind, but Haruhi curiously simmered down.

"We can't just show up at a shop like that without prior warning. They'd need to know your measurements beforehand. So..." Her eyes gleamed. This was going be an extra-special idea. "Tell me your heights and weights! And waist sizes!"

If that's all it takes, sure. Not like you knowing those numbers would bother me any.

But Koizumi seemed less than comfortable with this. Where he normally responded to any request with a flawless business smile, on this one occasion, he was abruptly left at a loss for words.

He pondered the matter a moment.

"You've done it again, Suzumiya," he said cryptically. That half smile suggested he'd worked through whatever was bugging him. "Mind if I tell you over here? I consider it a private matter requiring the utmost delicacy."

He glanced at me and then helped Haruhi hobble a few steps away. The two of them began whispering furiously. Haruhi was being Haruhi and making a grand show with her exaggerated, conspiratorial nods.

What need was there for secrecy? He's not a boxer getting ready for the weigh-in...

Then it hit me.

That number he'd muttered earlier: 775,249. The sum of three primes. A pair of two-digit numbers and a three-digit number.

Feeling eyes on me, I turned...

"........."

...and found Nagato staring at me. Seemed like she wanted to say something. Or wanted me to ask.

But I'm not always that desperate.

"Nah, Nagato. Don't tell me the answer. I can figure this one out myself."

"Okay," she said flatly.

She then rubbed out the numbers she'd written in the dirt at her feet.

A few days later...

Winter vacation was almost over, and my mind was starting to consider doing the warm-up exercises needed to survive the trip over the long hill that led to our beloved school.

On one such day, I was hanging out in my room, when my sister burst in (as usual, she didn't knock).

"Letter for you! From Koizumi!"

She handed it to me, then picked Shamisen up off my bed and took him away with her.

I flipped the envelope over. The sender's name was written on the back, in rather square handwriting. Definitely Koizumi's.

I ripped it open and dumped the contents out. Two photos fell onto my palm. No letter or postcard or anything, but this was plenty.

One photo featured me and Koizumi in our rented haori and *hakama*, surrounded by Haruhi, Nagato, and Asahina, each striking a pose in their long-sleeved kimono.

On the way from the rental shop to the next place of worship, Haruhi had found an old-fashioned photographer. The photos they'd taken had been sent to Koizumi and forwarded on to me. Man, I hate to admit it, but I had a really dumb look on my face. I can't pull off those clothes at all... Oh, I get it.

"*Everyone* in kimono, huh...?"

Impressed that Haruhi had gone to such lengths to fulfill Tsuruya's request, I picked up the second photo.

The framing, illumination, and photography skills were nowhere near as good as the pro's. This was just a printout of a photo taken with a cell phone, and it was clearly done surreptitiously, with no consideration for angle or light sources—clearly just Koizumi hastily grabbing the shot. I was in the photo, I could tell.

But something about it drew the eye, far more than the first photo. A tingle ran up my spine—possibly tickling out some memories.

"Not the look I thought she had..."

The square-framed photo showed me with legs splayed under the strain of Haruhi, my talkative burden.

I suppose Koizumi intended for this to be my prize.

SEVEN WONDERS OVERTIME

The air in the literature club room after school was not usually suffused with such grim tension.

Even with the windows closed, we could hear the baseball team at practice, shouting enthusiastically, the crappy trombones of the wind ensemble practicing, a few scattered birdsongs, and the telltale rustling of leaves blowing in the wind. But not a soul in the room was making a sound.

I was sitting across the table from Koizumi, our heads down, eyes locked firmly on the tabletop. Nagato was in her usual spot on a folding chair in the corner, her eyes never once leaving the dictionary-sized volume in her hands.

And Asahina…

Slowly, she gracefully reached out her hand, plucked a single card from the pile in front of her, and carefully flipped it over. She parted her pink lips to read the words written on it.

"'Now, in dire distress'…"

Koizumi and I both leaned farther forward, eyes straining wide.

"…'It is all the same to me! So then let us meet'…"

Asahina paused momentarily, looking from one of us to the other. She was in her usual maid outfit, but no matter how many times I saw it, it was magnificent, splendid, and affording of new discoveries—ones that I was currently not capable of searching for.

When neither of us reacted, the literature club's exclusive maid whispered, "'Even though it costs my life,'" drawing out the syllables theatrically.

Our eyes darted across the table. There were dozens of cards laid out before us, but our target was only one of many. I was muttering "Life, life, life" under my breath, but before I found the target…Asahina reached the end.

"'In the Bay of Naniwa.'"

Looking relieved, she softly put the card down.

"Whew," she said, then took a sip a tea from her mug.

Koizumi and I were still frantically searching for the card with the back half of the poem on it. The sound of Nagato turning a page echoed faintly.

"Got it!" Kozumi said, tapping one of the cards in front of him and picking it up. "Is this right?"

His smile didn't look too confident. We had both been wrong several times.

"I think so?" I said. I rolled my head, trying to ease the stiffness.

The game we were playing was known as karuta, which was based around a collection of one hundred poems known as the *Ogura Hyakunin Isshu* that had been assembled by the historical figure Fujiwara no Teika. Our goal was to be the first to grab the unique card that corresponded with the poem being read aloud.

"Okay. Next."

Silence descended once more. It was like the scene from earlier was on replay.

Koizumi and me glaring at the table, Nagato silently reading, Asahina slowly reaching out and picking up a new card.

She inhaled.

"'Coarse the rush-mat roof…'"

Neither of us moved.

"…'sheltering'—" A hint of concern crept into her voice. This next kanji was obscure. "Um, is this pronounced *an*?"

"*Io*," Nagato whispered instantly.

"'Sheltering the harvest-hut'… Uh, *koke*?"

"*Toma*," Nagato said.

"'Of the autumn rice-field.'"

Koizumi and I maintained our silence.

"*Waga…koromo…te*?"

"*De*."

Asahina restarted the line. "'And my sleeves are growing wet. With the moisture dripping through.'"

I was already looking for a card that started with *wa*, but my efforts were in vain.

"Got it." Koizumi found it on his side again.

Asahina was ready to move to the next card, but I held up a hand to stop her.

"Let's not," I said, addressing Koizumi. "Going any further would be foolhardy. And frustrating."

"Very true," he said. "I had hoped it would be a bit more fun, but…it's just too difficult."

He placed a finger on his chin, smiling ruefully.

I leaned against the back of my chair.

"We lack both the education and sophistication required to play competitive karuta. It's rude to even try! At the very least, we'll have to work improving our memorization."

I'd played a lot of board and card games with Koizumi, but we were clearly scraping the bottom of the barrel, so he'd brought in a battered old deck of *Ogura Hyakunin Isshu* karuta for a change of pace. Figuring it would help kill the time, we'd given it a shot, but as the preceding events proved, neither of us knew any of the poems by heart like you were supposed to and could only begin looking for the poems once the reader reached the back half—the amateur hour to end all amateur hours. No fun for anyone.

Truth was, I did, for some reason, remember, "In the cheerful light / Of the ever-shining Sun, / In the days of spring; / Why, with ceaseless, restless haste / Falls the cherry's new-blown bloom?" But Koizumi *also* knew that one, and watching him snatch the one poem I stood a chance of getting had been even more demoralizing than I expected. Hearing Asahina adorably stumble over the poems warmed my heart, but this was not conducive to smooth gameplay and ultimately wore the reader and the players ragged. Continuing the game was an insult to Fujiwara no Teika.

If we were gonna play any karuta, we should've used Yasutaka Tsutsui's parody of these poems, "Secret Ogura." Those were more fun, and we'd probably have a blast just messing around. If you're unaware of that work, I heartily recommend it. It'll leave you in stitches. I'd seen *Babbling Creation Chronicles* on the shelf in the corner, so I'm sure Nagato would agree. I doubt she'd so much as crack a smile, though.

Koizumi spent a few more minutes shuffling the cards, but then he sighed, put them down, and began reading his way through the stack.

Something about this made him seem ever so slightly disappointed, and that was when I realized I hadn't ever lost to him in any game that counted as a game.

He'd been winning at karuta, so if we'd kept going, he might have finally won something.

In other words, the games we played in this room might just be for killing time, but they were all zero-sum games, and this might well have been the first black mark on my record versus Koizumi.

Keeping all this off my face, I took a sip of Asahina's lovingly prepared tea. The SOS Brigade's formerly mysterious transfer student was back to his usual handsome self. He readied the deck once more and said, "What do you say? Since we've got the deck here, we could try a game called bozu mekuri. Asahina, too. Nagato, you in?"

"No," she said instantly. She moved her fingers, advancing to the next page.

Asahina handed the reader's deck over.

"What exactly is *that*?" she asked. "*Mekuru* as in…flipping cards? And *bozu*? Like a boy or…oh, a monk! Like the ones in the deck?"

What a very time-tourist way to divine the meaning of unfamiliar words. She looked quite pleased with herself.

"There's a lot of local variant rules," Koizumi said, "but let's go with a bog-standard version."

As he filled Asahina in, I turned my gaze to the vacant chief's chair.

When the end-of-day bell rang, Haruhi Suzumiya had shoved her bag into my hands, squawked, *"You go on ahead!"* like some screechy, tropical bird, and was out the door like a gust of wind. I had no clue what she was up to and didn't much care.

I had long since come to the realization that worrying was a waste of time. Concerning myself about things before they happened was exhausting, and I was better off only getting exhausted once some crisis actually took place. There was always the faint possibility that nothing would happen at all—yes, a particularly persuasive bit of self-deception, if I do say so myself.

A single card escaped the reader's deck that Koizumi was shuffling. It slid across the table to me. Lucky for me, it was a princess card.

SPRING, IT SEEMS, HAS PASSED, / AND THE SUMMER COME AGAIN; / FOR THE SILK-WHITE ROBES, / SO 'TIS SAID, ARE SPREAD TO DRY / ON THE MOUNT OF HEAVEN'S PERFUME.

The blossoms were gone, and the cherry trees blended into new greenery, but summer was still a long way off, and a chill hung in the air—likely because this was halfway up a mountain.

Two months into my second year at high school, in the last leg of May, and the SOS Brigade was as it ever was.

It wasn't like we were just killing time until Haruhi's arrival, but we did get to enjoy the entirely luck-based thrills of bozu mekuri for quite a while.

None of us had gotten the titular monk yet. This was only the first stage of the game, where we took turns drawing cards—and we all still had matching piles in front of us. Revealing a monk would force us to discard all of them. Whose luck would last the longest? Before the draw pile could determine our fates…

Bam!

…a loud noise came from the door.

"Huuuh?" Asahina jumped and turned toward it.

That was less of a knock and more someone ramming their shoulder into it.

Tap, tap.

This noise came from the bottom of the door. I had no idea who this could be, but it sounded like someone had body-slammed the door, fallen to the floor, and then began tapping it with their toenails. And this bizarre individual had business with the SOS Brigade. That narrowed down the potential suspects considerably.

If it wasn't someone from the computer club two doors down begging Nagato for programming tips, then maybe this was a third client following Kimidori's and Sakanaka's lead. Or perhaps it was Koizumi's fellow Agency member, the student council president, back with a new complaint. Tsuruya would never knock—she always burst in like she owned the place, even more than Haruhi herself.

Thud, thud, thud.

The shoe knocker seemed to be getting impatient.

"Oh, coming!" Asahina hastily got up and fluffed out her apron skirt as she reached for the doorknob. The portal opened, revealing the visitor beyond.

"Yo, is Haru here?"

A breezy question. One look explained the odd knock. She was carrying a huge stack of books and files and bundles of paper, leaving none of her hands free. Not sure kicking was the best solution, though…

"Mind if I come in?" she asked. Then she spotted Asahina dressed as a maid and gave her a long look, letting out a noise like she'd accidentally stepped on a jellyfish that got washed up on a beach. "I'd heard the legends, but…to think one of the wonders would be standing right here before me!"

What a cryptic statement.

Asahina flinched at this excessive curiosity, but her own curiosity got the better of her, and she asked, "Um, can I ask what brings you here?"

How very maid-like. I approve.

"Your boss asked me to bring the goods here. Actually, she may not have done that. But I brought 'em anyway! I'm just that nice."

Baggage and all, she stepped inside, glancing at Nagato, Koizumi, and me in turn.

"Hokay, Kyam! Take this stuff off me already. I want to use my arms again!"

Who and where was this Kyam fellow?

"*Kyon* is kinda hard to say, so I never liked that nickname."

I wholeheartedly agreed, but *Kyam* was equally terrible.

Neither Nagato nor Koizumi moved, so I caved and took the pile of stuff from her. There was a lot, and it was damn heavy.

"Um," Asahina said, tentatively raising an inquisitive hand. "Do you know her?"

"Yeah, she's a classmate." I said. "Class Five; a second-year like Haruhi and me."

Koizumi locked his gaze onto her. "What is it Haruhi asked you to do?"

I set the stack down on the table, which wasn't easy, since loose paper and books were all mixed together. The volume on top was called *Ghost Stories, Past and Present*. Below that was *Notable Tales, Old and New*, and what looked like a children's book? *Scary School Stories*? None of these titles were setting me at ease. It was clear what direction Haruhi intended to follow.

"So at lunch today," our visitor began explaining, legs set wide and firm, "I bumped into her outside the toilet, and she asked me something."

What?

"Whether I know about the school's seven wonders."

Why would she ask *you* that?

"I dunno. Probably has to do with the fact that I'm in the mystery research club."

I guess she did mention that when introducing herself at the start of the term. But how do the mystery club and the seven wonders connect?

"Okay, so her exact wording was…"

She launched into a Haruhi impression.

"*Does this school have seven wonders? I haven't heard of any, but maybe some stories about them have been passed down in the mystery club?*"

The impression was just good enough to be weirdly frustrating.

"Was it specifically *seven wonders*? Not the Seven Lucky Gods or something else she might've said wrong…?"

"Well, it certainly wasn't the seven blunders," she responded without any hint of a joke. "Honestly, it was confusing to even hear that schools have seven wonders, but I've figured it out!

Clearly, Haru is looking for spooky rumors. I imagine she thinks *mystery* and *occult* are synonyms."

I don't think that's quite it. Haruhi toured all the clubs when school started and was furious the mystery club had never actually stumbled across a murder.

"Oh yeah, I think I heard about that legendary visit from a senior."

Our classmate in the mystery club shook her head dramatically.

"I haven't participated yet, but the mystery club does have trips during the summer and winter vacations. But the North High mystery club's activity records show no instances in which the members were stranded on an island by a storm or suddenly snowed in and trapped in a ski lodge. A complete and utter shame."

I could see Koizumi spread his hands and shrug. Both those things had happened to us, and neither of them were particularly enjoyable experiences. I glanced at Nagato for confirmation, and to my complete surprise, the human interface had forgone her usual lack of interest in all things, closed her book, and had turned her eyes toward the uninvited mystery clubber like they were a pair of radio telescopes.

"Well, let's set all that aside," I said. "I think we know more than enough now about your club's wonderful activities. What was your response to Haruhi's question?"

Without batting an eye, she said, "I went directly to our club president and inquired about the existence of any oral tradition that might have preserved the seven folklores of this particular high school. He said no. I went flying back and informed Haru of that, and she said, '*Hmph*,' then promptly turned her back to me."

So North High had no homegrown seven wonders? Shouldn't that have been the end of the story? Why haul in this mountain of folklore?

"To be honest, I'm not really sure myself, either."

I was getting a headache.

"The club seniors told me to bring this over. So I came straight here, arms loaded high."

Thank you so, so much, mystery-club vets. How will we ever repay you...?

"If Haru's on the hunt for seven wonders, then we're on board to help! And the first step is naturally reference material. We got here a selection from the mystery club's library, and we printed out a bunch of supplementary info from the Internet."

Sorry, but I'm afraid all that hard work was for nothing. I hate to say this after you carried it all this way, but could you please take everything back? Especially before Haruhi has a chance to see.

"Why? We brought it for her! Kyam, you're saying she wouldn't want it?"

We have our reasons. And they're none of your business, mystery clubber.

She folded her arms, glaring at me. The gleam in her eyes was withering.

"How long you gonna just call me mystery clubber, huh? You know my name."

I knew Kunikida, Taniguchi, and everyone who'd been in our class the first year, but less than two months was not enough time to learn all my new classmates' names.

"Huh?"

She did not buy that at all. How should I explain this?

"You weren't even a student here last year."

"True."

Plus, your name was superlong, like if you said it quickly, you'd bite your tongue. Hard to remember.

"Then just shorten my first name. Everybody does."

Yeah, I'd rather not.

"That makes *no* sense."

She shook her head, clearly disgruntled.

"That aside," I said, seizing my opportunity, "how long are you gonna hang out here? If you're all done, could you head on back already? I thank you on Haruhi's behalf for bringing over the data on the seven wonders. Very helpful. Bye now."

I tried waving her to the door, but our classmate/mystery-club member showed no more signs of moving than a flamingo with its legs ensnared by vines. Don't tell me she's hell-bent on staying here until I said her name.

"Actually, I've got one other bit of business," she said.

She turned her entire body to face the corner of the room, where Nagato sat.

"I've been tasked with delivering a formal request to the president of the literature club."

Nagato looked directly at the mystery-club assassin. This was surprising enough. Nagato almost never stopped reading, no matter who stopped by.

"We read the magazine your club released."

Starting things off with a killer pass.

"…………"

Nagato slowly closed the book on her lap. I caught a glimpse of the title. *Dictionary of Symbols and Imagery*. Would you look at that? I said the massive thing was thick as a dictionary, but turns out it literally was one.

Wait, sorry, that wasn't the truly shocking thing.

Nothing was more astounding than the fact that Nagato had not only stopped reading but actually closed her book to listen to someone else. Asahina was too busy gaping at the mystery-club member to notice, but Koizumi was watching Nagato like an astronomer observing RR Lyrae variables from the Andromeda Galaxy with the naked eye.

But the mystery-club girl was oblivious to the cosmic significance of this miracle.

"Honestly, I can't say I was capable of objectively evaluating the content."

A fair opinion. Almost certainly correct.

"But putting aside its qualities as a piece of work, our club's leaders agree that putting out a magazine at all is noteworthy."

And that led to this request?

"The mystery club is planning to release a magazine of our own. We'd like you to contribute, Nagato. That's a pretty please with sugar on top."

She bowed low.

"I'm crazy for your dreamlike, poetic writing style, Nagato! And the others in the club agreed. Calling yourself the literature club president is no empty title."

Then maybe don't hit her up while here on other business. Make it a formal request. We put that magazine out a while ago. What has your president been up to in the meantime?

"He said he made the request at the club-president meetings."

Ah.

"And that your club ignored it."

That girl would.

"Well?" the mystery-club girl said. "We don't have a deadline set or anything. Just a vague goal to have it out in time for the culture festival."

That was in the fall, so quite a distant goal.

"We don't care what you write. Just give us one thing, one work of art. What do you say?"

Nagato rotated her head horizontally until her eyes met mine.

"…………"

After three full seconds of silence, she lowered her head two centimeters, and after a further three seconds, she raised it back up.

The mystery-research girl whispered anxiously in my ear.

"Yo, Kyam, can I interpret that series of movements as a yes?"

Yeah, I'll vouch for that interpretation.

"Thank you so much, Nagato!"

She bounded to her feet and moved so fast that she practically teleported over to Nagato, grabbing her hand and shaking it vigorously.

First, the computer club, now the mystery research club—Nagato might well be stealthily earning herself quite a rep here. She largely functioned as the literature club's own guardian spirit, almost like she was the resident *zashiki-warashi*. It wouldn't hurt her to broaden her social horizons. I was starting to think recruiting Nagato was the real reason this girl had been dispatched here, and delivering Haruhi's seven-wonders data had just been an excuse. If that was true, the mystery-club leadership were some crafty customers.

Having secured Nagato's participation, the mystery-club girl had made herself at home and was now sauntering around the room, inspecting the bookshelves. On a journey through the sea of spines.

"You've got great taste! Lots of fantastic mysteries here. This one's amazing! Ooh! Hmm? Mm!"

She'd frozen in her tracks, then yanked a volume from the shelf at lightning speed, flipping through the pages.

"I-is this is the Viking Press hardcover of Thomas Pynchon's *Gravity's Rainbow*?! The '73 first edition?!"

She held the book aloft to the heavens.

"Nagato, would it be possible for me to borrow this?"

"………"

I had no clue how valuable that battered old tome was, but Nagato placidly waited approximately six seconds before nodding once.

"Uh, Kyam, am I right to…?"

"That was a yes."

"Thank you so much, Nagato!"

She carefully placed the book on a nearby table, then bounded across the room once again, giving Nagato another vigorous handshake. If Nagato had not been sitting down, a hug might've entered the mix.

"I'll return it the moment I've finished passionately perusing the contents! I can just hand it off to Kyam, right?"

No. Bring it back yourself. To Nagato.

"Then I'll do that!" She nodded deeply and cradled the borrowed book under one arm. "Now, if you'll excuse me. Many thanks to all!"

She bowed with feline grace and danced her way out the door.

Leaving an afterimage of blond hair streaming through space.

"Whew."

That had been a long conversation to stand through.

Asahina had also been on her feet that whole time. She blinked a few times and then said, "Oh, I should have offered tea!"

Nobody had thought she would stay that long or be quite such a force of nature. There'd been no opportunity to inject hospitality.

And we'd blown our chance to reject the pile of folklore. We'd have to hide it before Haruhi showed up.

I checked around to see if there were any nooks or crannies where the contraband could be hidden out of sight and found Koizumi looking oddly dejected. Was the exchange student who had been placed in my class last month really that worrying?

"That's a concern, certainly, but…"

Then is it because she failed to mention the cat story you wrote for the magazine?

"Well…that doesn't really matter."

He peered down at the gift she'd brought us.

"The school's seven wonders are a far more pressing concern."

Aha.

Koizumi didn't seem to care for my reaction. He leaned forward in his chair.

"Suzumiya is investigating whether this school has any such legends. And like our visitor said, it would appear there is no such thing. Which makes matters simple. You know how Haruhi's mind works."

...If something doesn't exist, we just have to make it ourselves—her life motto.

"That is the next logical step, yes. And where that leads is clear. Sooner or later, Suzumiya will create a set of seven wonders for our school. Using the full force of her boundless imagination, she'll come up with occult phenomena that are downright disruptive."

Koizumi raised his hands in surrender.

"And it's entirely possible that one or all of these wonders will wind up becoming *real*."

I swallowed the last of my tea.

That's right. Haruhi had the power to make her wishes come true.

The SOS Brigade's chief had yet to appear. We had to consider it a stroke of luck she had not been present for the eccentric mystery-club girl's visit.

"That we should. This at least buys us some time," Koizumi nodded.

"Time for what?" I asked.

"Naturally, to think up this school's seven wonders. Before Suzumiya herself dreams up bizarre phenomena and plunges North High into the crucible of chaos, we must prepare a viable set of preventative measures."

We can't just do nothing, that's for sure.

"If it's something like cherry blossoms blooming in the fall, we can laugh it off as something caused by global climate instability. But the pigeons in the shrine turning out to be supposedly extinct passenger pigeons— Well, if biologists had found out, it would have been quite an event. A similar principle."

So just like when we filmed the movie.

The four of us had been repeatedly forced to hold emergency meetings. All SOS Brigade members, Haruhi herself excluded. But this was the first time we'd done that in the clubroom.

While Asahina was getting everyone a fresh cup of tea, I had Nagato leave her usual corner and join us at the table. She pulled a book of scary stories for children out of the mystery club's pile and quietly started reading.

Why did the mystery club's library have so many horror stories and old folktales in it? Did they have a spy from the horror camp in their midst?

"Horror and mystery are two sides of the same coin," Koizumi said, examining the stack of documents towering before him. "If the ghost turns out to actually be a ghost, that would be considered horror, but if it's just a dried flower or a weeping willow mistaken for an apparition, then it becomes commonplace. Taking horror-inspired phenomena, molding them with common sense, and providing logical explanations is a classic structure of mystery novels. John Dickson Carr was particularly famous for clever uses of this approach."

You should've brought that up while the girl was still here. She might have been impressed.

"I foresaw the distinct possibility that we might end up discussing mysteries for hours, so I resisted the temptation."

If he kept talking like this, I was definitely bound for headache-ville.

"The tea's ready," Asahina announced, bringing the tray of tea around. She served one to each of us and then took her seat.

Koizumi bowed to the club maid, then launched into the

briefing. "I explained as much during the film shoot last year, but the trick is to prepare sound reasoning that will prevent the state of the world from altering."

I could use a refresher. What does that mean in this case?

"I found a good example in the data your classmate brought us, so let us examine it together."

Koizumi pulled a book from the stack. A hardcover volume called *Notable Tales, Old and New.*

"This is a collection of lore compiled in the Kamakura era. It contains a vast quantity of stories and incidents that the author, Tachibana Narisue, either heard about or personally witnessed. It has become a valuable reference for the superstitions and attitudes of the age."

Classical Japanese was definitely not my forte...

"One story in here is so famous that it also appears in *Anthology of Tales from the Past.* It's a mystery tale that reads as horror. According to this, a certain grisly murder was perpetrated by a demon."

Muttering that he was sure it was in here somewhere, Koizumi seemed to be struggling with the index. Eventually, he located it.

"Here it is! August, third year of Ninna, pine grove east of Butoku Palace, a man transformed."

When was the Ninna era again? I could only remember the temple named for it.

"According to the author, the corresponding date on the Gregorian calendar would be sometime in early September 887 AD. Three court ladies were out for a nighttime stroll when they spied an attractive man beneath a pine tree. He took the hand of one of the ladies and drew her into the shadows."

I could only remember the temple named for it and that it was during the early Heian era.

"The two of them spoke for a while but eventually fell silent. The lady's companions grew suspicious and peered into the darkness, whereupon they found only the woman's severed limbs."

That *was* grisly.

"The two ladies hastened to the nearest guard post, and at their behest, the night watch raced to the scene, but all they found was the victim's limbs—no signs of her head or torso. Or the man in question."

Absconding with part of the body—the main part—was certainly the stuff of horror. And the man...?

"Yes, they decided only a demon could be responsible, and that the man in question had to be a demon in disguise—that's what the people of that era concluded."

There a follow-up?

"The account of the incident ends there, and the rest of the book covers other topics—it seems that same month had an unusual number of earthquakes and attacks by swarms of winged ants and heron flocks, alongside a number of other exceptional incidents."

Koizumi seemed indifferent, but for the Kyoto natives at the time, it must have been a real nightmare. They didn't have bug spray or handy nets to ward off unwanted birds. Earthquakes were a problem to this day. But it was hard to connect those to the murder.

"There are two basic conclusions," Koizumi said. "First is that the killer really was a demon. That's not particularly strange. In the Heian era, people were certain there were several species that fed upon humans, and all manner of unnatural creatures in the world at large."

My only window into the Heian era came from video games.

"The second is that the killer *wasn't* a demon, in which case he must have been human. Following this line of thought, there are several possibilities. One is that there was a murderer who cut off a woman's arms and legs and carried her head and torso away."

Even back then, it must have been quite challenging to kill someone, disfigure the corpse, then escape with the head and torso in tow without leaving any witnesses.

"The other possibility is that the two surviving ladies were responsible. They could have had their reasons to conspire and slaughter the victim. The disappearance of the head and torso could have been because of lingering evidence that the crime was their doing. Say, for example, the killing cuts were many and shallow, delivered by a physically weaker woman's hand. This would have forced them to completely remove the limbs, dispose of the remainder elsewhere, and file a false report of the incident."

Koizumi let out a short chuckle.

"Their report is difficult to believe, and the scene left behind even more bizarre. It's no wonder the guards concluded a demon did it. It was clearly not the work of mortal men. As you yourself suggested."

I feel tricked.

"But if you reach the latter conclusion, all becomes clear."

Koizumi picked up the mug with his name on it.

"The key to this explanation is that, however grisly the murder, *we* know demons don't exist. This is not a fantasy world, but the world we all know and live in."

He took a sip of steaming-hot tea.

"There's one other demon-based story in this volume," he said, clearly on a roll now. Which was quickly interrupted when he struggled to find the story he was looking for. "Ah, here it is. July, first year of Joan. *Izuno-kuni Okushima*, a demon ship, arrives. The contents are mostly what you'd imagine based on the title."

How long are we doing this? I hate dealing with old-school Japanese. Can we move on already? This is clearly just a way for Koizumi to vent frustration over not being able to chat about mysteries because of the issue surrounding the seven wonders.

"Unlike the previous murders, where the mystery man's demonic nature was pure supposition, in this instance, they believed from the start that demons had arrived."

Asahina perked up her ears, interested. No matter the angle, she looked every part like the Japanese representative attending the World Maid Symposium.

It was unclear if Nagato was listening or not. She was as silent as ever, but I realized she'd moved on to the second volume of children's horror stories. Perhaps she liked them.

Koizumi explained he would be paraphrasing and condensing the original text.

"In August of 1171, a drifting ship washed ashore an island near Izuno. The islanders assumed it was a wreck, but eight demons came ashore. When the islanders offered them sake, they drank and ate like horses. 'They spake not a word,' or so the text says. The demons are described as being eight or nine *shaku* tall, with hair dark as night, red skin covered in tattoos, eyes round like a monkey's, wearing naught but a simple cloth draped around the waist. Each carried a pole gauged to be some six or seven *shaku* long."

Didn't really sound like the islanders were particularly scared of these demons.

"One of them wanted a bow the islanders had, and when this request was refused, the demons roared and attacked. Five islanders were killed and four critically injured. The demons shot fire from their armpits, but when the islanders fetched blessed arrows and fought back, the interlopers were pushed back into the ocean before they took off on their ship. As they did, one of the demons lost his sash, and it was stored in the treasure chambers of Rengeo-in, more commonly known as Sanjusangen-do."

From what I'm hearing, these ain't your classic Japanese *oni*. Only the waist wrap really sounded familiar.

"Precisely. The incident itself does appear to have happened, and we know from Kujo Kanezane's diary that a report on it was indeed delivered to the Izuno court. Kanezane suggested the drifters were 'some manner of barbarian'—in other words, visitors from another country."

That seemed about right. It wasn't like they literally had horns and fangs, and if they were legit demons, the islanders would have been too scared to approach them. Instead, they all drank together.

"Yes. Assuming this was a ship blown off course by a typhoon or the like is a logical conclusion. They 'quaffed and feasted, horselike' because they were starving from their long journey. The conflict and murder that followed likely occurred because they didn't know a word of Japanese. A simple breakdown of communication between the natives of two nations."

What's up with the armpit fire?

"Based on their physical descriptions, there are theories the visitors were Polynesian, so perhaps that is an attempt to describe the torches used in traditional fire dances." Koizumi chuckled. "Unlike the grisly murder mystery, there would be nothing particularly uncanny about this incident—apart from the word *demon* coming up. There were plenty of witnesses, and everything that took place was entirely within the limitations of mortals. Sailors from abroad responded to conflict with violence, realized they had outstayed their welcome, and sailed away. Nothing more, nothing less."

And even when there were reports of demons appearing, people back then weren't so gullible that they just believed the first thing they heard.

"If anything, it seems like little separates us besides the many intervening years."

Koizumi was flipping through the book again.

"Another fascinating instance reveals itself in chapter twenty-seven, which deals with apparitions. Part of the preamble reads, 'That which is ever changing has been unparalleled since inception.

Ancient are the tales of apparitions bewitching the hearts of men, however improbable they may be.' In this case, the term *apparitions* is used to mean monsters—like the demons we've been discussing. The author is specifically calling out the unlikelihood that any such supernatural creatures were out there shapeshifting and playing tricks on humans. Even eight hundred years ago, people often thought these stories were quite suspect. One would think looking back from the future should provide us with a far more distinct advantage."

I wouldn't call it bewitching per se, but you did transform into a ball of light once, so I'm finding this all sort of unconvincing.

Koizumi snapped the hardcover book shut and placed it on the table. Assuming that meant the topic had drawn to a close, I attempted to sum up the point he'd been trying to make with this incredibly long-winded primer on historical anecdotes.

"So basically, we'll be using that same logic? No matter what Haruhi says the seven wonders are, we have to insist they were tricks of the eyes, rumors that were distorted in retellings, or false reports to begin with? Turn these wonders into something unremarkable?"

"I believe that's the simplest solution."

So even if an Elasmosaurus appeared in the school pool at night, and multiple eyeball witnesses spotted it raising its long neck and annoying the locals with its roars, we have to insist they're all just seeing things?

"If it comes down to it," Koizumi said as he nodded firmly. "I intend to stick to my guns."

Even if they had photos and videos and were spreading them online?

"That sort of thing can be easily doctored, so we'll simply insist it's impressive CGI."

You're getting pretty bold, yourself. Has Haruhi's way of thinking infected your mind?

I shook my head like a Sunshine Buddy.

"I don't think Haruhi'll buy that."

"Oh?"

It might set her off instead, leading to the birth of a super wonder so real and on such a scale that no weasel words would be persuasive, so insanely supernatural that anyone who saw it would know they were seeing it and not "seeing things."

"That would be rather bad."

I think it's better to not let her create anything in the first place. Trying to minimize the mysterious phenomena after they pop into existence is too risky.

Koizumi sounded impressed. "If that's doable, I would be all for it. But how?"

Flip the concept. Instead of waiting for her to dream the wonders up, we concoct our own wonders. North High already has seven wonders, and here's what they are! That argument is the best way to silence her.

"What if she doesn't like them?"

Once we get that far, the rest is a gamble, no doubt. But I feel like if we handcraft seven wonders for her, she wouldn't dismiss them out of hand.

"Then let us gamble on that chance."

Koizumi freed a pile of printouts from the weight of *Notable Tales, Old and New* and handed it to me.

"I imagine the references your class's exchange student/mystery-research-club member brought will prove invaluable."

At a glance, there were dozens of pages printed out (in color, even) from any relevant websites—and a lot of classic horror school stories were listed. These *would* be handy references.

"Still…"

Should we really be holding Haruhi Countermeasure Planning Committees here? She could come barreling through the door at any moment.

Koizumi glanced quickly down at his phone.

"Never fear. I'm tracking Suzumiya's present location and activities. We have time enough before she heads this way."

Did you put a GPS tracker on her?

"Well—the members of the Agency are Suzumiya experts, so we have our ways. Naturally, nothing quite that crude."

Not something to be bragging about, either.

"The student council members are not the only cooperators we have on campus. Should the need arise, our allies can slow her down—peacefully, of course."

I get it, okay? You and those countless red spheres are like Haruhi's tranquilizers. I'm long past doubting you on that front.

I tossed the bundle of loose printouts onto the table.

"Then let's formally commence the North High Seven Wonders Planning Committee meeting."

"Okay!" Asahina said, applauding alone. Our brigade's mascot girl/club maid/my personal source of comfort could be counted on to add a touch of delight to any given moment.

"By the way, umm," Asahina said, looking from one of us to the other, "by *wonders*, do we mean scary stories?"

Had we used it in any other sense?

"I thought *seven wonders* referred to historical buildings or ruins."

Then what did you make of all these old stories Koizumi was talking about?

"That was in ancient Kyoto, right? I remember Kyoto's supposed to be a historical landmark, with many old buildings that should still be standing today."

Was that how future people remembered it?

Then what about the second story?

"I thought that was about the island from *Momotaro*."

47

Putting Kyoto and *Momotaro* aside for the moment, sure, *seven wonders* on its own could refer to the wonders of the ancient world. The Colossus of Rhodes or the Hanging Gardens of Babylon, etc. But unless I'd misheard the mystery-club girl's demonstration of her mimicry skills, Haruhi was definitely talking about the seven wonders of our school. I mean, this was Haruhi we were talking about, so she was liable to add *of the world* at some point along the way.

"If that happens, then our summer trip will be international," Koizumi said, with a hollow look in his eyes. Like he was trying to ballpark how much that might cost.

The only ancient world wonder still standing was the pyramids, but Haruhi was perfectly capable of deciding to go dig up the ruins of the others and even stand a chance of being successful. I'd never heard her plans for the future, but it would've been fitting in a way if she wanted to be an archaeologist one day.

"I would not recommend it, personally."

Why not?

"Just imagine it. Haruhi picks up a random rock outside Giza, and it has hieroglyphs explaining the real reason for the creation of the pyramids."

A historical find. Mankind would rejoice.

"But what if the contents were not to mankind's benefit?"

Like?

"I daren't speculate. But we must prepare for the possibility and be ready to respond. For now, let's focus on the school's wonders."

Koizumi got right down to business.

"What's the first school horror that comes to mind?"

Without really thinking about it, I said, "Statues of Ninomiya Kinjiro."

I started flipping through the mystery club's printouts.

"Based on the data they found, stories about that rank first or second in most schools. Sounds like they're super standard."

Kinjiro was famous for being so hungry for knowledge that he read books even as he walked to work, but modern hand-wringing had led to newer statues depicting him sitting down. That was irrelevant, but it did bring a different problem to mind.

"Does this school even have a Kinjiro statue?"

"Not that I'm aware of."

"Well, if we don't, then does it have to be Kinjiro?"

"No, but like you said, Suzumiya might consider a Ninomiya Kinjiro statue to be an essential entry on any list of seven school wonders."

In other words?

"If Suzumiya firmly believes one of the seven wonders must involve a Ninomiya statue, then a statue of him will appear somewhere in North High. A weather-beaten, storied statue that looks as if it has been there since the school was built."

Wish she could manifest something more useful. Like AC for the clubroom.

"Hypothetically speaking, what sort of uncanny phenomenon do we think she'd generate from this statue?"

I considered this for a moment.

"Kinjiro flies around in a Superman pose. Because staying in the same position all the time is exhausting, and he needs the exercise."

"That is certainly the sort of leap in logic Suzumiya often makes. Well said."

Somehow, I don't really feel like I was praised very much.

"Let's consider a flying Kinjiro statue our starting point, then. The key here is to figure out how we can minimize the impact of this legend. More common stories involve statues that have glowing eyes, that change which way they're facing, that wave at passersby—maybe the book in his hands changes which page it's open to or the amount of firewood on his back changes."

Ninomiya Takanori (still the same guy) stories are all super mundane, huh?

"And all entirely dismissible as a trick of the eyes."

Koizumi pulled out a fresh sheet of A4 paper and began taking notes—awfully fast for handwriting. Who was the SOS Brigade's secretary again? I remembered him being the deputy chief, but...

I shook my head.

"Haruhi's not gonna accept any legend that cliché. We've gotta add a twist at least. Asahina, what would you have Ninomiya Kinjiro do?"

The maid from the future blinked at me. "It's a statue of that person, right? And it moves? How?"

The fact that a bronze statue is moving is what makes it a "wonder."

"Oh, I see! But does it have to be bronze? If we put an actuator inside a statue made of a kinetic metal, it would be able to move around just fine."

At that point, it would just be a robot. While I pondered how to explain this to her, Koizumi snapped his fingers.

"That would be one solution!"

If the Kinjiro statue were designed to move, there was nothing wondrous about it.

"No, not that, the material the statue is made from. Bronze is an alloy of copper and tin. The typical makeup is..."

"It's 85 percent copper, 5 percent tin, 5 percent zinc, and 5 percent lead," Nagato said, without looking up from the children's book. Guess she'd been listening, after all.

"What if those proportions changed once a year? For example, if it became 85 percent copper, 4.9 percent tin, 4.9 percent zinc, and 5.2 percent lead. The appearance wouldn't change at all, merely the composition. That would be rather wondrous, wouldn't it?"

Kinda weak. I considered it for a moment.

"What about 84 percent copper, 4.5 percent tin, 4.5 percent zinc, 4.5 percent lead, and 2.5 percent orichalcum?"

"Interesting. But that's an awfully high percentage for a metal that doesn't exist. Let's say 85 copper, 5 tin, 5 zinc, 4 lead, and 1 orichalcum."

Were we paying by the gram here or something?

"Well, we've settled on something rather restrained," Koizumi said. "Even if this does come true, it will have no lasting harm."

Having 1 percent of an unknown metal like orichalcum could turn out to be a huge deal, but let's just pray it doesn't.

"So that's one wonder down."

Koizumi's notes now read:

Legend of Ninomiya Kinjiro's Statue:

In the dead of the night on the full moon, the composition of the statue changes from 85 percent copper (ugh, skipping ahead) *to* (same) *1 percent orichalcum. Returns to normal when the sun rises.*

Adding the bit about the dead of the night was an obvious attempt at pretending this was properly spooky, but I had no objections to that.

Right, next.

"Almost as popular a theme are scary stories about music rooms."

The piano playing at night when no one was around—the sort of story anyone could dream up.

"Applying that mystery-novel-solution approach, it's likely someone left their phone or a recorder in the music room, and an alarm or ringtone went off at a scheduled time."

A bit too easy.

"If music's coming from the piano in an empty room," Asahina said, "then could it be a player piano?"

Possible, but nothing that fancy would be in the music room at a public school.

Asahina crooked her head like a songbird and asked, "What does it play?"

Did it matter? No, maybe it did. This was supposed to be a scary story, so the music had to be fitting. Schubert's *Erlkönig* or Mozart's Requiem?

"Oh," Koizumi said, snapping his fingers again. "I know just the number."

"Yeah? What?"

"*4'33"*."

Not sure if that was long or short.

"It's not the length of the track, but the title of a piece of music."

What a functional title. I figured it would be online somewhere, so why not pull it up? I moved to the laptop—spoils from a face-off with the computer club—intending to boot it up.

"Not necessary. I mean—you can't actually hear it," Koizumi said, smiling. "The performer sits in front of the keyboard for four minutes and thirty-three seconds doing absolutely nothing. Less music than performance art, perhaps."

Not functional so much as avant-garde.

"Very. Much has been written debating the question of whether it even qualifies as music, but there could be no composition better suited to a music-room horror story."

A soundless composition would be heard by no one even if there were a ghost to play it. What an astonishingly harmless specter. I felt almost sorry for it.

"Asahina," I said, on a whim, "in the future, have you uncovered any scientific evidence of ghosts?"

She looked momentarily surprised, but then she parted her full lips as she paused for a few seconds before saying, "That's classified. Heh-heh."

Why do you seem so pleased?

"When I can't tell you something important, it's really upsetting. But for something like this, where it's unlikely to make a difference if it's a yes or a no, my not being able to say anything is inconsequential, so I can say *'That's classified'* with my head held high."

The fact that she'd deemed the existence of ghosts inconsequential seemed like a solid hint toward what the answer was, but when our maid literally held her head high, it certainly emphasized her figure. I diligently averted my eyes. They found Koizumi shrugging.

He was awfully hell-bent on transforming horror into everyday mystery tropes. Maybe the whole Haruhi countermeasures thing was just a good excuse, and he was actually just a total wimp when it came to ghosts and ghoulies. That would certainly explain why he was so motivated about making Haruhi's seven wonders something unobtrusive.

He ran his pencil across the page again.

Mystery of the Music Room:

In the dead of the night on the new moon, the piano in the empty music room plays John Cage's 4'33". The music room is locked, with no way in or out.

"Do we need that last clause?"

"I was hoping it would add to the mood," Koizumi said. "Next…how about this? Your classic staircase horror, in which the number of stairs increases or decreases."

I'd certainly heard the like before. Some even incorporated puns, where it would only happen if someone was staring at you. Staring at you on the stairs. A rhyme just about anyone could come up with.

"Yeah," I said, considering it. What would Haruhi do with stairs?

Koizumi must have hit the same conclusion, because he jumped ahead of me and said, "Perhaps every staircase in the school becomes an escalator?"

Seriously, putting AC in every class would be way more useful. The lowest-bidding construction contractor had left us with flimsy walls that provided no protection from the heat or cold, and it was nearly always the exact same temperature inside as it was outside. We should fix *that* problem before installing any damn escalators.

"We're not proposing improvements to school amenities. Our focus is simply uncanny stories."

I was all in favor of turning this into a committee to steer Haruhi's weirdo powers toward manifesting stuff that actually benefited us. Nobody would be the least bit upset if AC and escalators appeared overnight. I imagined our schoolmates would be quite pleased.

Koizumi shook his head at me.

"Now that I think about it, if the stairs were replaced with escalators, that would just be dismissed as hasty construction work. The same goes for AC. Going to such extremes actually takes us further from *wonder*. Let's brainstorm something a bit more mundane."

The result of that storm?

The Staircase's Secret:

In the dead of the night on a crescent moon, the staircase leading to the roof of the southern building gains an extra step for one full hour. Whoever treads upon that stair will be briefly plagued by an ingrown toenail on their right big toe. Furthermore and hitherto, we can't dismiss the strange and uncanny possibility that all classrooms will suddenly have air-conditioning.

That bit at the end was entirely my doing.

"The first and last sections are entirely unrelated. Also, I think your misuse of archaic conjunctions will draw unnecessary attention."

Who cares?! Scary stories not making sense just makes them seem more real.

"I don't know if we want Suzumiya to think any of this is real."

Despite his grumbles, Koizumi was already leafing through more printouts.

"Mirror-based stories are relatively popular as well. Check one at a specific time and see your future self or be sucked in and get lost forever."

What mirror, though? I ran through all the mirrors I could think of in the school.

"There's a pretty big one in the bridge connecting the central building and the gym. Let's use that."

If it was raining, the baseball team would use it to check their forms. I'd seen people practice pitching in front of it. I dunno what other use the thing had; it certainly was sort of a mystery mirror.

What would happen to that in the dead of the night? Koizumi started us off.

"First thing that comes to mind is that your reflection's actions don't match your own."

Asahina?

"Um, what if your reflection steps out of the mirror?"

A doppelgänger, eh? Personally, I was sick of running across myself already, but...

Might as well ask Nagato. Any ideas?

Nagato's eyes had been locked on the children's book, but they slowly drifted upward.

"The person reflected in the mirror has all amino acids in their body changed from L to D."

A very scientific proposal. When I said nothing, she decided further explanation was required and said, "Enantiomers," under her breath.

I had no idea how this qualified as an uncanny phenomenon,

so I simply maintained my silence, pretending to take a sip from my long-since-empty mug. Asahina was definitely doing the same thing. Comrade!

"Oh, I see," Koizumi said with a single clap. Traitor! "Same principle as the statue. Your appearance doesn't change at all, but the composition of your very flesh is mirrored! Fascinating concept. And entirely harmless. A highly sensible wonder."

I didn't think *sense* had any business being mentioned in the same breath as *wonder*, but was it really harmless? Cool, let's go with that, then.

As Nagato went back to her reading, I could swear she whispered, "……jam," but there were no baked goods around, and our mugs certainly didn't have Russian tea in them, so I must have misheard.

Oh, my opinion? I was thinking looking in the mirror would reverse your personality. Give us a Haruhi who acted like Nagato or a Nagato who acted like Haruhi— Actually, just the thought makes me dizzy. Further brain stimulation would be too perilous. Let's not.

"How about this?" Koizumi said.

The Bridge's Backward Mirror:

In the dead of the night when the moon is waxing, if your entire body is reflected in the bridge's mirror, then the composition of the amino acids in your body is reversed. Also, if you perform routine two of the radio calisthenics, the reflection will go out of sync on the very last move. Perhaps the reflection will step out of the mirror, but probably not. Even if it did, it would vanish soon, so sayeth the rumors.

As he scribbled this down, I asked, "How many is that?"

"Four. We need three more."

I was getting tired.

"Shall we call it, then? There's only so long we can keep Suzumiya waiting."

I was curious how he was keeping Haruhi at bay, but let's leave that to the professional Haruhi minders. I was perfectly happy remaining an amateur in that regard.

Tea break time. Asahina made everyone fresh cups, and we relaxed for a moment. Then it was time to tackle the remaining three.

Koizumi put his mug down and picked up le report à la mystery club.

"What about an unopenable door that never opens? There's a door out there somewhere that *never* opens."

Didn't sound like the location mattered.

"Yes. At the moment, no such door exists, so it's just 'somewhere.'"

Why won't it open? Is someone keeping watch? Is it nailed shut?

"We want to keep this unobtrusive. How about a toilet stall that's always locked? Toilet horror stories are an orthodox school wonder."

An unopenable toilet stall. But, like, those doors have gaps around them, so you could always just...climb over.

"Nothing happens to anyone who enters that way, but though the door is always heavily locked, there are moments when the locks are gone—and some poor unsuspecting soul went in. And was never seen again. That's why opening the door became taboo."

Where'd the hapless victim go?

"Given Suzumiya's typical thought process, it's safe to assume a fantasy world."

And the first person the traveler meets in that new world would be super important. They'd get mixed up in a load of trouble that would decide the very fate of the realm, a journey filled with meeting new people, suffering tragic losses, and falling in love—a heroic saga the bards would sing about for eons.

"If a story on that scale commences, it would well and truly be out of our hands, so let's pick a more sustainable exit."

So the door's basically a warp zone? Maybe it connects to another toilet? What about the men's room in the North Gate Station?

"That would be a dramatic and unmistakable case of teleportation. Let's keep it closer, like…the next stall over. That way we could at least argue the occupant forgot which stall they went in."

Like the Bison Warp? In that case, why not just have them reappear in the same spot? Like, one or two seconds later, long enough for them to have clearly "vanished," but to an onlooker, it all happens in the blink of an eye. Totally wondrous from a physics standpoint.

"That could work, but it is a *little* dull."

Don't be picky. But you're right; I dunno if it would satisfy Haruhi.

I put my clenched fist to my brow, meditating on it. Then inspiration struck.

"I've got it. We can have them make that trip to a parallel world."

"Meaning?" Koizumi frowned.

Meaning you open the unopenable door, get transported to a fantasy world, and have an adventure with whoever summoned you.

"What sort of adventure?"

That's up to the individual. But whether they suffer like crazy or are crazy overpowered, the upshot is they resolve the problem and then get sent back to the toilet from whence they came.

"How?"

Some wondrous power at work. It's a fantasy world, right? Should be able to find a god or two over there. Ask them.

"Or perhaps a vague mention about the will of the world. The natural order of our world will not stand for having one resident missing for long, and some cosmic scale tips to restore them to their original location."

Whatever works. But when they return to our world, they lose all memories of their adventure. No matter how much time they spent over there, only an hour passes in our world.

"Let's at least limit the time they spent adventuring to a few months. If they spend years on the other side, they'd perceptibly age, and it would be awkward getting used to their original body again."

I'll leave those details in your capable hands.

"What about clothes? If they change over there, they might find themselves wearing the most outlandish garb and be rather perplexed."

Let them.

Asahina let out a little sigh.

"They'll forget everyone they met in that other world...no matter what good times they had or what precious memories they made. If those people only knew, they'd be very sad."

I hadn't expected her to take the scenario this hard.

"Don't worry, Asahina," I hastily added. "If there's a demand for a sequel, they'll be sucked back into that other world, be reunited with their companions, and regain their memories."

"Really? Oh, good."

She smiled like a poppy anemone transforming into an iris.

"Let's hope it sticks to a single sequel," Koizumi said as he flashed a wry smile. "But I suspect trilogies would be more likely."

He started writing.

The Unopenable Toilet Door:

A bathroom somewhere on the school grounds has a stall that is always locked and must never be opened. In the dead of the night when the moon was waning gibbous, one unlucky soul opened this door...and was transported to another world. They spent two months away, and when they returned, they found only an hour had passed in our world. And all recollection of the other side faded from memory. Details TBD. Sequels possible.

"…………"

Nagato was silently reading away. The children's book open on her knees was now the fourth volume.

Koizumi stopped rifling through the stack.

"This one has potential. The anatomical model that moves around at night."

Why were people so obsessed with making statues and models move?

"An anatomical model roaming the halls… Too typical?"

I might've just been getting desensitized, but it did seem a little boring.

The thing should at least do five hundred laps of the four-hundred-meter track or shooting practice on the handball court.

…Crap, now I feel like no matter what we make the model do, it won't be interesting.

Feeling like my train of thought was quickly going off the rails, I tried to come up with something better. Koizumi was pulling several sheets off the stack of printouts.

"Did you know our school has an anatomical model?" he asked.

Yeah, it's creepy as is. I'd spotted it before in the biology room a few times en route to another class. A silicone mass, muscles, organs, and blood vessels exposed, no eyelids so the eyeballs just stared back at you—not even its mother could call it handsome. It had a weird psychological effect where it conjured up so many splatterific images that you wound up laughing as a defense mechanism.

"But it would appear the model isn't *always* there."

It's stuck in the back of the room, so it was true I didn't see it all that often, but presumably that's not what you mean?

"The mystery research club's data included a report of a curious case."

A what now?

"It seems there is a bona fide mystery surrounding North High's very own biology-room anatomical model. They call it—the Terrifying Moving Anatomical Model. Not very imaginative."

Wait, hold up. This whole time, I thought we didn't have seven wonders, but now you're telling me we actually have one?

"It seems the mystery club viewed this purely as an everyday, real-world mystery, with nothing occult about it—just an ordinary trick."

So what's the case involve?

"According to le report à la mystery club…"

Don't steal my joke.

Koizumi ignored this. "One morning, a female student from the Sweets Appreciation Society opened the door to the home ec room, and—"

Wait, wait, wait. This is the first I've heard of this society, but more importantly, why was she in the home ec room first thing in the morning?

"Typically, the Sweets Appreciation Society operates in the home ec room after school hours, but the sweets they were making required prep work to be done earlier in the day. I believe they were making bavarian cream. The society itself appears to be a splinter group that was originally a part of the home ec club."

I don't care.

"In any case, she was rushing to put the ingredients in the home-ec-room fridge. And when she flung open the classroom door…"

Koizumi paused for effect.

"...her eyes met those of the anatomical model, posed right inside the door as if lying in wait. She almost bumped noses with it. So shocked she forgot to scream, the bavarian cream ingredients were splattered across the floor, gone to waste. That was the greatest tragedy of all, she said."

So the idea was that the model had snuck out of the biology room into the home ec room and then laid an ambush? That *did* sound like a horror story.

"But the story continues. The victim went directly to the faculty office, explained the situation to a teacher who'd also arrived early, and the two of them went back to the home ec room together. But once they reached the room, there was no sign of the anatomical model that had given the girl such a fright."

And then?

"And then they went to the biology room. That was where the model was meant to be, after all. And when they arrived, what did they find?"

Quit beating around the bush.

"The anatomical model standing forlornly in the corner, exactly where it always was. Nothing unusual about it at all."

Had it raced back? Or teleported? Why had it gone to the home ec room in the first place? A total mystery.

"Indeed. But on that note, look here." Koizumi ruffled through some loose pages. "There was a fish cut in three on one of the counters. It was later identified as mackerel."

Has the model been making fried mackerel for breakfast only to be interrupted by an unwitting early riser? Not a great punch line.

"Hardly. And this model has been spotted in other unexpected locations as well."

There's a whole series of anatomical-model terror incidents?!

"Two weeks after this incident, a member of the girls' basketball team came to the gym early for morning practice. It just so happened she arrived first. Figuring she might as well get ready, she opened the storeroom—"

And the anatomical model was waiting inside?

"Precisely. The basketball player first on the scene left the slightly old-timey statement, 'I went weak in the knees!' However, there was one key difference from the home-ec-room incident."

Koizumi held the second page aloft.

"This time, the model did not vanish. The rest of the basketball team arrived shortly after, perhaps cutting off its escape. The team members went to the biology room with a teacher who happened to have arrived early, and naturally, the model was not there. The team unanimously agreed to move their sinister intruder back to the biology room, and all cursed the name of whoever was responsible for this prank."

A prank... Well, that would be the first assumption. Was this the end of it?

"The third incident comes with a photo," Koizumi said, in the exact same tone of voice. "This time, it took place after school, as the sun was setting. According to a member of the school newspaper staff, work on the latest issue had run late, and they were only just ready to leave. As they were walking down the school corridor, they spotted someone moving about in a classroom in the opposite building. Since the lights in the room were off, they grew suspicious and looked closer—and noticed the figure was not in uniform. Or clothed at all. They squinted—"

And it was the anatomical model.

"The reporter hesitated but ultimately lacked the courage to investigate in person. However, he did have the presence of mind to pull out his phone and take a picture. Then he took that directly to the faculty room, found a teacher still there, and raced directly back to the biology room with them in tow."

Was it there or not?

"It was. The model was right where it should have been, in the back of the room, and the reporter had no choice but to doubt his own eyes. It had been mere minutes since the first sighting and their arrival at the biology room, which would mean someone—he did not know who—had moved the model from the classroom to the biology room, unseen, and successfully fled the scene."

Koizumi slid the reporter's photo across the desk.

The subject was far away, shot on a low-res camera and blurred by shaky hands, then printed out with a cheap color printer. There was no way I would've guessed it was an anatomical model without being told in advance. It seemed unlikely this could be used as hard evidence.

Before I could ask, Koizumi added, "The data has no record of a fourth incident."

So what conclusions had the mystery club drawn from all this?

Koizumi flipped the pages back over, skimming through them. "Nothing written here. I get the impression they drew up the facts but have yet to reach a solution."

Huh. Well, that's strange.

"Which one?"

Quite a few things are bugging me, actually. Not just the content of the story, but the fact that the mystery club passed this enigma our way. Judging by your response just now, I'm guessing you agree.

"Yes, well…there's a number of key points here."

Not to jump on your phrasing, but yes, the *key* is really jumping out at me here. The biology room, home ec room, and gym storeroom would all be locked, normally. If students needed access in the morning, whoever was the first to arrive would have to go get the key, and whoever was the last to leave in the evening would lock up before they left. None of these three stories mention whether the doors were locked, and I'm guessing you didn't just gloss over that, right?

"Certainly not."

Then we can assume the mystery club intentionally left it out.

One thing we can say for sure is that whoever was moving the model around was also in a position to open all three rooms whenever they pleased.

"Which narrows down the potential suspects considerably."

And all three incidents mention a teacher who "just happened" to be in the faculty room. Were these different people?

"No names are mentioned, so this is unclear. The way it's phrased, you could interpret it that way—or the opposite. But if this teacher is working with the culprit, the mystery is easily resolved. That would be much simpler than having a spare key made."

The other obvious revelation is that there are two anatomical models.

"What makes you say that?"

"Otherwise, we'd have to admit we live in a world where teleportation is possible."

In the first and third cases, the models seen by the early Sweets Appreciation Society girl to reach the home ec room and the lingering school-paper reporter were not the same as the model in the biology room. No matter how fast they dashed over there, they would find it waiting for them. Meanwhile, the culprit could calmly hide the second model once the witness ran off.

"Hide it where? They're hardly small enough to be easily hidden."

I'm not sure if this is true for the one in the biology room, but you can usually take apart those models. Disassemble it, stuff the pieces in an oversize duffel bag, maybe several. Easier if there's more than one culprit.

"That would make sense. Would that make the second case with the basketball team an attempt at camouflage? Did the culprits actually move the model from the biology room, using that as misdirection to disguise the fact that there were actually two models?"

Might be another reason, though.

"Namely?"

The home ec incident is the only anatomical terrorism incident with a perceivable motive. Since you mentioned the Sweets Appreciation Society had declared independence from the home ec club—any time two groups are using the same room, there's the potential for conflict, and the split itself might be the cause of it.

Either way, it wouldn't be at all surprising if the home ec club members had gotten fed up and decided to put the fear of biology into the Sweets Appreciation Society.

"And if they were all in the home ec room together, they could easily overhear when someone would be arriving early. But what significance does the fish have?"

That just served as a hint that the home ec club was likely responsible—so perhaps it was intended as an overt warning. That, or it was just done for meaningless shock value.

"Where'd they find an exact duplicate model?"

Probably got a used one in some online auction, or maybe they thought of this plan because they found one lying around in the first place.

"So the first case is the real one, the second a ruse to hide the method, and the third..."

Was done to play up the anatomical model's spooky vibe. Someone prone to believing in ghosts or ghoulies would definitely be at the front of the line for fear of moving mannequins. Perhaps the Sweets Appreciation Society girl in the first case was one of them. And the last witness being a reporter, planned or not, scored the story a lot of credibility—no better way to ensure the whole thing ends up in print.

"Ha-ha, so it started as somebody's prank, then the second and third incidents only served to enhance the supernatural aspects, and as the uproar grew bigger, the more scared everyone became. Well thought-out."

"By the mystery club, that is."

Koizumi's faint smile showed no doubt.

"I know you've picked up on it."

"Have I?"

Please. There's no dated article on the terrifying anatomical model case. No clue when this took place—but it certainly wasn't after we enrolled. No way something like this would happen without reaching Haruhi's ears. But we can safely assume this wasn't in the past, either. Why? Because that's exactly the sort of school horror story—or wonder—that Haruhi is looking for. Even if they classified it as a mystery that only appears like horror on the surface, if they had something like this in their files, they'd have told her about it at lunch when she asked.

"This is a fictional tale created by the mystery research club," I concluded. "Probably the work of the president or the club seniors. Haruhi's messenger bird brought the question to them at lunch, and they wrote this up in the meantime, then sent it along to us via the same bird. Effectively a pop quiz directed right at her."

And you're the one who said it was a trick, not anything occult, Koizumi.

"They snuck an occultish school mystery of their own creation into the pile of seven-wonders data. How droll. When did you first realize it was fiction?"

The moment they failed to mention the key. If they clearly stated the rooms involved were locked, then any idiot would suspect the teacher. Once you realize that, the rest is easy to figure out.

Of course, my solution might be off base, and maybe the person who recorded the details had been too lazy to take note of everyone fussing with keys. It *would* have broken up the flow of the story.

"That said, I'm impressed they concocted this so quickly. Even providing a photograph."

They even invented the Sweets Appreciation Society. I doubt any such group actually exists. As for the picture, let's just make impressed noises about modern photo-doctoring techniques.

"That leaves us with one problem."

Koizumi placed a finger on his brow.

"If this is a challenge from the mystery club to Suzumiya, you've just ruined it. What do you say to that?"

Oh, that hadn't occurred to me. Still…

"My answer might not be the final truth. There could be several other twists hidden, and I got fooled by one of them. Let's hope Haruhi's wits get us through the final round."

"If Suzumiya asks, then you should go over your deductions once again."

The Terrifying Moving Anatomical Model:
For details, reference the report drawn up by the mystery research club.

Koizumi's notes were definitely getting lazier. I got sick of looking at his smirk and turned toward better-looking pastures.

I thought she'd been awfully quiet.

"…*Zzz*…"

Asahina had her elbows on the table and was resting her chin on her hands, sound asleep.

"………"

Nagato was now on the sixth volume of juvenile horror stories.

Perhaps this was simply proof they were both bored.

"Now we have only one of the seven wonders left."

Why look so disappointed?

Koizumi flipped through the pages. "Popular school-horror tropes we've yet to touch upon include dancing old books, the bust of Bach in the music room changing expressions, the *Mona Lisa* in the art room yawning, basketballs bouncing in an empty gym, something grabbing your leg when you swim in the pool at night, a school version of a *zashiki-warashi*, etc."

Old books that moved were too similar to the anatomical model. The art things were just optical illusions designed to look weird from different angles. The invisible/chameleon man wasn't doing anything but dribbling and therefore too dull even with the supernatural twist. If there really was something lurking in a freshwater pool, then it was probably a *kappa*, and we could just bribe that classic folktale creature with some cucumbers. And that last bit about a homebound guardian spirit already described a member of our brigade.

"How about this?" he said, grimly examining the last page of the report. "Nobody knows what the seventh wonder is. If anyone finds out, they vanish."

Sure you just can't be bothered to think of a seventh? I mean, dreaming up six was pretty hard work, so it's not like the rest of us are bursting with ideas.

"If nobody knows it, wouldn't that make her want to know it all the more?"

We were obviously referring to Haruhi.

"That's hardly an issue," Koizumi said. "In the scale of phenomena Suzumiya has generated, wishing to know what must exist is far preferable to creating what does not."

Are those two concepts that different?

"Consider it this way. Which impacts the world at large more? Making something never seen before? Or locating something that has been lost?"

Only gods and con men could do the first. Although, the possibility of a summer archaeological dig was sounding more and more plausible.

"And I'm worried that not leaving her at least one mystery to create herself will lead to trouble."

Yeah, making sure she stayed content could be tricky. I was

starting to get the hang of it, but I wasn't particularly pleased about that. Spending over a year under the human personification of arrogance meant I was getting awfully good at predicting how the boss would react.

Koizumi and I went into a huddle, and the seventh wonder ended up like this.

Nobody knows the seventh wonder, and nobody should. That is the wonder of the seventh wonder.

"A bit too succinct, perhaps?"

Good enough for Haruhi. The fact that nobody knew was the whole premise of this wonder, and the condition that kept it fantastical. The moment it became known, it would cease to be a wonder, destroying the seven wonders themselves. You could only have seven wonders if there were seven, after all, so one of them had to be something nobody knew.

"Russell's paradox? Most apt. That should help convince Suzumiya."

Apt my ass. That said, if *you're* convinced, I'm good. Give this Russell dude my regards.

"We just have to type up a clean version of this and print it out, and we'll be ready."

Koizumi had managed to fill two pages with handwritten notes, and he spread them out on the table, then massaged the back of his neck.

"............"

Nagato seemed to have finished her reading. She picked up the notes, moved over to the laptop the computer club had paid her off with, and started typing at eye-watering speed.

I doubt it took more than a minute.

A few seconds after Nagato tapped the "enter" key with a certain finality, the inkjet printer in the corner hummed to life and started working.

She may have seemed like she was just reading, but I guess she'd been paying attention after all. Whew. Then again, that level of multitasking was well within her specs.

This was a far cry from Asahina, who was totally dozing, but any situation that required Asahina's help was dire indeed, so let's call that a good sign. Asahina in a maid outfit devoting herself to menial tasks around the clubroom was my barometer for world peace.

The printer finished up its job and went into cooldown mode. Koizumi thanked Nagato as I got up to retrieve the results.

End of May, SOS Brigade's Selected Seven Wonders of North High

The wonders are as follows.

   1. Legend of Ninomiya Kinjiro's Statue
   2. Mystery of the Music Room
   3. Secret of the Staircase
   4. Uncanny Mirror on the Bridge…

I'll omit the rest, but the sheet had the full details of the seven wonders created by the SOS Brigade (sans Haruhi) by dint of Koizumi and myself rambling on endlessly and Nagato and Asahina chiming in with specific and timely advice. The document read like a proper report, and the recipient was a given.

Koizumi had been closely monitoring his phone's screen, but that seemed to have reached a decisive end because he slipped it back in his pocket, caught my eye, and winked.

A moment later, I heard footsteps approaching at Mach speed right before the door slammed open.

"Listen up, people! I got good news!"

Our chief, Haruhi Suzumiya, beamed a smile at us that would shame the sun god at high noon.

Just the sight of this expression felt like it raised the temperature in the clubroom by 0.5°C.

*　　*　　*

The noise of the door and Haruhi's mouth were loud enough that Asahina was yanked back from the world of dreams. She jumped, let out a weird yelp of "Hnauu!" and hastily scrambled to her feet.

"O-oh, Suzumiya!" she said. "Good morning!"

"Mornin', Mikuru," Haruhi said, clearly in an excellent mood. She strode over to the chief's desk, then spun back to face us, waving her index finger like a conductor's baton. "I realized something this morning!"

When nobody else spoke up, I reluctantly asked, "And that was?"

"We've been busy searching for the seven wonders of this world, but despite showing up here every day, we've never once thought to ask about the seven wonders passed down in the halls of this very school!"

Are there any? Passed down, I mean.

"I looked into it, but apparently not! But if you think about it for a moment, this is only natural. This is a public school and hardly boasts much of a history. But that's the good news!"

She was now pacing back and forth.

"All we have to do is make our own seven wonders! For the benefit of all students to come! Having wonders will enrich every student's school life!"

What the enriching properties of spooky stories were supposed to be was anyone's guess, but I suppose they did at least add flavor to your day.

Before Haruhi could say another word, I stopped her.

"First, there's something you should see."

"What?"

Haruhi looked around, sensing something different in the air.

Nagato was frozen at the laptop, her finger still on the "enter" key. Asahina was holding the tray like a shield in front of her, looking nervous. Koizumi had messed up his expression selection big-time, and the result was indescribably odd.

I slowly reached out and picked up the printed report we'd left lying on the table.

"We figured you'd suggest something like that," I explained.

Then I handed her the proposal the rest of us had drawn up.

"What's this?"

Haruhi glanced over it, and her expression changed instantly. She was never hard to read. She looked like she was imagining what bugs would taste like if you deep-fried them.

"Aha. The mystery club, huh?"

She'd already figured out the cause. There was no doubt that Haruhi was quick on the uptake.

She glanced at *Notable Tales, Old and New* and the files of loose papers piled on the table, and she narrowed her eyes like a sleepy spectacled caiman.

"Guess I shouldn't have asked *her*," she muttered.

No use regretting the choice, whatever the outcome—that girl had turned out to be far more productive than anyone could have imagined. You'd have to be Sherlock Holmes to realize an off-the-cuff question would lead to them turning over a mountain of data *and* a mystery of their own devising that very afternoon.

"I may have underestimated the mystery research club," Haruhi admitted.

Then she gave each of us a glare that suggested mercy was not in the cards.

"But you all worked awfully fast, too. I suppose I should be proud! It's a chief's duty to praise the growth of her brigade."

She didn't look all that pleased, though.

"Well, you sure took your time getting here. What have you been up to?"

"I thought the principal might know some old stories," Haruhi grumbled. "I went to pick his brain, and somehow, we ended up playing shogi, and my king ended up chasing his around the board all the way to the far edge."

Ah, Entering King. That *would* take a while...

I shot Koizumi a sidelong glance, and he had an innocent smile plastered on his face. Cooperators beyond the student council, huh? Guess that included the principal.

"I guess I should have just had tea and a rice cracker before coming right to the clubroom. Dammit."

Haruhi couldn't find a proper target to vent her frustration on. You didn't often see her at such a loss. She curled her lips this way and that, like they were fighting to keep words from spilling out.

What is it? Bottling it up isn't good for you.

"Argh!" she yelled. If she'd been alone, she probably would've stamped her feet. "You all had fun without me!"

She was waving her hands all over now.

"I wanted to be part of this!"

Go on, let it out.

I was thoroughly enjoying this.

"So we going with these seven wonders or what? I mean, your brigade did handcraft them just for you, putting ye olde three heads (plus one) together, pooling all the inspiration, imagination, and innovation we could muster."

"Okay, fine," Haruhi said, sighing through pursed lips. She had come to terms with the situation, but only just.

Come to think of it, I think this was the first time we'd so thoroughly gotten the jump on her.

Normally, Haruhi just blurted stuff out, and we were all dragged along in her wake, hastily trying to resolve whatever phenomenon she caused, so it wasn't often we got to preempt that.

Perhaps this would be an effective strategy going forward. Predict what schemes Haruhi might concoct next, then make sure we were ready. The moment she blew the kickoff whistle, we'd be ready to call no side and bring it to an immediate close. I wasn't sure if it would make a noticeable impact on our workload, but having several strategies ready was the foundation of any war planning. All that being said, we'll have to proceed with caution, since there's always a chance that we could get outplayed despite our best intentions and end up exacerbating the chaos.

"I've got some gripes, though. What's this crap about Ninomiya Kinjiro? We don't have a statue of him here!"

I am shocked to hear such a pragmatic concern from you. Excuse me while I shed a tear.

"Huh? Don't be stupid."

Just because she'd approved of the list in principle didn't mean Haruhi was so amenable that she'd leave the specifics unchallenged. She flicked the printout of our seven wonders with one finger, giving her take on each.

"A ghost playing *4'33"*, huh? We've got a band room, too, with all the wind instruments you could want. Instead of just a piano, let's add a bunch more instruments and go with the orchestral version. That'll liven things up. Should be more fun for the ghosts."

A full wind orchestra playing a silent piece of music. And all performers were ghosts. That certainly sounded a lot less lonely. Apparently, Haruhi had something against ghost stories that were sad.

Haruhi was quickly working her way through the third entry.

"Air conditioners in classrooms? That's just wishful thinking."

Can we make it happen?

"*I* certainly can't! I guess I can mention it to the principal next time I see him."

Let's call that a faint ray of hope.

"I was wondering about this mirror myself," Haruhi said. She considered Nagato's proposal. "If we ended up with D-amino acids, wouldn't that prevent us from absorbing protein? I suppose that would speed diets up. If word about this mirror gets out to the overeaters, it'll have clients lining up! It oughtta charge a hundred yen each and make a killing. But we wouldn't want it being too effective, so let's put a generous time limit on the effect, like, say, forty-eight hours."

I thought she'd be interested in the trip to a fantasy world, but instead…

"What's this about sequels? Anyone who doesn't have the guts to do their best with the first go-around doesn't get to have a series. And you're giving these people way too much plot armor. The basic idea is fine, but you can come up with a better story than this."

"Certainly," Koizumi said, his smile so strained that I thought he was gonna pull a cheek muscle. You could see both strained rage and strained joy—there should be a better way to explain this. If only *strage* and *stroy* were real words.

As for the sixth wonder…

"The mystery club did it!" she declared immediately. "At least, they did on a meta level. But if we consider the story on its own merits, I have to assume the true culprits are the secret society known only as the Friends of the Anatomical Model. These serial acts of anatomical terror would definitely have continued unabated. After all, this secret society is—"

Deciding that was an inherently dangerous key word I could not risk following up on, I point-blank ignored her.

"Oh, whatever," Haruhi said as she tossed our report on her desk. She crossed her arms and turned back toward us.

No comment about the seventh wonder, then?

I saw a brilliant smile creeping back onto her face and quickly grew concerned. Before I could identify the source of this concern, Haruhi spelled it out for me.

"I'm gonna think up an eighth wonder all on my own!"

"Huh?" I said reflexively. "Can you read? Nobody knows what the seventh wonder is, so if there's suddenly an eighth one, the setting'll be inconsistent!"

"The seventh one still exists; it just isn't yet known. That's fine, whatever. It's esoteric."

Yeah, but…

"Look, Kyon. Nobody knowing something is totally different from it not existing. Nobody knows what the 9,999-quadrillionth digit of pi is yet, probably, but we do know that's definitely a number between 0 and 9."

Yeah, but…

"The seven wonders of North High! That list is complete as is. I respect that. The report also shows how much work you guys put in."

How nice of you say.

"But nothing can stop me from making an eighth wonder."

But then there won't be seven wonders.

"The Four Heavenly Kings get a fifth member all the time!"

In what world? You don't wanna piss them off, do you?

"I'm talking about the originals! There's basically five of them."

Haruhi started counting on her fingers.

"*Jikoku-ten, Zocho-ten, Komoku-ten, Tamon-ten, Bishamon-ten.* See? Five."

I almost nodded, but…

"One of those is someone's alter ego. Right?"

"They say *Tamon-ten* is another name for *Bishamon-ten*, but that's just a trick to fool people in the next life. In actual fact, *Tamon-ten* and *Bishamon-ten* were twins! Maybe one of them was actually a split personality of the other. Or the two of them were playing the same role. Doesn't matter! It's more dramatic that way!"

I dunno what kinda drama this was supposed to be, but we probably shouldn't say things that might offend Buddha. Or whatever the Four Heavenly Kings were. Besides, why in the world would *Taishaku-ten*'s entourage need to trick people in the afterlife by disguising how many of them there actually were?

"Don't let your thoughts get calcified! The future demands flexibility! Don't fall behind the times now! The new era will have eight wonders in it."

An age of eight wonders, huh? Yup, still made no sense.

I looked around, hoping someone else would back my opposition, but only Koizumi even met my eyes, and he simply raised his hands, palms turned upward. Clearly a sign of unconditional surrender.

Asahina was hastily moving toward the tea-prep area, like she was fleeing tentacles emerging from Haruhi's mouth. Nagato had moved on to the next volume of the children's horror series.

This is not fair, people.

Wrestling with seventh wonder number eight until it became something unobtrusive was gonna fall completely on my shoulders.

If every school in Japan had eight wonders the following day, this would be all Haruhi's fault.

She flung herself into the chief's chair.

"Mikuru! Tea."

"Coming!"

"Make it strong as night."

"How about a hot double helping of plum kelp tea?" Asahina said, happily scurrying about her task.

Haruhi was flitting from the report typed up by the SOS Brigade's reigning WPS champ, Nagato, to the data provided by the mystery research team, and back again, pausing only to make vaguely brooding sounds, grin wickedly, or scowl furiously. Best not to interfere.

I returned to my own folding chair, and Koizumi leaned in to whisper something to me. We keeping secrets now?

80

"*I* don't mind saying it louder, but...," he murmured. "There is one thing I've been wondering about beyond the seven wonders."

He paused for effect.

"Namely, why you object to addressing that girl from the mystery club with a nickname."

No reason.

"Really?"

What's your point?

"Suzumiya has had a nickname for you this whole time. In other words, this signifies your disposition."

I dunno what you mean.

"That girl calls Suzumiya *Haru*, right? Rather like how you—"

Okay, don't finish that thought.

"—regularly call Suzumiya by her given name. No titles or honorifics."

I need a way to shut him up. Right now.

"A given name sans honorifics is undeniably a sign of affection, but not quite on the same level as a nickname. However, you have no nickname for Suzumiya, so you're reluctant to address any other women by a nickname instead, correct? Perhaps you aren't consciously aware of that fact, but if you are—then it's a deliberate choice."

I had no response to that.

"I have no opinion on whether calling someone by their name alone is any more or less intimate than a nickname, or whether you can read much into their relationship without more information."

Even if you did, you don't have to share it.

"Suzumiya has called you by a nickname from the get-go, so I hardly think it would be inappropriate for you to call her Haru. Try to imagine yourself calling her that."

I did. Huge mistake. Walked right into his web of crafty words. Before I could stop myself, my imagination was already spooling out that scenario, guesstimating Haruhi's reaction and expression— I felt sick.

Seeing me turn pale, Koizumi let out what can only be described as a snicker and said, "Pace yourself."

I dunno if that was a warning or a portent or merely a considerate word, but he left me with that, grabbed the pages he'd been taking notes on, and began brainstorming more details for the fifth wonder's fantasy setting. How many submissions would it take before Haruhi's standards were met?

I need a favor from you.

Come up with an amusing nickname for Haruhi. If I find one I like, I might consider calling her that. Address it to North High Literature Club, attn the SOS Brigade. I will announce the results at a later date.

With no one to talk to, I looked around and flipped over the top card of the deck from the abandoned bozu mekuri game.

THOUGH, INDEED, I LOVE, / YET THE RUMOR OF MY LOVE / HAD GONE FAR AND WIDE, / WHEN NO MAN, ERE THEN, COULD KNOW / THAT I HAD BEGUN TO LOVE.

I'd been hoping these would work like a tarot deck and give me a sign related to my current state of mind, but this was clearly unrelated. I'd have to try another.

WOULD THAT THIS, OUR WORLD, / MIGHT BE EVER AS IT IS! / WHAT A LOVELY SCENE! / SEE THAT FISHERWOMAN'S BOAT, / ROPE-DRAWN, TOWED ALONG THE BEACH.

I started to reach for a third…then thought better of it.

Drawing fortunes until you got one you liked wasn't very sensible. And since the cards failed to include a modern translation, I wasn't even really sure what they were saying.

I'd have to remind Koizumi to restrict the games he brought to ones we could play without needing a whole lesson first. Didn't matter if they were foreign or domestic—and that thought reminded me of something.

Right. I'd better pass that on. The mystery club had asked Nagato for a submission. Nagato was in the literature club, so technically that might not concern us, but it *had* been Haruhi who'd headed up our magazine project.

"Yo, Haruhi."

"What, Kyon?"

She raised an eyebrow over the brim of her double serving of plum kelp tea.

No clue when she'd moved, but Nagato was back on her chair in the corner, wrapped in silence, reading once more. Having apparently polished off the entire series of children's horror stories, she'd taken up her massive dictionary again.

Asahina was boiling more water, hemming and hawing over what tea to brew next. She had a tea canister in each hand.

Koizumi was prodding his brow with the butt of his mechanical pencil, muttering ideas for the fantasy world under his breath. Not his usual vibe at all, and honestly a bit creepy.

Haruhi was in her usual seat, radiating burning passion like she was trying to remind the air in the room what temperature it should be.

"The mystery club wanted a favor from Nagato."

"Oh? What sort of favor?"

Spring was slipping by, and crouched beyond this season of new green growth were dazzling sunshine and tropical temperatures. The SOS Brigade truly was as it ever was.

TSURUYA'S CHALLENGE

This is a recent development, but lately, after school, in a corner of the North High literature club, I've heard a number of worrying conversations.

Lots of ominous phrases, like *alibi trick, impossible crime, somethingsomething murders, the tragedy of whatchamacallit,* or *XYZ-phobia.* Or even more enigmatic expressions, like *iodine tincture bottle, the Birlstone gambit, red herring, Y's mandolin, the Ackroyd twist,* and other jargon that no amateur had much hope of understanding. It was a small room, so it was hard not to overhear.

There were three main participants in these discussions. They centered around Nagato, but all she did was sit on her folding chair in the corner with a book open on her lap, silently reading. Her lack of movement was so distinct that it would've been convincing if someone claimed she was set in paraffin wax, meaning the other two participants were deliberately choosing to stand and talk in her vicinity so she only had to literally occupy the center between them. The majority of the conversation was carried by Koizumi and a rare honey-blond guest, while Nagato uttered no more than the bare minimum required to communicate…which only happened on exceedingly rare occasions.

While Nagato maintained a facial expression best described as an absence of emotion, the other two were flinging around the aforementioned phrases with blinding smiles and voices full of delight. I gotta admit, it was unnerving. Discussing murders, dismemberment, and headless corpses with cheery smiles? That's the domain of fanatics, if not outright lunatics.

Turning my gaze in the opposite direction, I spotted a charming maid.

Clad in a springtime maid outfit, the SOS Brigade's chamomile bouquet, Asahina, was staring at a grid laid out on the long table. It was a 4×4 grid of round spaces, with a number of wooden pieces on them. She had one such piece held in her fingers.

"Um…hmm…?"

The noises she made while deep in thought were adorable. She'd been thinking for a good five minutes now, her head tilting, her brows furrowing, her lashes batting against the air, examining the board from every possible angle. It was hard to believe this maid was a year above me, but I could never get tired of watching her face. It had the same soothing effect you'd get from watching a sleeping kitten. The remaining tea in my mug had gone cold, though.

"A question for both of you," Koizumi started, addressing Nagato and our guest. "Of all the orthodox mystery novels you've read, what would you deem the best?"

"You want to know the greatest-of-all-time story that I've ever read?" T asked, poking her chin with one finger, blond hair swaying. She was from the mystery research club. "That range is way too broad. I can't possibly narrow it down that far. Plus, I must admit I'm hardly an expert on *Japanese* mystery novels."

"………" Nagato said nothing, never even looking up from her page.

"Then let's go international. And to narrow the scope, what would you say is the finest work by John Dickson Carr? However, since *The Three Coffins*, *The Judas Windows*, and *The Plague Court Murders* are all in the hall of fame, I'd prefer you choose from the remainder of his oeuvre."

Who ran this hall of fame?

In response to Koizumi's proposal, T brushed back her bangs. Must be a habit of hers.

She normally let her blond locks spill onto her brow however they pleased, but today, for once, she had an unadorned hairpin holding them back. She flicked aside a single strand that had escaped that pin and said, "I applaud the direct simplicity of your inquiry. Naturally, I have not read every work by him, but from what I have, I'd have to go with *The Emperor's Snuff-Box*."

"Oh? Both surprising yet perhaps not."

"Too obvious a choice? I just like what I like and refuse to deny those feelings. Koizumi, your turn."

"If I must pick one, it would have to be *The Burning Court*. The admission in the epilogue hit me like nothing else. A masterful fusion of horror and mystery, a real testament to his writing chops, and a flawlessly constructed plot."

"Oof. Hard to argue with that," T said. She peered down at Nagato. "What's your pick, Nagato?"

"*The Problem of the Green Capsule*," said a flat voice below them.

"Huh," said Koizumi.

"Oh?" said T.

They glanced at each other.

"That is unexpected. I wonder what— No, perhaps a trick like that, at that time? Plus, the thing."

"Ah yes, the thing with the— That must be it. Hard to beat *that*."

I had no idea what they were talking about, but they seemed to all be on the same page somehow, which was frightening.

Honestly, I thought the greatest mystery here was that Nagato had responded to a question from someone *not* in the SOS Brigade, but I suspected neither person talking above her head would agree.

"Then let me ask," T said with delight. "What is your favorite Anthony Berkeley? Limiting your answer to the works published under that name. I assume you've read them all?"

"It has to be *The Poisoned Chocolates Case*," Koizumi said without hesitation. "You?"

"*The Poisoned Chocolates Case*. Nagato?"

"...*Poisoned Chocolates*."

Koizumi and T both groaned.

"I suppose that's to be expected. If we eliminate that option... then either *Top Storey Murder* or *The Second Shot*."

"We can't dismiss *Trial and Error* or *The Wychford Poisoning Case*. Both are quite a riot."

A thoughtful silence settled over the area around Nagato's chair.

"I suppose that covers Berkeley. One of those authors whose most famous work has such impact that it's like the sun while the rest are mere planets. The comparisons of popularity and significance are far too lopsided."

"Mm-hmm. The rare mystery novel you can confidently recommend to both hardcore fans and beginners."

Were they coming up with a staff-favorites display for a bookstore?

T placed her fingers on her hairpin. "Who's next?"

"........."

Nagato silently turned a page.

"Allow me to make another suggestion, then. We cannot discuss orthodox mysteries without mentioning our favorite Ellery Queen. Yours?"

"I have a proposal," T said, raising a finger. "Let's limit it to titles with the name of a country in them. I'm ashamed to admit that, at present, I have yet to read many of the rest. Beyond *X* and *Y*, obviously."

"So that eliminates *The Tragedy of Y*?" Koizumi said, seeming rather happy about that. "Fair enough. The nationality mysteries are a treasure trove in their own right."

"To answer my own question, I'd have to go with *The Egyptian Cross Mystery*. There's a certain elegance in simplicity."

"I am firmly in *The Siamese Twin Mystery* camp. Yes, yes, I know! I'm aware of all the objections. It certainly has its share of flaws. But that climax! The characters placed in extreme peril, as Ellery makes his deductions and pinpoints the culprit, and the miracle that saves them just as their doom seems inevitable! Right as the finale draws near, Inspector Queen delivers a simple line, a statement of pure fact that ends the whole tale. The curtains fall in the most beautiful resolution I've ever seen."

"So you value it less as an orthodox mystery and more for its pure entertainment value? They do say *every book its reader*, but that emphasis on the final scene does certainly seem like a very personal preference. Fascinating. Nagato, I'd love to hear your answer."

"*Greek Coffin*," Nagato muttered.

"Really? *The Greek Coffin Mystery*? A surprisingly banal choice for you."

Nagato's fingers twitched at T's comment, pausing mid-page-turn.

Koizumi smiled. "I think it's very Nagato. It's the single thickest volume in the series."

I wasn't sure that helped.

"It receives every bit as much praise as *The Dutch Shoe Mystery* or *The Egyptian Cross Mystery*," he added. "I have no objections."

"That said, Ikki Koizumi, there are very few who would recommend *The Siamese Twin Mystery* in the same light."

"Perhaps. But if nothing else, that's more than you can say for *The Chinese Orange Mystery*."

"Oh my god, that one… Yeah. Come to think of it, *Siamese Twin* is also famous for lacking a Challenge to the Reader. The rest of the books in the series all contain one right before the final solution is revealed. I have long suspected this is because the authors lacked confidence in the logic of the case in question. You can't tell me they simply forgot to include it."

Koizumi nodded, his gaze wandering over to the bookshelf nearby.

"Naturally, the lack of a Challenge in *Siamese Twin* was a conscious choice on Queen's part. However, this is not due to any vagaries in the deductive reasoning. The reasons are detailed in Kaoru Kitamura's Ellery Queen pastiche, *The Japanese Coin Mystery: Ellery Queen's Last Case*. A copy of which happens to be right here!"

He plucked one of Nagato's possessions off the shelf, flipping through it.

"I'll avoid spoilers, of course, but I'd like to quote one of the characters in this novel. Starting in the middle of a speech, I'm afraid.

"A set of deductions is prepared for each arrest. The story is composed of shifting logic. The source of fascination lies in the ever-changing hues, and in wondering where it will wind up, and how far it will go. Thus, a Challenge to the Reader flies in the face of that fundamental ethos. Placing that in the table of contents would be tantamount to announcing all deductions before that point are flawed.

"Later, it says:

"In *Siamese Twin*, it's the culprit's own actions that prove decisive in identifying them. Naturally, there are clues and deductions to be found. But the final result is achieved without reasoning. It is not that this story lacked a Challenge. *Siamese Twin* was never a work that could have contained one in the first place.

"What do you say to that? Compare these two passages against the plot of *Siamese Twin*. Makes sense, does it not?"

Koizumi was looking at Nagato. She was staring at the book on her lap, but I could tell her head was tilted ever so slightly to one side, like, only measurable in millimeters tilted. It soon reverted to an upright position. Evidently, she had engaged in some rapid processing and finally arrived at a conclusion. She promptly went right back to reading.

T threw her hands up.

"I am adrift in a sea of fog," she said. "Ikki Koizumi, I demand further explanation. Make it more dolce and adagio."

Was that cooking jargon or something?

"Kaoru Kitamura explains it using terms like *the process of temporary elimination* or *circular analysis*, but if you'll excuse the gross oversimplification, he's saying *the Challenge to the Reader is not only unnecessary for the effective identification of the culprit, but it is actively detrimental*. That would be the gist of it."

I couldn't speak for T, but I did not follow any of that.

"Perhaps you have to read it to understand. But before you do, you must read *The Siamese Twin Mystery* while pondering the question of why it is the only book in the nationality series to lack a Challenge to the Reader. If you then read *The Japanese Coin Mystery* as a supplement to that, I am sure you will make new discoveries. Anyone out there who has not read both, I heartily recommend doing so."

No one's going to do anything that convoluted. People should be able to read however they want.

"A fair point," Koizumi said, putting the book back on the shelf. "However, I believe there is one other reason *Siamese Twin* lacks a Challenge."

"Oh? What's that?"

The SOS Brigade's certified most handsome member flashed a smile at T.

"*Siamese* takes place in a mountaintop home encircled by a forest fire. It is the one closed-circle mystery in the nationality series."

"Come to think of it, that's absolutely right. But what of it?"

"Consider the benefits of the closed-circle trope. The characters involved are unable to leave, and no additional characters can appear. In other words, the number of potential criminals is finite, and the number of suspects is correspondingly limited."

"No unnecessary characters."

"Another advantage, yes. Too many characters merely add to the chaos. Especially when the setting is overseas."

"I have way more trouble remembering Japanese names! But what relation does the closed-circle thing have to the Challenge to the Reader?"

"When the suspects are trapped somewhere, their number is limited, and the scope of deduction need not expand beyond that circle. In *Siamese Twin*, the culprit *must* be one of the people trapped in the residence with no means of escape. I believe Queen assumed the case was too simple, and no challenge was warranted."

"I see. Islands cut off by a rainstorm or snowed in lodges provide plenty of atmosphere, limit the head count, and streamline plots, which is exactly why they're effective— Is that your point, Koizumi?"

We'd done both stormy islands and snowed-in lodges before. I'd prefer this conversation between Koizumi and T not give Haruhi any more ideas on how to create closed-circle situations. Fortunately, she was not currently present.

"Let's get back to basics." Koizumi smiled again. "What purpose do those Challenges serve?"

"They're telling the readers, *If you've read this far, the truth should be evident, so go on, try to figure it out! Naturally, the mystery I've concocted will be far too difficult for an oily sardine head like you to solve, mwa-ha-ha-ha-ha!* Basically bragging about how confident they are."

"I think there are precious few writers who add challenges with quite that much arrogance."

"In that case, what else is there?"

"I would think the opposite is more common."

"How so?"

Rather than answer immediately, Koizumi's eyes became unfocused.

"This notion was inspired by an orthodox mystery I read recently."

Stick to the point.

"Stick to the point," T said.

"This mystery was quite heavy on the puzzler aspects, one of those classic works famous for its emphasis on strict logical underpinnings."

He turned his gaze to the bookshelf once more.

"The detective named five conditions that the culprit must meet, and only one person—A—met all five, thus A was the culprit. A very Queen-style process of elimination. However…"

Koizumi seemed to be running his eyes across the spines of Nagato's paperback collection.

"Certainly, we readers knew only A met all five conditions. No one else had been described that way anywhere on the page. But how did the detective know this?"

"Aha." T grinned. "The readers can flip back to the cast list at the front, but the detective is part of the cast and can't do the same."

"Put simply, yes. The scene was not a closed circle, so no real limit was placed on the cast. Perhaps there was some third party out there who met all conditions but simply wasn't in the book. So how did he eliminate that possibility?"

"Good question."

"There was no real explanation. But this struck a chord with me. How does a character in the novel—not a writer or a reader, merely a member of the cast—know, out of all the countless people who met the conditions required to be the culprit, it must be one of the cast members?"

"Hmm. The so-called late Queen problem."

"Exactly." Koizumi was nodding, but what the hell was that?

"Someone has summarized the problem most adroitly, so allow me to bring them into the mix."

He plucked another novel from the shelf.

"Toru Hikawa's *The Penultimate Truth* has the detective—also named Toru Hikawa—explain it as follows.

> "...The Challenges to the Reader in the nationality series is largely unrelated to the chivalry Edogawa Ranpo examines. It is purely a product of logical *necessity*.
>
> "In brief, the author operates on a meta level within the work, which means they have a capacity for arbitrariness that makes anything possible. But if they exercise that potential, the aspect of 'fair play' crumbles. The Challenge is a device to forbid that arbitrariness—or more accurately, a means by which creators announce they have restricted themselves from using it.

"Furthermore:

> "...Based on a specific clue, the detective deduces A is the culprit. But this was in fact a clue left by the real culprit, B, who was aware it would mislead the detective into making that faulty deduction. The means to logically deduce this *only* exists outside the world—and the detective is merely a character who exists only

within the work and has no access to such means. That leads immediately to one vital conclusion—in the world of the story, it is *impossible* to logically deduce there is only one possible culprit. This is the destructive conclusion Norizuki—and Queen—arrived at.

"Well? Clear as a bell, right?"

Who the hell is Norizuki?

"Rintaro Norizuki. A mystery writer known as the modern-day Ellery Queen and a talented critic to boot. And the man who invented the concept of the late Queen problem."

Koizumi put the volume back in place and fished out another.

"To learn more, please consult the essay 'On Early Queen' included in this, *Rintaro Norizuki's Mystery School—Foreign Works—The Art of Complicated Murders.*"

Man, what doesn't that bookshelf have? Perhaps it's made from fourth-dimensional materials from the future.

"The Challenge to the Reader doesn't just bind the author's hands. It also has an undeniable effect on the reader. Norizuki writes that the Challenge functions to restrict the reader's ability to guess, to roll the dice, to intuit the logical culprit the author has constructed. He said, 'Only with this mutual restraint is a closed formula, or the self-contained gamespace of a puzzle created.'"

He couldn't have said that in a way I might actually understand?

"Basically, somewhere along the way, readers start to get a vague idea that someone *might* be the culprit, but even if they're *right*, the author can smugly insist the *reader* hasn't won. They're demanding that the reader deduce the culprit with elegant logic, not just a hunch."

No clue what the point of this conflict is, but I'm getting a clear sense of deep-seated love for this specific formula.

"If you understand that much, consider me satisfied."

Koizumi grabbed yet another book.

"There are many ways of examining the late Queen problem. Like the short story 'A Walk on New Year's Eve,' included in Alice Arisugawa's *Insights of Jiro Egami*. The following is a conversation between the fictional Alice Arisugawa and Egami.

> "But if a fake clue made it so the detective couldn't make flawless deductions, wouldn't that be bad?
>
> "If any information remains hidden, logical deductions and reasoning are necessarily impossible. This is true beyond the world of mysteries, too. But information contained within a novel is always finite, so this deductive impossibility is a greater factor in the real world. Yet out there, no matter what trouble arises, everyone's lives go on; perfection and infallibility may not exist, but the police and courts continue to function, and I can't imagine any of those people are concerned about the nature of mysteries.

"In other words, you need not feel overly conscious of it."

Does being a mystery writer mean you have to think about all kinds of nonsensical crap and not just tricks and logic? Sounds rough.

Koizumi was busy swapping out books again.

"We can sum up Egami's proposal in brief. In Kouji Ishizaki's *A Killer of Record*, there's a serial killer attempting to act according to a bizarre set of principles, and the following dialogue occurs as the characters attempt to profile the killer.

> "But what if the killer understands profiling? If their actions and the traces they leave behind are all done to bait us into profiling someone else entirely, what then? The investigators have no way of telling if a clue is intentionally left by the killer.

"The fictional Kouji Ishizaki hears this and responds:

"That's the Gödel problem. The orthodox mystery's dead end. The perennial conundrum.

"But yet another character responds:

"The Gödel problem arises through manipulated profiling. That means the Gödel problem crops up in real-world cases—and as a result, it inevitably occurs in orthodox mysteries as well.

"Pretty much the same conclusion as Egami, but framing the idea with the concept of profiling makes it easier to follow. Even when it's fiction, if you're basing the work on the real world, then the rules of your world follow those of the real one. It may seem self-evident, but there are many works where that isn't the case, so it is far from meaningless to discuss it explicitly."

I'm assuming the Gödel problem and the late Queen thingy are the same?

Also, is it, like, normal to have a character named after the author? Are orthodox mysteries I-novels by another name?

"We'll discuss characters who share the name of the author another time."

With that, Koizumi put the novel back and, this time, pulled out a B6-sized magazine.

"For a look at a more extreme opinion, Reito Nikaido's column, Logic Excalibur, said:

"No matter what qualities the detective might possess, the late Queen problem is simply an excuse for the writer and detective's laziness. Additionally, the detective is merely a genre device designed to carry out thought-based actions called 'deductions,' so this problem does not actually exist in any meaningful way.

"Quite dismissive, as you can see."

Very blunt, but refreshing. I hate getting caught up in a tangle of thoughts. Better to not think about anything and just look for the next move. Like I'm doing in this game with Asahina.

"Occam's razor? Certainly effective in the right time and place, but what you call 'a tangle of thoughts' is an enjoyable intellectual exercise for die-hard fans of the genre. Although, I certainly admit these topics tend to matter little to anyone outside the community."

I guess if you realize that, you aren't *too* far gone.

"For a much odder take, we have Reiichiro Fukami's *Inspector Oobeshimi's Case Files*, chapter seven, 'The Serial Tetrodotoxin Poisonings,' in which a detective yells:

> "In the mysteries to come, the cast will be required to have flexible thinking! To avoid falling into a late Queen problem, they'll be forced to question if they have all the facts, or if those facts are correct at all! Forced to constantly doubt themselves! And on occasion, required to do whatever they can to move beyond the boundaries of their own thoughts!

"Naturally, if you take it to this extreme, it's more of a joke than anything else. The detective is aware of being a character in a novel and capable of ignoring all metalevel considerations. In fact, if you don't go this far, your characters wouldn't be able to discuss these subjects in the first place."

But, uh, do you need to? Are orthodox-mystery writers like

penitent monks, deliberately choosing to put themselves through torment?

"Ultimately, the late Queen problem is derived from the mathematical concepts of Gödel's incompleteness theorems, but whatever value it may hold as a philosophical conundrum, there are many critics who argue against incorporating that discussion into the plot of an actual mystery novel."

Koizumi returned the volume he'd been reading from to its rightful position on the bookshelf.

"Back to the original topic..."

What was that again?

"The raison d'être for the Challenge to the Reader," T said. Guess one of us remembered. "Herr Koizumi. Say we have a mystery that is *not* a closed circle, and the logic employed is unable to narrow down the potential suspects to a specific set of people... Would a Challenge have a role there?"

"The Challenge is most effective in exactly that type of mystery. You want to limit the possible suspects to the cast, but the circumstances and setting do not allow it. One false move, and you might end up with everyone in the world as a potential suspect. So what then?"

"You can just drop in a Challenge. Phrase it right, and it solves all the problems! Make it sound like you're being both considerate and fair, while clearly stating the culprit is a definitely a character in the cast."

"No need to be so obvious! Just having a Challenge is enough to shape the readers' thoughts. Common sense dictates that the culprit won't be a third party whose name has never once appeared in the book—the author issuing a Challenge would never make the solution so arbitrary! But what if the author's goal is to trick them into that assumption? Unlikely. If the culprit was someone unrelated to the story itself— Well, if they were going for a curveball like that, then they'd never include a Challenge in the first place."

"So what would normally be an implicit understanding between the author and reader is being made explicit?"

"Exactly. Limiting the field to the cast in no way disadvantages the author; it simply prevents the reader from considering unnecessary suspects. This is an acknowledgement that the author had been unable to find a way to completely rule out the possibility of an unnamed third party being the true culprit."

So it's less of a challenge than an excuse.

"I wouldn't go that far," Koizumi said. "And there is one other factor—for mysteries that include a Challenge to the Reader, it's preferable that one member of the cast be named after the author. And the Challenge should be issued in their name."

"When the namesake is the narrator, we have both the Queen pattern and the Van Dine pattern," T pointed out.

"Either is perfectly acceptable," Koizumi said magnanimously. "It is clear that orthodox mysteries with a Challenge included are an intellectual game played between author and reader. And since it is the author who prepares the problem, the Challenge must likewise be issued in his name. However, if the author's name appears abruptly in the text, this adds an metatextual element to the work, which inevitably reduces immersion in the story itself. It pulls you back into reality. But if either the detective or a Watson-type share a name with the author, it becomes possible to seamlessly transition between the real world and the world of the story, or at least, effectively suggest as much."

We all pondered this for a while.

"Mr. Koizumi, I definitely get that you've imprinted the Challenge to the Reader into your mind as a serious obsession," T said with a rather lopsided grin. "But I would have to disagree at least some of the time. I wouldn't say it makes much difference to me whether there's a Challenge. Even if it's a straightforward who-dunit or one of Ellery Queen's works."

"Queen himself only insisted on the Challenges within the nationality series and *Halfway House*," Koizumi said, shrugging. "But personally, I insist you can't call it 'orthodox' unless it's the sort of hardcore puzzler that could accommodate a Challenge to the Reader."

"A little too fundamentalist for me! I can feel my hackles hockling."

I wasn't sure that was an actual word.

T turned her gaze downward. "What would you say are the conditions for an orthodox mystery, Nagato?"

"Not unfair," Nagato said, short and sharp.

"Does that mean it has to be fair?"

"………"

Koizumi posed a question but received only silence in reply.

"Oh, I think I get it! *Not unfair* and *fair* are not the same."

T had apparently decided to speak for Nagato.

"In other words, as long as the text doesn't actively lie, she's fine with it. Or even if it does include lies, that isn't a problem as long as they are lies that you could reasonably detect."

Koizumi held the palm of his hand out toward the mystery clubber.

"If the story has a first-person narrator, a certain degree of falsehoods and unreliable narration is acceptable, but surely not with omniscient third-person narration."

"Nagato's statement does not rule that out, either. Even if that third-person perspective includes feints, I'm sure she would see right through them."

"That's a radical position. If there were a Curia-like administration supervising the world of orthodox mysteries, they'd surely brand her a heretic."

"At Nagato's level, reading the author's intent between the lines is easier than twisting a three-year-old's arm." T let that statement hang for a moment, then added, "First- and third-person narrations are ultimately one and the same. First-person perspective embellishes the narrative with the character's point of view, while third person is merely first person from the author's perspective. It merely pretends to omit subjectivity."

"So you're suggesting a first-person perspective is an interplay between the author, character, and reader, while third person simply eliminates the character's perspective?"

"Rather," T said, "omniscient third person is just another term for the author's first person, so they can embellish the descriptions as they please, and some authors will take that as an opportunity for misdirection."

"Surely, that's a liberty too far. If we concede that deceptions hinging on misleading narration are viable, it's not impossible to reach that conclusion, but if you ask me—"

Any moment now.

Asahina tightened her lips, like she'd made up her mind.

"Hah!" she said, placing her piece on the board. Then she reached for the lid we were keeping the pieces in and fiddled around with the bits of wood inside, examining them from every angle.

"Okay, here!" she said grimly, handing me one of them.

I could still feel a trace of her warmth on the piece and would have loved to savor that for, say, three minutes, but we were in the final stages of the game. I couldn't exactly drag this out any further. Without really thinking at all, I plopped the piece down on an empty square, completing a row of four pieces with a common trait.

"Ah!" Asahina yelped, leaning forward, eyes round and shapely as the yolk of an egg fried by a top chef. "Oh, you had friends over there! I lost again."

That sad smile hit me hard, but the game didn't end until you declared victory, so I said, "Quarto."

*　　*　　*

On the cusp between spring and summer, with the first whiffs of the rainy season approaching, the clubroom currently hosted the SOS Brigade, minus the chief, plus one outsider.

Asahina and I had finished our fifth play of our board game, and she was now hustling about, getting tea ready.

She first collected everyone's mugs, including the guest mug T had been holding, then put the kettle on the gas burner, clutching the tea caddy that held our best leaves as if it were a precious treasure. Seeing this delightful maid at work was the highlight of my after-school experience.

Koizumi had brought in Cockroach Poker the previous day, and we'd tried it out, but Asahina was incapable of lying, so if she laid down a card and said it was a fly, you could easily tell if it was true or false. I tried playing without looking at her face, but I could tell from her voice alone. Clearly, I had become a certifiable expert in all things Asahina.

"Here," she said with a smile, placing a mug in front of me. She then headed off to serve the group engaged in an increasingly fruitless and extremely specialized exchange of ideas in the corner.

Koizumi and T accepted their tea and thanked the maid, all while still standing. They quickly resumed adding to a stream of ominous jargon no ordinary person could possibly comprehend. Nagato, meanwhile, never even glanced at the tea placed on the table near her. I don't think I've ever actually witnessed her drinking tea, but the contents of her mug did eventually vanish, so she was either draining the mug while no one was looking or consuming it via some incomprehensible cosmic art.

But just how long was T planning on hanging out here? She'd popped in right after classes ended to return Nagato's book and struck up a chat with Koizumi and Nagato...well, mostly

Koizumi...over tea, but was everyone in the mystery research club this laissez-faire?

Asahina finished her rounds and rejoined me at the table, holding her own mug in both hands. She blew on it several times, took a sip, and said, "Suzumiya's really late."

"Not unusual," I said, glancing over at the chief's chair. "In class, she said something about being late today. Beautification-committee meeting, I think?"

"Oh, she likes to keep things tidy? That's a new discovery!"

"Our class drew lots to decide who was on what duty, so...it was pure chance."

Still, this was Haruhi, so she may have unconsciously manipulated the draw to make herself part of that committee. Hopefully, she wasn't up to anything...

We soon learned she wasn't.

"The beautification committee will *not* shut up!" roared our chief, Haruhi Suzumiya, as she flung the door open. "Stuff we could take care of in three minutes took forty-five! That takes real talent! I fell asleep, which helped, but when the first-year next to me woke me up, they were still going! I couldn't believe it! Must have been a real nightmare for anyone actually taking it seriously."

She, on the other hand, had clearly not been taking it seriously at all. This whole speech had been delivered with a scowl on her way from the door to her chair.

"Mikuru, tea, please. On the warm side. Oh, T, you're here? Go on, have a seat. We got enough folding chairs for guests. Koizumi, you can't strike any decent poses with a mug in one hand. Yuki, you're in a good mood! I approve. And you, Kyon!"

The torrent of words seemed to have cleared away her frustrations with the committee, and by the time she turned to me, she was her usual self again. She fired up the computer on the chief's desk, asking, "Anything interesting happen while I was gone?"

I wondered how exactly I should report the futility of the last hour, when the computer chimed, "You've got mail!"

The voice sampled for this was Asahina's. We'd actually recorded several such sounds. I'll show you the rest in due time. Probably. Or at least, that was my intention before—

"Oh? That's unusual." Enough so that it even surprised Haruhi. "Someone actually used the SOS Brigade's e-mail address?"

Since the dawn of our website's operations, it had served basically no function at all. I was worried that someone had been inspired by the SOS Brigade's stated interest in all things strange and been strange enough themselves to actually e-mail us about it, but...

"Oh? It's from Tsuruya. Why bother using this address?"

Haruhi tilted her head quizzically. My own head yawed on a distinctly crooked angle.

The Tsuruya? E-mailing? And to the virtually unused SOS Brigade address?

She was usually the first person to just burst right in here without so much as a knock, so why take such a roundabout approach?

At my question, Asahina gingerly raised her hand.

"Tsuruya's been out for a few days now," she said. "N-not, like, sick or anything. Traveling, she said. Family business, couldn't get out of it... She got permission from the teachers."

"Huh, okay," Haruhi said, grabbing the mouse. "Then she's e-mailing from wherever she is now? Sending photos in lieu of souvenirs?"

She took a sip of Asahina tea, then leaned in closer to the screen.

"Or not, I guess? There's a file attached."

Curious, I moved around behind her, quickly reading the e-mail.

And almost let out a groan.

The timing was uncanny.

I glanced toward the side of the room, at Koizumi, Nagato, and T.

Of all the things she could have sent us, Tsuruya had gone with a Challenge to the SOS Brigade.

Haruhi read the e-mail out loud.

"Heya, SOS Brigade!

"How's it going? I'm all revved up and ready to go!

"So I've been tagging along with my hyper dad and letting him drag me all over the map. You know, mostly stuck at parties, sitting next to Dad, forcing a smile, but that's, like, so dull, I could die. Can't relax like a real vacay, and I'm not allowed to wander off alone, which leaves just, like, awkwardly killing time. I know the meet and greet is, like, a big deal, but man, I ain't your replacement or your proxy, so don't treat me like one.

"So while all that's been going on, I stumbled upon a case you might find interesting. Yes, it's exactly what you're imagining. Anyway, I kinda mixed in a travel story, figuring I'd write it up and send that over, too. Start with the scribblings in the attached file. I've got the problem listed at the end, so put your heads together and figure the solution out for me!

"Buh-bye!"

Haruhi's imitation of Tsuruya was so perfect that I could have sworn it was her real voice, and I caught myself wondering if this was foreshadowing a trick that would make another appearance later on. Maybe I'd been listening to too much mystery chatter.

"Aha," Haruhi said, eyes glittering. "Well done, Tsuruya. Sending us a quiz from distant lands! Hunting the strange and mysterious is the perfect extracurricular activity. Kyon, you should take tips. She's not even in the brigade but still delivers in spades!"

We'll see about that. Given her personality, I didn't think Tsuruya was particularly trying to entertain Haruhi here, and she certainly wasn't obligated to keep us posted on her status or anything. That line about how she "stumbled upon a case" had me worried. Plus, she'd used the words *problem* and *solution*.

Haruhi moved the cursor and opened the attached document file.

"So this is the problem? Can't wait to see what mysteries it holds!"

She began reading aloud.

*   *   *

This was in a party venue at a hotel somewhere, okay?

I was bored. My dad dragged me here, and I guess I'm used to that, but dull is still dull.

Nothing but old men and women as far as the eye could see, and after doing the meet and greet with everyone, there's nothing left for me to do. I mean literally; that's my entire job. Dad didn't even say *well done* or nothing. He just chattered away, champagne in one hand, with people who were either important or acted like they were. I'm used to that, too, and frankly, glad to be left out of it.

Anyways, I had this glass of orange juice and was stomping around this huge-ass banquet hall. In this fancy-ass party dress that was getting on my last nerve. My dad picked it out, so it had, like, frills all over it, ugggh. I told him it was completely wrong for me, but does he listen? No.

I found a wall that was just one massive windowpane, and I stopped to look at the view but got bored after, like, two seconds. I think we were on the third floor? Only an idiot would expect a decent view that low to the ground. Maybe it was different at night, but the sun was still doing its thang.

So I found a row of chairs lining the back wall and figured I'd take a break on one. Sitting still was boring, but I wasn't hungry, and the buffet here was not getting on with my tongue too well. Sometimes, throwing money at a problem wasn't enough.

But when I got to the corner, I found it occupied by another girl.

She was probably having the same problem I was. She had her hair all done up in fancy layers with a sparkly headdress and sat with a lady who was a bit older, probably her minder. The girl was as decked out as I was, but the older lady was in a drab pants suit, so I could tell she was here serving the girl. The lady was doing her best to engage her charge, but the girl was hella sulking and kept shaking her head. I feel ya, kid. I am just as bored by all this.

So I decided I was gonna be her friend.

I left my juice on a nearby table and went right on over. Up close, I could tell she was no regular customer. Total princess vibes radiating everywhere. So I was like—

'Sup!

And launched right into small talk.

Your dad drag you here? Mine too. Grown-ups, amirite? They all think their daughters are like trophies they won on the golf course, ya know? Putting all these frills on me ain't gonna turn me into a jewel or nothing. You're awfully pretty, though. Nah, I ain't hitting on you. Just speaking facts. For real, though, you're the only other person my age around here, so we should get along. What do you say?

I rattled all that off and then went for a handshake.

And the eyes on that cute face shot open, and then she giggled. I didn't say nothing funny! The lady with her was giving me the weirdest look. I didn't do anything to deserve— Argh, whatever.

The girl took my hand and stood up.

Her smile was mega-adorable. Humanity is definitely better off when people smile openly rather than maintain a poker face.

"Nice to meet you," she said.

I knew she'd have a cute voice.

Mmkay, let's go!

Still holding the girl's hand, I led her right out of the hall. The lady with her didn't follow. Maybe she was caught off guard when the girl followed me so easy? Or maybe she knew who I was. Either way, we got outa that stifling party without anyone stopping us.

We just kept walking, hand in hand. I realized my stride was a bit longer than hers and was careful to slow myself down a bit. We hopped on the escalator toward the first floor, and as we rode, I turned back to her.

You good at sports? Wanna play tennis?

She looked unsure but said she had before. That was good enough for me.

We cut across the lobby to the front desk. All the other guests in the lobby were staring for some reason. Probably 'cause she was cute.

I made a few requests to the snazzily uniformed concierge lady. She managed this perfect balance between friendly and elegant, and she gave us the stamp of approval with a smile that seemed genuine instead of businesslike, so me and the girl whose hand I was holding bowed as she started making a call somewhere, and like that, we were out the front doors of the hotel.

The hard soles of our shoes tapped out a steady rhythm in unison.

Too easy? Well, the hotel people *definitely* knew my name. It sure sped things up when I could just let my name talk for me without me having to justify any requests. Course, that ain't my accomplishment, and I ain't proud of it, but I put up with enough crap because of it that I didn't mind abusing the perks sometimes, too, you know? Not like I was gonna go changing my name anytime soon. That'd be a real pain in the neck.

Anyway, there we were on the hotel tennis courts. I'd spotted them earlier from the window back at the party venue.

We went in the locker room next to the courts, and there were tennis clothes, shoes, and rackets all laid out for us. Damn, concie-lady. You ain't working at a first-rate hotel for nothing. You really get stuff done. And the tennis shoes were just my size, too.

The girl held up the matching tennis clothes, grinning. Before she went to put them on, I stopped her with a suggestion.

Why not play like this? Not like we get a chance to every day.

"In these gowns?" She blinked.

Yup. I mean, the shoes have to change, but yeah, I'm thinking we play like this. Everyone can watch us play tennis in these frills! Prove we ain't dolls, but girls still young enough to wanna jump around. Sounds fun, right?

She stared at me with those strong-willed eyes of hers...and then she broke into a smile.

"Okay," she agreed.

Glad I got through to her.

We grabbed rackets and headed out to the courts. No one else was playing, so we had them all to ourselves. Shame we only needed a single court.

I decided to let her have first serve, did a few stretches, and got ready on the baseline of the clay court.

In the far corner, she bounced the ball with her racket a few times, like she was adjusting to the sensation—then she looked at me.

Anytime, kid.

She read that sign no prob, threw the ball high, hit a serve with *fine* form—and caught me by surprise. If I'd reacted 0.2 seconds later, she would've aced me.

It was all I could do to return the serve, and it just barely landed inbounds. Whew! She seemed pretty shocked by that but still nailed a backhand return. Yeesh, good hit. Can't believe she did that while her gown was wrapping itself around her legs.

I managed to catch up to her crosscourt shot and aim it back toward the center. Her second return was a bit more forgiving. I returned the favor, hitting it where she could easily reach. We didn't need words to communicate this intent. The fun here wasn't in the struggle to score—both of us just wanted to savor the simple joy in keeping a rally going.

As we played, I stole a sidelong glance at the hotel towering over us. I could tell several people were gathered at the windows of the party venue, watching us. Maybe people who'd found themselves without anyone to talk to. Two girls playing tennis in fancy dresses was a fine chaser for their drinks. I'd expected as much.

Both of us missed a few shots, and we took turns serving into the next rally. The crowd watching us from the venue was growing. I couldn't tell if my dad was among them or not, but he was long past being surprised by any antics I got up to, especially minor stuff like this. That went both ways.

The two of us played tennis for quite a while, our skirts whipping this way and that all the while. Long rallies had been the goal at first, but we eventually got more heated as time went on. Returns started coming hard, aimed for the singles sidelines. I was past maintaining my cool, and I chased those balls hard. Putting a spin on the ball was definitely something best left for serious play, not messing around in these getups—which meant it was probably time to call it.

The girl hit a drive shot at my side, and I knocked it straight up, catching it with one hand as it fell.

That baffled her for a moment, but then she smiled. Great minds.

"It's gotten so late."

You don't need a watch to tell you that. The sun was setting. There were still some people watching from the party venue, but it was definitely time to wrap things up.

"That was fun," she said, still a bit out of breath. We shook hands across the net, completing the whole *good game* bit.

You sure are good at tennis. You got a pro as a coach or something?

I was joking, but she straight-up nodded.

Oh, I see. One of those cram-your-schedule-full-of-tutors deals? Tennis, piano, violin, ballet, horseback riding, swimming, the works. Totally unimaginative list of rich-kid lessons.

"More or less," she said, looking depressed.

We headed back to the clubhouse and made a beeline for the showers.

Shucking off that gown felt like I was fairy freeing its wings. And with that headdress gone and her hair flowing free, no clothes at all, I thought for a second the girl *was* a fairy.

We washed the dust and sweat off, wrapped towels around ourselves, and were back in the locker room. After toweling off and running dryers through our hair, she reached for that gown again with a glum look.

Not that thing! Let's put the tennis clothes on.

"You mean, we play tennis in the gowns and wear the tennis clothes after?"

Exactly! Sounds like fun, right? Besides, after that workout, the gowns are kinda grimy...

"They *are* dirty now."

We both grinned and slipped on the tennis gear the hotel concie-lady had arranged for us. Way more comfortable than that glossy gown fabric. Shoes, too.

We could totally just ditch the gowns and dress shoes here, but...

Lemme see yours for a sec.

I reached for her hair decoration. Just a standard-issue headdress made of pure silver metalwork. Probably safe.

I looked over her shoes next. Elegant in their simplicity, no fussy decorative bits. Probably also clear.

What about the gown itself, then? There were buttons on those sleeves. Pure decorative buttons, no actual function, three on each side, six in all.

I held the sleeve to my face. Nope, couldn't sniff it out. I tried flicking each button in turn. Oh, one sounded a bit different? What could that mean?

Clearly, there was something else inside this button.

"No," she said, looking close. "A bug?"

If that was her first thought, it spoke volumes about the life she led.

But no, they aren't listening in. Probably just a GPS tracker.

"A what?"

It uses the Global Positioning System to broadcast your location so somebody can keep track of you.

"Oh…"

A hand elegantly placed on her lips. She made that pose look good.

"How'd you know?"

I used to have similar crap planted on me a lot. I always dumped it the second I found it, though. It ended up becoming a battle of wits between me and my dad—actually kinda fun, looking back on it! All kinds of transmitters hidden in all sorts of places for me to find and discard.

I thought it was silly anyone would go to that much effort, but I'm clean now. Long as he didn't plant one inside my body without me knowing, that is.

Clearly, both our parents are overprotective. Like, I get that all parents worry about their kids, but damn.

With her permission, I removed the transmitter button from her sleeve. Snapped the thread holding it in place with my teeth, a sight that made her laugh out loud, one hand daintily covering her mouth. Was that too uncouth?

"So now what?"

Back to the hotel. I'm parched! Gotta grab something to drink.
She looked slightly dejected. Did she think I meant the party?
'Cause I sure as hell didn't.

I leaned in and whispered that in her ear.

This brought her smile back, so we picked up our shoes and
dresses and left the clubhouse.

I looked up at the hotel on the way. Couldn't see the venue from
here. So they couldn't see us, either. They could see the courts,
but the route to the clubhouse was hidden—a fact that I'd noted
before leaving the party.

We went right in the front doors of the hotel. Two girls in
matching tennis outfits carrying ball gowns sure drew a lot of
glances. There was an older dude carrying a trunk toward the
door, must have just checked out. He smiled at us, so I smiled
back.

As we brushed past him, I slipped the transmitted button in his
pocket. I counted to three, then looked back. He was gone, and
nobody was looking at me. If they played the camera feed back in
slo-mo, they could probably catch the handoff, but for now, we
were clean, Mr. Bean.

Acting like we owned the place, we waved over to the concierge
from before, thanked her, and asked her to send the dresses out
for cleaning.

Oh, and heads-up? One button came off, but don't worry about
that.

She readily accepted, super professional about the whole thing.
Good-bye, party dress. Do *not* wanna put you on again anytime
soon.

Then we hopped onto the elevator, and after a brief battle with
gravity, we were in my room. I purposefully avoid sticking the
card key in the slot to turn on the room's lights.

I grabbed a bottle of grapefruit juice from the fridge, poured a glass, and handed it to her. She waited for me to pour myself one, then we both chugged.

We sat down on the bed and chatted for a while. About our homes and whatever. That's all, but it was a real blast. I'd have gladly talked forever, but how much time could I buy? When they found the transmitter on a stranger, my dad would totally know what was up.

Maybe we should hide under the bed.

"What?" she said.

I didn't know her eyes could go that wide.

Yup, only a matter of time before they show up here. Hiding under the beds is a primitive approach, but that might turn out to be an unexpected blind spot. Let's call it the purloined-letter stratagem.

Wriggling on our bellies like lizards, we slid under the bed. She was laughing pretty hard.

"I've never done anything like this," she said.

I'd hidden in all kinds of places, so it was getting a little old hat for me.

Facedown, shoulder to shoulder in the darkness, we kept talking, moving from one topic to another. Man, it was fun.

Eventually, I got sleepy. I hadn't slept much the night before and had been fine up till now, but lying still in the darkness like this got me good.

I must have drifted off.

When I woke up, I was on top of the bed, with covers drawn over me. It was night.

She was gone.

The only proof she'd ever been there was the pair of empty cups on the table, looking like, uh… Nope, can't think of any good similes.

I pulled the covers over my head and closed my eyes.

As I drifted back to sleep, I thought…

…*I hope we meet again.*

* * *

As Haruhi finished, a veil fell across the entire literature club with *silence* written on it in big letters.

In the distance, we could hear sports teams getting way too into practice, and the racket of the wind ensemble.

No one said a word, so I spoke for everyone.

"And?"

"And nothing. That's all there is!"

Haruhi clicked around a bit.

"No other attachments, nothing else in the e-mail itself, no links or nothing. No follow-up e-mails."

Wait. The e-mail said, "I've got the problem listed at the end, so…figure the solution out for me!" but where did she do that?

"Good question. I mean, there's some odd things in here," Haruhi said. She thought for much longer than she usually thought about anything. "Koizumi, what do you make of it?"

"Hmm," he said. He was still standing with a tea mug in one hand. "It was certainly very Tsuruya. Positive, forceful, active, witty, and impish all at once. A true delight."

"I wasn't asking for your book report," Haruhi snapped. She chugged her Asahina tea, clearly lukewarm by this point, and added, "How long are you and T gonna stand around? Sit the hell down."

Koizumi grabbed a guest folding chair from the corner, unfolded it, and waved T into it. Only when the mystery-club girl with dazzling hair had taken a seat did he move to his own chair.

T was definitely here for the long haul, then. Hmm, okay…

"By the way, do you actually know Tsuruya?" I asked.

T was an exchange student, in the same class as Haruhi and me.

"Of course," she said, glancing my way. "That is a verified fact. She's famed throughout your North High. I would imagine the total sum of people who do not know Tsuruya is *nobody*."

I'd never heard of her until she showed up at the pickup baseball game.

"Kyam, that's just part of what makes you priceless."

She made this sound like lousy ad copy. And please stop with the Kyam thing. Not like I love being called Kyon, but *Kyam* just makes me want to crawl into a hole.

T shrugged off my protests and took a sip from the guest mug.

"Would you prefer *Kyami*?"

What we have here is a complete breakdown in communication.

As I was teetering on the verge of giving up...

"I've got it!" Haruhi yelled, knocking her chair over.

Her eyes were gleaming like she had Sirius, Canopus, and Arcturus trapped in them, and she waited a moment to see if anyone would ask what she'd got, but nobody did, so I took one for the team.

"Got what?"

"This is a narrative trick!"

The term Haruhi dropped made the mystery trio's ears twitch.

"A what?" Asahina whispered. I could swear I saw question marks going off over her head.

"You remember that pseudo love story Kyon wrote for the magazine last year? That kinda cheap crap."

You're the one who picked the genres. Your fault for making me write a romance.

"*Cheap* is hardly a fair descriptor," Koizumi said, with his most gentle smile. "It's a pedigreed literary technique that dates as far back as the *Nihon Shoki*, in the chapter on Empress Jingu. You can see clear signs of the people compiling that history struggling to make the facts match Chinese records like the *Records of the Three Kingdoms*."

118

Rather than judging this statement on its own terms, I was inclined to be skeptical of the underlying premise.

"So what part of Tsuruya's writings is the narrative trick?"

"I read the whole thing Tsuruya-style," Haruhi said, "but that's where Tsuruya's trap began!"

Looking extremely proud of herself, our chief declared:

"The narrator of this passage *isn't* Tsuruya!"

"Aha. Coming from that angle, I see," Koizumi said. A rather loaded statement. "So you believe the trick lay in the very opening?"

"I'm sure she knew I'd read the thing in her voice. And I fell for it! Well done, Tsuruya. You aren't an honorary SOS Brigade member for nothing!"

Seemed more like a dishonor, but let's put that aside.

"But is that really true? I mean, all the details in that story really make the narrator sound like Tsuruya."

"But her name is never mentioned," Haruhi said. "That proves it! It's all *I* and *her*—not a single name anywhere! Entry-level narrative-trick stuff."

I dunno if it was entry-level or an advanced technique, but if the narrator wasn't Tsuruya, then who could it be? Why would Tsuruya send us a story that didn't even happen to her?

"No, Kyon, this is definitely a true story Tsuruya herself experienced."

By what logic?

Haruhi waved a finger back and forth in front of my face.

"Don't you get it? The girl the narrator meets at the party and hangs out with is only ever called *the girl* or *she*. But that was actually Tsuruya!"

Ridiculous. I refused to believe that. Please elaborate on your basis for this claim.

"If you insist…I'll call it a hunch!"

That's not proof. As far as I can tell, the first-person narrator of this essay is clearly and obviously Tsuruya herself.

"That's the point! It was specifically written that way to create a false assumption. Otherwise, it wouldn't be much of a trick, would it?"

Even so. If your theory is right and the girl is Tsuruya, no matter how I look at it, I can't see her being Tsuruya at all.

"On what basis?"

Haruhi looked quite pleased to turn that around on me, knowing full well I couldn't hit back with a hunch.

"For starters, I can't imagine Tsuruya sitting quietly on a chair in the corner of a party venue."

Haruhi's smile never wavered.

"She might hide her true nature in public. And she was at this party doing her bit for her family, right? If her father was there for work, and she was there with him, she might be forced to act with decorum."

"Secondly, she barely talks at all. I can't imagine Tsuruya being a girl of few words. And she just seems way too genteel. What part of Tsuruya makes you think she could ever play this role?"

"Even Tsuruya would be forced to class up her act in high society. People are complicated!"

Yet it says she was sitting in a corner looking sullen.

"She does that, too! If the mood strikes her."

"Third, and this is the biggest reason," I said, moving on. "Let's say you're right, and the other girl is Tsuruya. Which in turn means the narrator is someone else."

"Isn't that obvious? What's your point?"

"That would mean this world contains a second person with Tsuruya's energy and enthusiasm, who also talks just like her. I find that difficult to believe. One of them is more than enough."

"Fair." Haruhi conceded that point. "Then how about this? Neither one of them are Tsuruya."

This was another huge leap in logic.

"Huh...?" Asahina said with a face so surprised that I wanted to photograph it and register the image as the official illustration for the online dictionary entry on the word *surprised*. "Does that mean Tsuruya didn't write this?"

"No, I think Tsuruya definitely wrote it. I'm not taking Kyon's side, but I definitely doubt anyone but her could reproduce that distinctive speaking style."

"Er...then why would Tsuruya write a story about two people who weren't her and e-mail it to us?"

"No idea!" Haruhi flopped back in the chief's chair, realized her mug was already empty, and said, "Mikuru, can I get a refill? Somewhat warm."

"Sure thing!"

Asahina went right into servant mode, which clearly banished all memories of the question she'd asked a moment ago. Clearly, Mystery Solving < Tea Serving in her book.

Haruhi stuck her chin in her hand, glaring at the screen as Asahina scurried about getting the pot on the burner. Koizumi and T both had their arms folded, staring at the ceiling. They sure were two peas in a pod.

Nagato was still melting into the corner of the room, reading in silence.

Feeling like this topic was well on its way to getting dropped, I said, "Wait."

Asahina froze in her tracks, so I hastily assured her I didn't mean the tea.

"Let's question the base assumption. Is this story actually the 'problem'? What would the 'solution' be? Still no follow-up from Tsuruya?"

Haruhi clicked once.

"Apparently not."

If there was a mystery hidden in Tsuruya's story, perhaps we should consult people who knew more about these things than Haruhi or I did.

Fortunately, we had a mystery-research-club member right here. An expert on this exact type of problem.

"You want my opinion?" T had been sipping, birdlike, from the guest mug, but she put that down and said, "I'd like to get Nagato's take first. Got anything for us?"

Nagato slowly looked up from the yellowing rectangular pages of the book on her lap.

"......Nothing yet," she whispered.

Then she returned to her best impression of a statue reading.

Someone interpret.

"Kyam, how is it *you* fail to understand her intent? She said as of right now, the range of possibilities is far too vast, and she has insufficient data to narrow it down to a single truth."

Can't help but be impressed at your ability to weave anything that long and complicated from two words, but Nagato could have just said, *Not enough information.* Plus, your first line was entirely uncalled for.

T shook her head at me. Like she pitied my failure to comprehend the merits of Nagato-ese. It was legitimately a miracle that anyone outside the SOS Brigade was capable of conversing with Nagato on any level, so I would quite like for T to understand *she* was the exception here.

T's headshake was making her hairpin and bangs sway, too. Looking closer, that hairpin was less for keeping her hair in place and more a fashionable accent.

Seemingly growing tired of radiating disappointment in my direction, T turned her back on me and said, "Koizumi, surely you have some line of reasoning you can present us with?"

"Well," he said, flicking his bangs. "I think there has to be some sort of narrative trick included in this passage. However, I think the assumption that the first-person narrator is not Tsuruya is going a step too far."

Here, he made eye contact with me.

"I think this narrator is undeniably Tsuruya herself. I simply don't think Tsuruya would use such a mean-spirited deception. We should take her role at face value."

"Hmph," Haruhi said, accepting a fresh mug of tea from Asahina. "Then what's she up to? Is there a trick or not?"

"I doubt she would send us something that was *just* intended to read like an ordinary passage from her diary."

It's true that she *was* always up to something.

"Perhaps we should focus on the text of the e-mail itself. She states in advance that she 'stumbled upon a case.' Yet while the adventures of these two girls are a bit eccentric, can this heartwarming tale of bonding really be called a case?"

"The only thing remotely case-like is that the narrator stuck a GPS transmitter on some random stranger."

"And if we're qualifying pranks as mysteries, then certainly. But I think we should examine her e-mail closer. She says, 'I kinda mixed in a travel story.'"

"Oh," Haruhi said, snapping her fingers. "Then the part about these two girls is just an anecdote?"

I'm lost.

"Kyon, you should know better! She said she'd put the problem at the end."

Maybe I hadn't been listening. I didn't remember anything like that at all.

"That's the point!" she said, leaning back in her chair like a big shot. "Tsuruya's writings don't end here. There's more to it! We haven't reached the end yet! There oughtta be a follow-up e-mail any minute, and that will present us with the final problem."

Why create a time lag like that?

"So she could trip us up! It worked, too. We were totally over-thinking! Don't really feel bad about it, though."

Doesn't quite add up. Would she really send a story like that just to confuse us? Something's bugging me.

"Indeed," Koizumi chimed in. "I'm of the same opinion. Surely, the problem has yet to arrive. However, I think we would be hasty to assume this initial Tsuruya salvo is a straightforward piece of writing."

"Fair," Haruhi said, then grinned at us. "So what's wrong with it?"

Koizumi smiled back. "We can safely assume the narrator is Tsuruya. And in light of that, it calls into question the actions of her companion, this mystery heiress. Specifically, her actions are much too childish."

"Yeah, hiding under hotel beds to avoid discovery isn't exactly doable when you're in high school."

"I believe even Tsuruya would hesitate to play tennis outdoors, in a party dress, in full view of spectators. But this other girl readily agrees, which again, indicates the time frame of this tale is not the present."

I dunno about the other kid, but I feel like no matter what point she was at in life, Tsuruya would not give a damn what she was wearing whether she was playing tennis, basketball, or *sepak takraw*. And she definitely had the skills to do all that action without accidentally flashing anyone.

"This also applies to the GPS tracker. We can assume both girls are similarly affluent, but no matter how worried you are, hiding a tracker on their clothes is a bit much. Especially without their knowledge. I would think a high school girl would be well aware and involved in such decisions."

"But since she wasn't…," Haruhi said.

"That's where I began to suspect something was afoot." Koizumi nodded. "Could this really be a recent incident?"

Okay, even I got it by this point.

Koizumi folded both his arms and legs.

"As Suzumiya's intuition suggested, there was, indeed, a narrative trick at play. But this was not to disguise the characters involved—the deception lay in the time frame of the narrative itself! This is not a recent incident Tsuruya experienced, but something from the much more distant past, likely when she was in elementary school. Yet written and presented as if it were something that had just happened on her current travels."

Kids that age could easily fit under a bed, and it wouldn't be at all weird if they fell asleep. I could totally see my sister doing that. Sadly, her life was bereft of tennis and high society, so she didn't really map well to this rich girl in the story, but I had definitely found her asleep in a closet with our cat, Shamisen, on a number of occasions. Why it was always *my* closet was an eternal mystery.

"She didn't write a single false word," T muttered. "But neither does it present any clear clues. Yet nothing so far could be declared unfair—right, Nagato?"

Nagato failed to respond to this in any way. She merely turned a page with her slender fingers.

Haruhi locked her fingers behind her head, reclining in her chair and scowling at the screen.

"Well, I'm sure we'll know more soon enough. The next e-mail…"

"You've got mail!"

It was like she had eyes in the room.

Asahina's daffy digital voice announced the arrival of Tsuruya's follow-up.

Haruhi read it aloud.

"Heya, heya! Sorry for the mass e-mail attack! The last message had a travel tale attached, but I bet you figured it out—that all took place seven years ago! I got kinda bored, then remembered another boring day and wound up taking a trip down memory lane! Figured it was as good an excuse as any, so I wrote the whole story down and sent it to you. Had no one to share the piece with, and the waves of melancholy were getting kinda high, so basically, I just wanted someone to listen! Simple as that. And out of everyone I know, Haru-nyan's brigade has the most free time on their hands, so I figured you might get a kick out of it. What did ya think?"

Koizumi had been right.

But the SOS Brigade's most handsome member showed no signs of pride. He merely listened to Haruhi, shaking his head. T had her arms folded, eyes focused on the air, and Nagato never once looked up from her book.

Asahina alone was going "Huh? What?" and blinking at everybody, clearly lost.

I tried to picture Tsuruya seven years ago. My sister was in the sixth grade, so not that much different. But try as I might to imagine a miniature Tsuruya, my brain didn't seem to want to lower her age at all. I just felt like she wouldn't really have changed that much.

"But I figured if it was *just* an old story you'd all be like, *Wut?* so this time, I sent along a story from last fall. Me and the girl from the previous story have been running into each other now and then ever since. Once again, we'd both been dragged along by our dads, but for once, we got to spend a bit of time together and hang out, which was nice. This one's a hot-springs episode! We hit up the baths together. Sit back and enjoy the tale! Buh-bye!"

Haruhi read that far, then fell silent. She moved the mouse, clicked the attachment, and opened the document file.

"Let's hope we get to the case this time," she muttered. Then she took a breath…

…and read Tsuruya's second salvo.

*   *   *

We were in the outdoor bath at some hot springs.

I was leaning against a natural rock formation, enjoying the water.

The sky above was clear and blue, not a cloud to be found. It was kinda nice taking a bath in broad daylight sometimes.

"Thank goodness the weather's so nice," she said, making waves with her hands next to me.

Yup, I said back, trying to bore a hole in her smile with my gaze alone.

Same girl as before. Last story was the first time I met her. Family business led to us running into each other any number of times, so we grew pretty close. We were mostly just our dads' plus-ones, so once we'd played our part, we were free to hang out together.

If there were games or facilities, we could kill the time easy, but sometimes, there was nothing but the hotel rooms and the party venue, nothing you'd normally take a kid to see.

And when that happened, our favorite pastime was real hide-and-seek.

Rules were simple. All we had to do was evade the grown-ups' notice. Nothing more to it.

We'd start by checking each other over, finding where they'd hidden GPS trackers. Couldn't get much hiding done with those things still on us.

But like I said last time, odds were high I was tracker-free, but since there was always a chance they'd try and slip one on me once my guard was down, we always checked. She nearly always had one. It was kinda impressive, really. You could see the technological improvements growing by the day. That was pretty cool in its own way. Scientific progress driven by overprotective parents.

Each time we found her trackers, they were smaller.

The trickiest ones were embedded in her shoes. Since everything she wore was custom-made, they were designed from the start to hide devices the size of a grain of rice. You couldn't find those things unless you took the whole shoe apart. Like, why go that far, seriously?

There was one time we just couldn't figure out how they always found us, so we actually tried just wandering around naked wearing only shoes, and her minders were on us instantly, so we realized then it had to be the shoes.

Once the hiding place was pinpointed, it was easy enough to handle. You just had to microwave the shoes. This sort of gizmo can't handle that at all. Best trick when we couldn't just swap out her shoes. But! Good kids shouldn't try it at home. I mean, *your* shoes don't have GPS trackers in them.

Anyhoo, after that, they stopped putting them in her shoes. In retrospect, I think it was less because we kept destroying the trackers and more because her walking around wearing nothing else was frowned upon. The follies of youth!

But that didn't mean they'd given up trying to keep tabs on her location. They just changed up their approach. The two of us got a firsthand look at just how fast the tracker industry was evolving. Every tracker we found impressed us all over again.

And we played the trick of planting the trackers on random people one too many times, so it stopped working. They just started ignoring trackers that ran off in some inexplicable direction.

So one day, we used that to our advantage. We left the tracker on and just straight-up went outside. The purloined-letter stratagem: phase two.

Our dads thought it was the same old trick, ignored the signal, and just kept searching the area.

Meanwhile, we hitched a ride with some strangers, ditched the constraints of parents and family names, and cried freedom. Naturally, we offered up the ultrahigh-quality trackers as a gift to the nice driver as we got out.

Several hours later, after eating and shopping to our heart's content in some place we had never been to before, her minders and my dad's secretaries surrounded us. Apparently, they even had helicopters out looking for us. Maybe we went a bit *too* far. We made a show of at least looking sorry.

What's my point? Well, freedom isn't free, I guess. We had to work for ours. I feel like that's a cool thing to say.

"How right you are," she murmured, looking rather forlorn. The way she gently brushed the wet strands of hair off her forehead was a sight to behold. "I envy you, Tsuruya. You always seem free."

That's 'cause I make a point of enjoying life's freedoms every chance I get. Doesn't mean I'm as free as it looks. I mean, even this trip to the hot springs is for family business. But if it weren't for that, I'd never get to see you, so take the thick with the thin and the snow and the rain.

"Yes, getting to know you has been a blessing. Accompanying my father before this was always so tiresome. Even if it isn't every time, I'm always grateful for the time I spend with you."

Same here! And thanks for playing along with the hide-and-seek thing.

"Not at all. I look forward to the things you talk about. You seem to really enjoy your schooling."

School's all right, yeah. But that place just has an extra helping of interesting people. Almost like someone specifically gathered 'em there.

"Tsuruya, you're not a member of any specific club, right?"

Mm, yeah, I'm just not the joining type. I'm more into going my own way without a specific goal. Leaves my feet unfettered, so I can stick my head in wherever seems most fun. That makes it easy to talk to anyone and let me make the most of my time.

She sighed. Her shockingly long lashes drooping.

"Your drive toward freedom is what makes that possible. I wasn't even allowed to choose my club."

What club you in?

"Classic poetry recitation."

Like Li Bai and Ikkyu Sojun?

"No, Goethe, Baudelaire, and sometimes Brontë."

But you don't actually like reciting Western poetry?

"No. My father forced me into it. I'm not *obligated* to obey, but he donated a considerable sum to the chairman and principal and pushed me into it."

He a poetry fan, then?

"I've never seen him read a single sonnet. I think he just chose the most harmless-sounding club. Myself included, it's all girls. So as my sole means of resistance…"

Here, a glimmer of a smile appeared.

"…I started calling it the Dead Poets Society."

I think this was a joke of some kind, but I didn't get the reference.

Still, I said. It's not like you hate your dad, right?

"No," she said, not hesitating at all. I liked that about her. "He's very strict, but that comes from a caring soul. I have much to be grateful for and could never turn against him."

No matter how many times I escaped with her, he never tried to keep us apart and never complained to my father, either. That generosity was worth respecting. He forgave it all with a smile. I quite liked the guy.

"But I *do* think I should at least get to pick my own club."

Even her sad face looked pretty.

"My school is notoriously uptight. Even during club activities, we're not allowed to cut loose."

That sounds so dull. But there's this girl and boy a year under me who weren't the least bit fazed by school rules. They just made their own original club and spent the whole dang year doing weird stuff that looks like a hot mess, but even that turned out be an understatement. Now it's actually total bedlam, and everyone and anyone who gets sucked in like there's a tornado passing through gets turned topsy-turvy. Right, you two?

"I'd love to hear more about them. From the way you describe them, they seem most admirable."

Well, we just had a school festival before I came here. They got up to all kinds of mischief. I got a bit involved myself, but, well, I didn't even know I could go through so many emotions that fast. Surprise, laughter, the works.

"Heh-heh."

She put the second knuckle of her index finger to her lips with a heart-stopping smile.

"Your school sounds like so much fun. I envy you."

Hmm, I dunno about them, but I'm not sure me or the school are worth getting jealous over. The grass is always greener beyond the yellow brick road.

But she clearly had undying love for the "freedom" status effect. I'd known her long enough to get that.

I looked past her, to her right. On her other side, someone was half submerged in the water, trying to maintain a poker face.

We'd all been at this long enough to be fairly used to one another, and her minders followed her like shadows, never letting their guard down.

You'd think they'd at least let her hit the baths on her own.

This was why she always feels trapped.

If they said this was a countermeasure against our constant prison breaks, then all we could do was laugh.

"Miss," the minder said, breaking the silence. "I believe you have enjoyed the waters long enough. I recommend emerging before they start to take their toll on your health."

"Fine," she said, sinking up to her chin. "I'll consider it. Good enough? And stop calling me miss. Especially in front of people. It's embarrassing."

"Miss," the minder said, not budging at all. "The beautification effect lauded by the waters of this particular spring has long since had time to render the desired effect. This is certain beyond all doubt. It is clear even to my eyes that the gods have wreathed both your bodies in the light of their blessings."

"You don't say."

"Should you seek any further beauty, you would surely incur the jealous wrath of every goddess who art in heaven. Were we in ancient Greece, they might well have already descended from Olympus to bring calamity upon you."

This was just a super roundabout way of saying *Get out of the bath now*, but I kinda dig the turn of phrase.

"This isn't Greece, nor is it the age of myths," the girl said curtly. "Am I not even allowed to decide when I get out of the bath on my own?"

"Miss...," the minder said, exasperated enough to shoot a glance my way.

Not the first time this had happened. When the girl was being extra stubborn, the minders would check to see if I felt like helping. We'd never actually specifically discussed it, but somewhere along the way, her staff had decided sending me an SOS was okay. Apparently, she was much more prone to these fits when she was with me. Was I a catalyst of some sort? Maybe. I guess it didn't hurt to do my bit sometimes. As a catalyst. I only felt a little manipulated.

But it was also true we'd been in here a long time. Our schedules were still totally fine, but hanging out in hot water all day wasn't exactly ideal, either.

I remembered hearing that at one point along the path of evolution, humans were semiaquatic, like otters, but I don't believe a word of it.

"…If you say so, Tsuruya."

Somehow, that got through to her.

As reluctant as she sounded, she certainly stood up fast enough. "Let's go."

The silhouette of her body was so beautiful that I couldn't help staring.

Before the ripples reflected back toward us, me and the minder followed her out.

She headed straight to the changing room, and while her back was turned, the minder directed a quick head bob toward me.

The minder had a rockin' bod, too. Walking between these two made me feel like a string bean or a stalk of horsetail.

I waggled the fingers of one hand, listening to the sound of our bare feet.

The fall breeze on my postbath body felt dumb cold. If I didn't get something on fast, I'd be shivering uncontrollably in no time.

I sped up, catching up with the girl.

The minder hung back, following us—at first, but then swooped past us before we reached the building, heading into the changing room first. Probably wanted to make sure to be ready to leave before we were.

The girl and I exchanged glances, took measure of each other's smiles, and stepped into the changing room.

The next bit was your standard postbath routine, so I'll breeze through it.

We toweled off, ran dryers through our hair, put our clothes back on, drank some fruit punch, and went outside to find the minder waiting for us in pretty casual clothes—likely dressed with the intention of constantly being on the move.

Always so efficient. Like we'd be in the wind if any time was lost. I mean, we had priors, so maybe her staff were right to be concerned.

Anyway, the three of us departed the bathing area. Our driver was waiting for us—he'd been provided by the hotel we were staying at. The girl seemed accustomed to having drivers hold doors open and help her in. She settled onto those leather seats with real grace and no wasted motion.

The girl and I were in the back seat, and the minder in the front passenger seat. When we were all buckled in, the driver pulled out—he'd kept the engine running. We drove down country roads for a while.

The minder kept glancing at the clock, trying to hurry the driver up. Basically urging him to break the speed limit.

"We should have plenty of leeway before this evening's gathering," the girl said. "Let's take our time and enjoy the scenery."

I could tell the driver had eased his foot off the gas, even without looking.

"Miss," the minder said, voice like the clear waters of a mountain stream. "This was an unplanned excursion to begin with. If we consider the possibility of unexpected accidents, my heart is called far from the realm of comfort, forced to wander, lost, in the darkness of the woods beyond. We agreed in advance to minimize deviations from your notoriously intricate schedule."

"This hardly counts. We're staying near proper hot springs! Even if I can't stretch my wings, at least allow me to stretch my legs."

"Miss, does this qualify as 'near'? It is a half day by horse-drawn carriage from the hotel you ladies are staying at. We must all be grateful the internal combustion engine has saved us from the trials of the centuries that preceded the Industrial Revolution."

"I don't see any need for why any trips should be measured by horse-drawn carriage in this day and age, but out of curiosity, who are we giving our thanks to?"

"Jean Lenoir and Nicolaus Otto."

"I offer my most sincere thanks to both those gentlemen. Satisfied?"

"Thoroughly."

They might bicker like this, but she and her minder were actually quite close. Certainly nothing as distant as mistress and servant. When I said that, the girl made a face, but this was clearly an acknowledgment. Despite the girl's polite griping, the minder had swiftly made arrangements for our little hot-springs jaunt.

After we drove for a while, the trees and mountains outside fell away as the car reached civilization. It was more a village than a city, and one that lived hand in hand with nature.

No sooner did we enter the village than the driver abruptly slowed down.

Wondering why, I leaned around the front seat to peer out the windshield.

"What's wrong?" she said, doing the same thing.

There was a crowd in the street. A group walking together, dressed quite oddly. Like a costumed parade.

"It doesn't seem to be a mistimed Halloween celebration. Some local festival, perhaps?" the girl said, looking around. She was clearly very interested. "Driver, can we stop here?"

"Miss," the minder snapped.

But...

"According to my watch, we still have a good two hours to spare. If we head back to the hotel now, I'm more likely to fall asleep waiting for the party to begin. Do you want to drag me around to greet my father's friends looking like I just woke up?"

I doubt my dad would even care.

"Just for a few minutes, then." The minder made a show of reluctance but didn't actually fight us on it, which I took as more proof these two really were quite close.

The driver found a spot to park, and the two of us exited through our respective doors.

Outside, there was lively music playing, a bright and simple melody we both immediately fell in love with. Clearly being played live somewhere nearby. We could hear the crowd cheering, too.

We headed toward the rear of the parade, and the minder followed after us.

I wasn't really sure what concept these costumes were based on.

There were kids in witchlike capes and cone-shaped hats, like they were holding a Sabbath, but then others were just dressed like medieval European country girls.

Burly men were carrying big cages made of woven bark, laden with what looked like fruit.

The sticks in the witch kids' hands were pointing at those cages, then waved wildly around, and they were apparently chanting some sort of spell. I didn't see any pumpkin heads, so I was pretty sure this definitely wasn't an off-season Halloween deal.

We joined the procession, walking with them as the music and cheering got louder. We soon worked out what kind of event this was.

We'd neared the town square, and there was a temporary arch waiting for us at the entrance. The procession passed under the arch, dancing to the music.

There was a wooden sign nailed to the arch, and it said:

Autumn Festival: Grape-Stomping Girls Pair CONTEST! Late Entries Welcome!

A crowd of…villagers, I guess…were greeting the arrival of the procession with smiles, shouts, and music.

There was a huge barrel-looking vat in the center of the square, and the men were dumping their baskets into it. The fruit inside was all plump grapes, ripe and ready. Apparently, the witches' chant was supposed to be a charm to enhance the grapes' flavor.

There was an even bigger cheer.

Two girls in traditional clothing had stepped into the barrel, barefoot, and were dancing to the music—it was definitely dancing—stomping all over the grapes.

I've heard of this! You crush the grapes this way, making juice or wine. Of course, the stomping is just a spectacle these days, and they've got better ways to crush the grapes for actual production. Right?

This whole thing was really accentuating the exotic atmosphere. It was hard to tell if that was done deliberately to try to hype the thing up or if this was a storied, historical tradition of the locals. Could be either. Both possibilities were entirely possible.

Regardless, seemed like we'd lucked into seeing the local harvest festival.

She was watching them avidly. Bare feet crushing grapes, juice spurting out—I could tell it had captured her curiosity.

"Surely not," the minder said, sounding more stunned than appalled. "You aren't thinking of joining this ill-mannered revelry, are you?"

"Tsuruya."

Sure.

"Let's join in!"

Hokay.

Once decided, there was no time to waste. Before the minder could stop us, we skittered like squirrels over to the entry desk. When the girl said she wanted to join in, the woman at the counter smiled and handed her a clipboard. Seemed like all you had to do was write your name.

We both wrote out our real names, and she pointed us toward a long, thin building that looked like some sort of community center.

The minder followed right behind us, muttering something. Sounded like philosophical ruminations on the decorum (or lack thereof) in young women, present or past. I'd have to ask what the conclusion was later.

The girl knocked on the door.

Someone answered, the portal yawned open, and we slipped inside.

The community center was pulling double duty as a changing area and a closet, if that makes sense.

There were several women there, chattering and changing.

There was a rack full of the outfits the grape stompers wore, and the woman in charge of those eyed the two of us up for a good thirty seconds.

Then she handed us each an outfit, and we were told to change right here, so we did and were surprised to find the clothes a perfect fit.

The rack lady looked proud of herself, so we exchanged high fives. I took a good look at the girl in her new outfit. There were no mirrors in here, so I couldn't see myself, which meant the only way to scope the costume out was to look at her.

"Well? Anything seem out of place?"

"You look like you've stepped out of an impressionist's painting, miss."

Definitely just like a lady dressed as a medieval European village girl. Looks totally natural.

She tied her hair back with a scarf, smiling with only one side of her mouth. Good trick.

"You look very good yourself, Tsuruya."

These clothes seemed perfect for doing the schuhplattler, and I remember thinking I'd love to see Mikuru in them. She'd look way better standing next to this girl than I did, I'm sure.

The lady minding the rack said to wait here until they called our names.

Every now and then, they'd shout a pair of names over a crackling megaphone.

The girls in front of us headed out the doors with an embarrassed giggle.

We went to the door with them so we could watch what they did.

Between the door and the barrel was a mat that looked like what you'd have left after transmuting a red carpet. They walked across this barefoot and then washed themselves thoroughly in a basin of knee-deep water. Preparations complete.

Their names were read again, a cheer went up, the music started, and the grape stomping began.

As the new pair hopped into the barrel of grapes, plenty of new grapes were added.

Nice. We could stomp fresh grapes to our heart's content.

Two more pairs went before us.

When our names rang out, we stepped through the doors, unable to repress our smiles.

It was somehow fun just walking outdoors barefoot. The hemp-like mat felt good on our soles.

We both raised our hands, answering the cheers, and headed toward the barrel, and the crowd of spectators.

We washed our feet as instructed, and then we hopped into the barrel. Fresh grapes squished beneath our soles. It was a sensation like nothing I'd ever felt before. Neat.

The band began playing a tune bright and encouraging. Matching the beat, my feet began moving on their own. Clutching my skirt, swirling the hems, copying what I'd seen others do, ad-libbing a bit, but most of all, I was dancing in the barrel of grapes.

She followed my lead, her body rocking. The way she held her skirt was much more elegant, and there was a real grace to her footwork. She grinned and stomped those grapes real hard. Like she was taking all her life's frustrations out on them.

Juice went flying everywhere, and both our feet turned purple.

The minder was at the front of the crowd and nearly fainted at this sight.

"Oh, miss! This is most, most improper!"

"Don't call me that here!"

"If your father saw you like this, whatever would he say?"

"Oh, give it a rest!" She giggled and was soon laughing so hard that her shoulders shook.

Even as she laughed, she was letting the music guide her. Dancing like the fairy of the grapevine. And stomping them grapes. With evident delight.

I did my best to match her pace.

There was no trace of the stiffness she carried with her when she was all prettied up for the ballroom.

A simple dance, down-to-earth, derived from the core of human lives, celebrating the bounty of the seasons. Like a glimpse into the shamanistic heart of things.

Or at least, the sort of vibe that makes you wanna dub that narration over it.

It was over all too fast.

We could only dance while the music played. I think it was a solid five minutes, but before we knew it, only echoes remained.

We were both out of breath. Quite a workout!

I glanced down at her feet, and she at mine. We both pointed, laughing.

To the sound of clapping and cheering, we stepped out of the barrel, washed our feet in cold water, and went back to the community center.

The minder followed like a shadow, tapping that watch and gesticulating at the heavens. Perhaps worried the goddess of plenty had grown envious. The sight of the girl throwing herself into grape stomping must have been just that alluring.

We ignored the minder's grumbling and slipped back through the doors.

We chatted with the rack lady a bit, and she said after every-one had done their grape dance, the judges would announce the results.

There were still several pairs left, so it would be at least an hour.

There was a lovely prize and a wad of cash for whoever won. What do you think?

"I'll bow out of the contest," she said, taking off the costume. "We've got places to be and need to go. Sorry. But it was a real pleasure."

She bowed her head to the lady and turned away.

"If the opportunity presents itself, I'd like to join again. Will we be able to fit it in next year?"

"A year is enough time to adjust any plans. But what your father will make of this, I could not begin to say."

"My father will approve of anything as long as he knows his daughter is doing it together with Tsuruya."

What an honor! I've been making mischief since I was little, so the fact that he doesn't call me a bad influence is either a testa-ment to his generosity or a sign I need to up my game. Maybe both. Then again, I think we're both getting a bit too old to get our kicks out of harmless pranks.

We might need to take things to the next level, get some real devious skills. Okay, I dunno *why* I think we need that, but...

No, that's not right. I do know. It's just more fun that way. That's all that matters. I'm sure all of you get that, right?

When we finished changing, we returned the grape-girl cos-tumes and made sure we were presentable.

Man, we sure were changing clothes a lot today. And since we had a gathering or party or whatever tonight, we'd have to deck ourselves out in something else. Definitely something not as comfy as the grape-girl gear, that's for sure.

The ruckus outside went up a notch. The next challengers must have entered the barrel. The music shook the whole building.

If we went out the front, we might distract the dancers. Dancing in a barrel of grapes was a rare experience. It would never do to interfere. Best to avoid drawing attention.

So we snuck out the back doors.

The square was all gussied up, but the back road was quiet, lots of shade. We went the long way around the square as we found our way back to the main road.

It took us a bit to locate our ride, and we found the driver with his seat back, taking a nap. We knocked, woke him, and hopped on in.

As the car drove off, she turned to gaze longingly out the back window. For a moment, she savored the lingering effects of the strange little festival, then she sat back down, glanced my way, and winked.

"Any further stops you'd like to make, miss?"

For the minder to say that here could *only* have been sarcasm.

"No," the girl said. "We'll stick to the schedule from here on out."

"Then we shall proceed as planned."

The driver knew where to go. The wheel was in his hands.

It didn't take us all that long to reach the station.

We bought tickets and went through the gates to the platform. It was a pretty long wait before the train came in.

Once we'd settled into our seats, we watched the view passing by outside. It felt like our first chance to relax in a while.

"I feel like a dip in the hot spring would have been perfect *after* the grape stomping," she said.

True, but I bet that autumn festival was a holy rite practiced in that village since days of yore. If we consider the springs a ritual cleansing prior to a ceremony, then it wasn't a waste at all. It might have even been a boon! I bet Dionysus would be thrilled to drink wine pressed by the soles of postbath maidens.

"We definitely aren't in Greece, but let's hope so."

The outdoor bath and the unique, local grape harvest festival…

Leaving the source of these pleasant memories in our wake, the train sped away, carrying us to a city far, far away.

* * *

Haruhi's long recitation ended, and a renewed silence settled over the room.

The soccer, baseball, and track and field teams were still going all out in the school yard, and way off to one side, we could hear shouting from the handball court. The gym was closer to the club building; and the stereo sounds of the basketball and volleyball practices were totally drowning out the table-tennis team, and the wind ensemble was still producing noises like the angels sounding the dissonant fanfares that heralded the apocalypse.

Blotting all these quintessential school noises out of my mind, I said, "And?"

To this déjà vu query, Haruhi responded, "And nothing. That's all there is!"

Clearly following established precedent.

"If this is the problem, it sure seems…like there's a whole lot of nothing. But, uh…"

It was rare she had to think this hard about anything. She even put a hand to her chin.

"The whole thing just feels wrong. Even as I was reading it, I felt like Tsuruya was pulling a fast one on me."

Did Tsuruya's writing have magic powerful enough to defeat even Haruhi's intuition? Maybe we should have her write a charm to ward off crows and stick it to the dumpster.

I glanced around the room. Nagato was staring at the paperback on her lap as if she hadn't heard a word. T had her arms and legs folded and her head tilted all while fiddling with her hairpin.

Asahina was still blinking and going "Huh? Huh?" and searching our faces for clues.

Koizumi spent a while pondering this, but then he snapped his fingers.

"Aha! This is one of *those*," he said.

And what would *those* be?

"I'm starting to see the pattern. At a glance, the story appears quite ordinary, yet there is a mystery hidden within—and the fun lies in figuring out what."

So is this *also* not the case Tsuruya initially mentioned in her first e-mail?

"Likely not. I'm unsure of her intent, but instead of dealing with the fallout of that case, Tsuruya has sent us two stories about this friend of hers, each with something hidden. While we wait for the next e-mail, we shall have to ponder what. I suppose that's the goal, at least."

The last e-mail immediately spilled the beans, yeah.

"Kyon," Haruhi said, standing up and jabbing a finger at the screen. "Print out enough copies of this file for everyone."

We all have our own laptops, so you could just transfer the data. I guess that would leave T out, but I was surprised Haruhi was being that considerate. I assumed the chief's chair, ordered the printer to run six copies of the second attachment, and only then did I realize I'd forgotten to yell at Haruhi for failing to master basic computer functions.

She probably hadn't read my mind, but Asahina eagerly announced, "I'll do the rest!"

Without delay, she scooped up the pages from the printer, dividing them into six stacks and binding each into little booklets with paper clips.

Apron frills ruffling, she handed them all out, leaving her own copy on the table before turning her attention to new cups of tea. Clearly far more important to her than deciphering Tsuruya's writings.

Meanwhile, Haruhi swapped seats with me, allowing me to return to my own. Once there, I started reading through the ten pages of text-laden A4 paper.

It was impressive how well Tsuruya had captured her own voice in print. Haruhi's flawless impersonation of her might have helped. Since I'd already heard all this before, I was able to skim through pretty quick.

As Asahina poured water into the pot, the rest of us flipped through the material we had received thus far.

MysClub T was the first to look up.

"I still know but the barest teaspoon of modern Japanese. So might I ask—is Tsuruya writing in anything resembling a conventional literary style?"

"They're written in a distinctive colloquial voice," Koizumi said, "but that's not unusual for first-person writing. There are certainly a few places that tripped me up, but...let's put that aside. I have a proposal."

Smiling breezily, he raised an index finger...and then his middle finger, too.

"What say we refer to the story set in her childhood as Episode One, and the hot spring and grape-stomping adventure as Episode Two? It seems likely an Episode Three will arrive in due time, so this will make it easier to distinguish between them."

No reason to oppose that. Only thing bothering me is how many of Tsuruya's travel episodes we were gonna be stuck with. I dunno where she is now, but I hope this all wraps up before school closes for the evening.

"Then it's decided," Haruhi said. She had a ballpoint pen and was already inscribing dramatic check marks here and there on the printout. It seemed like there were more things bugging her toward the end of the story.

Her expression was significantly more serious than it had been five minutes before our last Japanese class exam, so clearly, she wanted to unearth the problem Tsuruya had hidden within Episode Two.

A mystery as to why she cared so much.

"Simple, Kyon," Haruhi said, not looking up from the page. "I feel like I'm helping prop up her trick."

She seemed to be going through the dialogue with a fine-tooth comb.

Koizumi raised a hand.

"As a preliminary assumption, my theory is that Episode Two, like Episode One, contains some sort of narrative trick."

Nagato, Asahina, T, and I all nodded.

"Since Episode One disguised their ages, Episode Two made the time line perfectly clear. Tsuruya specified that this took place last fall. And the text of the story itself mentions the harvest festival."

"That's true, but...still..."

Haruhi seemed dissatisfied. She was tapping the base of her ballpoint pen against her brow.

"Mikuru, I'd like to hear your pure, honest opinion. When you reached the end, what was your first thought?"

"Huh?"

The maid had been going around the table, filling each mug in turn. She stopped in her tracks, cradling the teapot.

Haruhi picked up the chief's mug, carefully ascertained the contents' temperature, and added, "Especially about the ending. Anything strike you as odd?"

"Um...I guess so." Asahina crooked her head, eyes shifting as she searched her memories. "They got on a train and went somewhere, right? But where did they go? I thought they were going to a party."

"That's it!"

"Eeeep?!"

Asahina levitated a centimeter off the ground but fortunately maintained her grip on the teapot.

"Amazing, Mikuru! A perfectly uncomplicated doubt! And right on the money to boot! Kyon, you should take a few tips; learn the value of a pure heart."

Asahina's purity levels were beyond question, so I said nothing.

Haruhi pointed at the end of Episode Two with her pen.

"They just go to a station and board a train. But that makes no sense! Tsuruya and the nameless girl went to the hot spring from their hotel. See, right here, 'Our driver was waiting for us—he'd been provided by the hotel we were staying at' (P134)."

Maybe they had some reason to take a train back instead?

"What reason? Did a landslide block the road? Then why not say that?! No reason to hide it!"

"And there are passages that allow us to estimate the travel time between the hotel and the hot springs," Koizumi said, jumping on the back of her horse. "'It is a half day by horse-drawn carriage from the hotel you ladies are staying at' (P134). It is unclear why this minder chose to bring horses into this estimate, but that would make it approximately…"

He did a quick search on his laptop.

"Let us assume a horse and carriage have an average speed of ten kilometers an hour for simplicity's sake. A half day is twelve hours, and they would cover a hundred twenty kilometers in that time. Assuming an average speed of sixty kilometers per hour, their driver would get them there in approximately two hours. You could shrink that down even more by assuming they took an expressway. Either way, I see no logical reason for them to board a train. The girl even says, 'We're staying near proper hot springs!' (P134), so I think it's safe to say this is a bit of a drive, but no more than that."

"So it's inconsistent! At the end of Episode Two, she's all, 'The train sped away, carrying us to a city far, far away' (P143). If you could just drive there in a matter of hours, you wouldn't say 'far, far away'! Clearly, this train is not taking them to the hotel they've been staying at."

So what did that mean? The minder seemed to be hell-bent on getting the girl and Tsuruya back to that hotel as soon as she could, so why is she accompanying them on a train that's apparently bound for some entirely different destination?

"She isn't!" Haruhi said, as if she'd just figured it out. "See! Only the girl and Tsuruya are on the train. They've ditched the minder and the gathering. They aren't going to the hotel, but somewhere totally different!"

"Then I suppose that makes Episode Two's narrative trick clear."

Koizumi seemed sure of himself, but it wasn't clear to me at all. When and where did the minder vanish?

I flipped through the pages, reading the ending.

The minder certainly doesn't get any lines after they reach the station, nor does Tsuruya mention her specifically. Did they lose her between the car and the train?

"Nope."

"Not at all."

Haruhi and Koizumi spoke as one, and he gestured, conceding the floor to her.

"Kyon, when I read this aloud, how did you know who was saying what?"

Well, you helpfully changed your voice up for each line. You nailed the Tsuruya impression for the narration, and while we can only imagine what the girl and her minder look and sound like, you made them all distinct, so I never got tripped up.

"Exactly!"

If sighs had sisters, the one Haruhi let out would be the youngest.

"That's where she got me. Reading it aloud only made it more confusing! She baited me into it. Well, probably not intentionally; it just worked out that way, but I hate that I ended up contributing to the misdirection here."

Haruhi had somehow expressed remorse and pleasure in equal measure.

I turned from her to Nagato, who had put Episode Two aside and was reading an unusually oblong, yellowed volume.

Should I interpret this resumption of her typical silence to mean she'd already solved everything or to mean it simply didn't interest her? I wasn't sure.

Meanwhile, the real expert on these things, MysClub T, was still flipping back and forth through the pages.

"Ugh, so many different character sets, all mixed together!" she grumbled. "How do you keep them all straight? Phonograms and ideograms all piled on top of each other—whoever dreamed up this system is *insane*. Do you really need *both* katakana and hiragana, really? Can't believe someone made up a system this complicated and had the gall to leave it for the world to come. He or she is my mortal enemy."

She'd been reduced to cursing our ancestors.

Once she was sure my gaze had completed the circuit around the room and was back on her, Haruhi said, "Do you know what these two episodes have in common? As far as distinctive writing tics, I mean."

Tsuruya's dialogue never has any quotation marks?

I hadn't directly seen Episode One, but based on Haruhi's performance, it was likely written the same way.

"It was! And the way Episode One blended Tsuruya's dialogue into the rest of the narration was itself a trick designed to pull the wool over our eyes when it came time to read Episode Two. During the sight-reading, I totally fell for it."

Where exactly did you fall? And where did the minder vanish?

"Those two questions have the same answer, which makes it

easy." Haruhi took a deep breath, paused dramatically, and said, "I thought it was the minder talking, but it was actually Tsuruya!"

It took me a minute to digest that.

I looked down at the printout. It was open to the last page.

"Then this line here, 'Any further stops you'd like to make, miss?' (P142). Who says this?"

"Clearly, Tsuruya." Haruhi grinned as she replied.

"Same for 'then we shall proceed as planned'?"

"Also Tsuruya."

She seemed confident.

"When did this start? And why is Tsuruya talking like the minder? And why do her lines suddenly have quotation marks?"

Countless question marks were pouring out of my brain and spinning through the air around my head. Haruhi and Koizumi had matching grins, which was extra annoying.

I took another look at these two Tsuruya lines, wondering if there was a hint hidden somewhere. One line caught my eye.

"Hang on. The sentence right after 'Any further stops you'd like to make, miss?' Tsuruya writes, 'For the minder to say that here could *only* have been sarcasm' (P142). Doesn't that prove the line before it is the minder's dialogue?"

"That's the exact moment where Tsuruya's trick is revealed!" Koizumi ran his finger along the relevant passage. "This line actually contains a subjunctive mood. Grammatically speaking, this structure is used to describe a hypothetical situation and outcome. If we examine this line carefully, it's actually saying, '*If* the minder had said this line in this situation, it would have sounded very sarcastic.' But by the same logic, it means the minder did *not* actually say anything. She wasn't even there! Tsuruya deliberately omitted the word *if*. And the result is that, at a glance, it doesn't appear to be a subjunctive."

"A subjunctive?" I said, brightening up. "I get it now!"

She stared at the line awhile.

"So to paraphrase it, this is actually saying: *This was obviously sarcasm—or would have been, if the minder were actually here to say it!* Right?"

"Past perfect subjunctive." Koizumi nodded.

This didn't sit right with me. It felt like a cheap trick. But you're okay with this, T?

"I would call it…not exactly safe. More like as close to going out-of-bounds as you can get."

That sounded like an out to me.

Koizumi turned toward T. "I think you're getting that impression because you're translating the passage into English as you go. Tsuruya is employing a specific quirk of the Japanese language to create this illusion. Japanese is notorious for failing to distinguish between singular and plural and occasionally does not even make it clear if a verb is present or past tense. Especially if things are written colloquially. I'm sure you've been tripped up by these things in novels before."

I've never really noticed, so can't say I relate.

"Tsuruya is likely writing this with the intent of toeing the line between *fair* and *unfair*. Here, she says *ittara*, which is key—it can be read as either an abbreviation of *itta to shitara*, or simply a replacement for the present tense *iu to*. She'd deliberately employed a colloquial writing style to make both interpretations viable."

Maybe so, but this *was* Tsuruya. We can't rule out the possibility she just wrote this for shits and giggles. I turned to the literature club president for a second opinion.

"Nagato, what do you think?"

"Can't call it unfair," she whispered, then went back to reading a paperback with a title that sounded like something a Greek philosopher would perform on the lyre.

"If Nagato says so, then I'll join her camp. I revise my earlier statement. It is as close to safe as you can get without being safe."

I wasn't sure T's subtle adjustment actually moved it in the direction she intended.

Koizumi was still running the show, though.

"Let us take a closer look at where Tsuruya's dialogue acquired quotation marks."

"Mm-hmm, Kyon had a bunch of good questions, so let's get into the nitty-gritty and take a closer look."

What did I say again?

Spokesman Koizumi took over.

"Up to this point, Tsuruya has consistently left her own dialogue as narration, yet somewhere in Episode Two, she begins putting quotation marks around it. This begs several questions:

"1. When, exactly, does this begin?

"2. If this is Tsuruya speaking, then why is she speaking like the minder?

"3. Why was it necessary for these lines, and only these lines, to receive quotation marks?

"For off-the-cuff questions, these certainly do get to the heart of the matter."

Good job making it not sound like a compliment.

Koizumi shrugged that comment off, flipping through the pages in hand.

"Let us begin by defining which lines we are certain belong to the minder," he suggested.

Haruhi had already checked for this.

"I think we can safely say everything from the first 'miss' in the hot springs (P132) to the bit about 'ill-mannered revelry' (P137) right before they join the grape-stomping festival is all actual minder dialogue. Plenty of these lines specifically say 'the minder said,' leaving no doubt about who the speaker is."

"So the lines after that are in doubt...like the scene where they're changing."

We were all flipping through the pages now, and the sound of pages rustling filled the room. It felt like we were in Japanese literature class.

Koizumi found them first.

"'You look like you've stepped out of an impressionist's painting, miss' (P138). This isn't clearly attributed to a speaker. I'd say that's the answer to the first question."

"It ends in 'miss,' which taken on its own would seem to suggest it's the minder speaking. And up to this point, all of Tsuruya's dialogue has been indistinguishable from the narration, which makes it unlikely anyone could tell at a glance."

Haruhi had certainly not read that line in Tsuruya's voice, or the girl's voice, but as a third party. That had made it even harder for us to tell, but if you looked closer at the lines that followed... Hmm, it did kinda start to seem a bit suspicious, maybe?

"I'm grateful for it, Haru," said the one non-Brigader member, T. "I'm still struggling to read Japanese text. It's much easier for me to follow it by ear. Also, Haru, your voice is clear beyond compare. It's like I'm listening to a radio drama."

I completely agreed with this point. No matter what she tried her hand at, Haruhi was inevitably top-tier.

"Thanks, T," Haruhi said, not the least bit bashful. "Anything minder-like after that point?"

"Let's list them out," Koizumi said, dedicating himself to following her lead. "'You look very good yourself, Tsuruya' (P138). The speaker here is technically unclear, but based on the conversation's flow, it seems likely to be the girl's line. From that point on we have..."

"...'Oh, miss! This is most, most improper!' (P140).

"'If your father saw you like this, whatever would he say?' (P140).

"'A year is enough time to adjust any plans. But what your father will make of this, I could not begin to say' (P141).

"These three lines. In addition to the two we've covered before...

"...'You look like you've stepped out of an impressionist's painting, miss' (P138).

"'Any further stops you'd like to make, miss?' (P142).

"'Then we shall proceed as planned' (P142).

"Six lines in all. Surprisingly few, but the story itself isn't particularly dialogue heavy."

The bulk of it is just Tsuruya describing things in her distinctive speaking style.

"But of these lines, how do we tell which are the minder's and which are Tsuruya's?" I asked.

Haruhi snapped her fingers. "No need!" she said, then chugged her long since lukewarm tea. "They're *all* Tsuruya's lines," she added, slamming the mug down on her desk.

Asahina swiftly grabbed the teapot and filled her mug again. Her earnest pursuit of the maid ideal was now so polished that it no longer felt at all unnatural to have her dutifully serving us. When T had first visited the club and marveled at her, it had served as a harsh reminder that a literature club with a maid was actually a baffling thing to most residents of the world.

This might not be the best time to record my observations of Asahina in her natural habitat.

I should probably mull over Haruhi's words.

But, well, uh...what did they mean?

I reviewed the last few pages of Episode Two again.

"So everything after they went into the community center to change...is actually Tsuruya talking to the girl?"

"Yep."

And the minder didn't say anything when she heard Tsuruya imitating her?

"How could she? She wasn't there."

What?

"Specifically, I mean in the community center. Or in the car after they left, or the train at the end."

That was a lot of places not to be, I thought, but I elected not to say that out loud.

Koizumi ran his finger down the page.

"Look closely. When they first went into the community center, it says, 'Someone answered, the portal opened, and we slipped inside' (P138), but in this case, 'we' is Tsuruya and the girl, and the minder didn't enter with them."

How could you tell? And why? Wouldn't she have just followed after them? The story makes it seem like she's not only keeping her on schedule but also her bodyguard. Kinda doesn't work if she leaves the girl's side.

"So now we have a fourth question! Let's put a pin in that for the time being."

I thought I detected a note of spite in his grin and raised an eyebrow at it.

"If you must have a reason, we could simply say only grape-stomping dance entrants were allowed inside, but…"

Naturally, you think there's another reason?

"Yeah, we can leave that point for later," Haruhi said.

An unexpected burst of suppressing fire. When I saw just how broad her smile was, I got a sinking feeling in my chest.

"Koizumi, I leave the rest to you," she intoned, and took a sip of her tea, assuming an observer's stance.

"Then let us follow the remaining stretch of story," Koizumi said, spreading Episode Two out on the table before him. "We'll pick up at the moment they enter the community center. At this point, the minder has not entered with them. Tsuruya and the girl change, barrel dance in full view of the minder, and return to the center to change once more. At which point, they slip out the back doors."

Even I got this part.

"So that's where they gave the minder the slip?"

"It would appear so. This is where it becomes clear that the minder was not present in the community center. Which tells us that the line about 'A year is enough time...' (P141) is Tsuruya talking. After that, the girls leave, but because they wanted to 'avoid drawing attention' (P142), they 'snuck out the back doors' (P142). Naturally, it was the minder's attention they did not wish to draw."

Then the car they got in to get away from the minder was...

"Not the driver the hotel provided, but an entirely difficult vehicle. The evidence is here. 'It took us a bit to locate our ride' (P142), but if it was the same ride, they should've known right where he was parked. This was a vehicle they hadn't previously used, and they only had a vague idea where the car would be, so they needed some time to track it down. Either Tsuruya or the girl had arranged for the driver to pick them up without the minder's knowledge, telling him to wait for them in that village at a specific place and time."

So the girl had only been pretending she didn't know about the festival and wanted to stop and check it out.

"It seems certain she and Tsuruya knew there was a festival taking place on the route between the hotel and the hot springs, and about the grape-girl contest."

It seemed slapdash at first, but they were actually on a pretty tight schedule.

"Indeed. Tsuruya describes them as being very unconcerned about the time and contrasts that with the minder's constant fussing, but it seems likely their plans required much more careful timing than it appeared."

Even then, they'd wound up keeping their second driver waiting. After all, they found him "with his seat back, taking a nap" (P142).

"That, too, was a clue. The driver of the car that transported them to this village would hardly do something that uncouth. After all, he's described as holding the door open and helping them climb aboard (P134). This contrast is a hint that there are two drivers involved."

And the second driver has no clue how rich Tsuruya and the girl are.

"There's not much else worth mentioning. Having ditched the minder and the first driver, the girls elect not to return to the hotel or the intended 'gathering.' Instead, they seek freedom, boarding a train bound for some distant land."

Didn't really seem like they had a destination in mind. I looked back at my copy of Episode Two, reading again from the start.

I found references to "real hide-and-seek" (P127) and "we hitched a ride with some strangers" (P129).

"It establishes at the start of the episode that they often found ways to slip away from the supervision of the minder and the GPS trackers and escape the burdens of their respective families' businesses. And this proves to be yet another such escape. A dash toward freedom."

With that grand conclusion, Koizumi reached for his neglected tea.

Well, that explained what Tsuruya was writing about. Basically, she just wanted to avoid her responsibilities. But the doubts swirling in my mind remained unresolved.

"Your second question, Kyon," Haruhi said, sticking her beak back in. "Why was Tsuruya talking like the minder? Koizumi, your theory?"

"Judging from the writings in these two episodes, we might assume Tsuruya always talks in the same frank manner as she does with her close friends. But perhaps that is simply how Tsuruya thinks, and she is actually speaking quite politely, as seen in

these quoted lines. No one but Tsuruya herself can know defini-
tively if this narration is what she actually says aloud."

But even then, would it really sound so similar to how the
minder talks?

"That, I dunno. Maybe if this girl's family outranks Tsuruya's
by a lot…but personally, I bet Tsuruya was just goofing around.
Making a joke by imitating the minder. Poking fun at her, but
in an affectionate way, you know?" Haruhi pointed to the page.
"Look at the conversation during the barrel dance. That one's the
most obvious."

Her ballpoint circled the lines in question.

> *Juice went flying everywhere, and both our feet turned purple.*
> *The minder was at the front of the crowd and nearly fainted*
> * at this sight.*
> *Tsuruya: "Oh, miss! This is most, most improper!"*
> *The Girl: "Don't call me that here!"*
> *Tsuruya: "If your father saw you like this, whatever would he*
> * say?"*
> *The Girl: "Oh, give it a rest!"*
> *She giggled and was soon laughing so hard that her shoulders*
> * shook.*

"From her answers and reactions, we can tell they were joking
around. If we assume that was always the vibe, then that explains
why Tsuruya maintains this polite demeanor for the rest of the
story."

I felt like objecting but couldn't find the right words. What was
this? What was bugging me here?

"Yuki? *Yes* or *no* will do."

Nagato didn't look up. "No problems."

"See?" Haruhi said, looking back at me. Proud of herself.

What about you, T? You're a mystery-club girl. This solution doing it for you?

The blond exchange student rose to her feet with all the flourish of a stage performer and placed her hand on Nagato's shoulder.

"I'm on the same page as Nagato. Count my vote as another yes."

The cloud in my mind wasn't clearing up, but I had to go with the majority. I knew from experience that we were usually better off following Nagato's lead on these things. But I had hoped there would be at least one other person on my side here.

Asahina had clearly abandoned any attempt to ponder and was busy making an original blend of Japanese teas, which might well be the correct approach to avoid winding up with frayed nerves.

"Next," Haruhi said, using her ballpoint pen as a fidget spinner. "Onto Kyon's third question. The reason why Tsuruya's dialogue suddenly acquired quotation marks, huh? But, Kyon, is this something we actually need to specify a reason for?"

I mean, it doesn't make sense. If she's got lines, might as well put them in quotes from the start or stick with the no-quotes style till the bitter end.

"That's *your* opinion."

Well yeah, obviously.

"Look at it this way—there's no rule against it. Who cares?! Tsuruya can write this any way she wants. I don't think it matters in the slightest."

Don't get apathetic on me.

"I would say it's an intentional attempt to mislead us," Koizumi said, stepping in. "I can't see any other justification for it."

"I don't read a lot of mysteries," Haruhi said. "Do they do this sort of thing a lot?"

"Narrative tricks weren't designed to allow the culprit to fool the detective—they're both members of the book's cast, after all—but as a way for the writer to directly fool the reader. Naturally, the reader winds up feeling 'tricked.'"

"But that's not against the rules?"

"I hate to drop an ultimatum, but I don't believe there *are* any rules—not just in mysteries but in novels at all. Personally, I have a marked preference for the type of mystery that drops in a Challenge to the Reader and encourages you to guess the culprit, but I am not so arrogant as to demand my tastes become the global standard. For one thing, I don't see how you can enjoy reading if you're worrying about *rules*."

Keeping one ear on their conversation, I looked at Nagato.

Well, Nagato? What do you think?

Her gaze slowly drifted up from the pages of her book. For a very long second, she seemed to consider the question.

"Can't say there's always a problem."

With that unusually long utterance out of the way, she went back to her book.

"Same!" T said. "Agreed with everything Nagato says!"

Are you her worshipper now? It's entirely valid to interpret her as a cosmic horror, so maybe not the best choice for investing your unconditional faith.

Koizumi was doing his meeting-leader thing again.

"With Nagato's seal of approval, let us reach a conclusion."

I'm amazed that you counted *that* as an approval.

"It appears as if there are three characters present, but there were, in fact, only two. The narrative trick was designed to disguise the cast size. That is the deception built into Episode Two."

He let this last sentence hang, and Haruhi took the hint.

"But that's not the end of it! Right, Koizumi?"

"Quite right. I suspected you'd picked up on it."

Quit patting each other on the back.

"Your fourth question, Kyon. Why wasn't the minder with

them in the community center? You're the one who brought it up, so don't tell me you forgot."

Since this minder also seemed to be some sort of bodyguard, it was weird she took her eyes off them, right? Even if they were only allowing entrants in, she could easily have just insisted on being an exception. After all, she'd joined them in the baths, and a village community center was hardly a high-security area. It would make more sense if she'd forced the issue and made them decide between letting her follow them in or not letting them do the barrel dance at all.

"Right? Yet the minder *didn't* join them. Before or after the grape stomping."

The story certainly said as much.

"What did Tsuruya and the girl do in this community center?"

That was obvious.

"They changed."

"Exactly!"

Haruhi picked up her tea like she'd proven her point. Sipping away, she glanced over at her computer screen.

"We should be getting the answer e-mail soon," she muttered.

Koizumi was playing innocent, the smile on his lips so faint that I could barely identify it as one. Nagato was reading. Asahina had finished a pot of her house blend and was taste-testing it. T was grinning in a way that made it no less clear to me whether she understood, apparently leaving any further questioning in my hands. I hated to play along, but the explanation had clearly been inadequate, so somebody had to.

"What does 'exactly' mean here?" I asked, emphasizing those scare quotes.

"Do you know the difference between Tsuruya, the girl, and this minder?" Haruhi asked.

Students and adults.

"Not that."

162

Employer and servant.

"Not that, either."

Tricker and trickee.

"You're getting colder."

Does this spot-the-difference riddle have a right answer?

"It's not so much spot-the-difference as much as it is figuring who's the odd one out. And the odd one out is the minder. The minder has one trait that puts the other two in a completely different category."

Haruhi flashed me a highly eco-friendly ten-watt smile, then snorted.

"The hint is the changing. Even a third-rate mind like yours should get it by now."

While Tsuruya and the girl were changing in the community center, the minder stayed outside. Or was forced to stay outside. Because coming in would be inappropriate.

"You mean..."

"Mm-hmm. I think you've got it."

"...the minder's a man?!" I said. This was as loud I ever got. "This whole time?!"

"Why did you think the minder was a woman, Kyon?"

Because the story started with the three of them in a bath together. And because you—

"I know! I read the minder's lines in a woman's voice. If I'd known he was a man, I'd have voiced him accordingly. Tsuruya herself is easy to imitate, but I can only guess what the girl and her minder sound like. She had me fooled the entire time!"

Haruhi shook her head but was clearly enjoying herself.

"I bet Tsuruya knew I'd read both of these out loud. Did she do anything to encourage that?"

"That would be a big assumption," Koizumi said. "I don't recall anything in the e-mails themselves that would influence your choice to read them out loud. However, Tsuruya knows your personality well. It's likely she knew the odds were in her favor but wasn't counting on it."

"My personality?"

You're far too impatient to forward the e-mail to everyone or wait for it to be printed out. Reading it out loud would skip all that.

"I mean, yeah," Haruhi said, baffled. "Reading it aloud is way faster! Episode One wasn't even all that long."

That might have been the first trap.

Koizumi nodded emphatically. "If you read the first story out loud, you're likely to read the second the same way. If this was a psychological tactic, it's a pretty accomplished one. It's certainly a gambit, but the trick itself would still work well enough even if it failed."

If we'd printed out the story and read it that way, would we have figured it out any faster?

"Perhaps."

"Let's print out Episode One, just in case. Kyon, you're up!"

She leaned back in her chair, not even trying to get out of the way, so I was forced to lean in from the side and grab the mouse, making her wishes come true. To be fair, I wanted to take another look at it myself.

Asahina put everyone's booklets together. For some reason, T helped.

Koizumi picked up the hot-off-the-presses sheaf of papers.

"Episode One clearly says she 'was sitting with a lady who was a bit older' (P109), and 'the older lady was in a drab pants suit, so I could tell she was here serving the girl' (P109). Both of which specify a gender. This may also function as a setup for the later deception."

I quick skimmed both episodes, but nowhere did it specify the two minders were the same person. Perhaps this is why Nagato said it wasn't a problem.

Haruhi locked her hands behind her head, grumbling, "I wish I could delete my memories and read it from the top. Silently."

That was a terrifying concept. Please abandon it.

"Can I say one thing?" T said, showing us her right palm. "Do we have firm evidence that the minder from Episode Two is male? Is there a specific clue anywhere in the story? I could use some assistance here, given my Japanese-language shortcomings."

She had Ep2 in her left hand and was waving it about.

"Isn't the fact that he wasn't watching them change enough?" Haruhi said.

I felt that needed a rebuttal, so I started paging through the booklet again.

"He was in the outdoor bath with the girls, so should we assume that was mixed bathing?"

"It's likely. I can't imagine any of them were actually naked. Tsuruya herself probably wouldn't mind at all, but..."

An image of Tsuruya in the baths began forming in my mind, but thanks to years of training, I now had the self-control to brush it aside in time. I doubted there were any telepaths present, but it was best to avoid thoughts you wouldn't want anyone to read.

Haruhi ran her eyes over the opening of Ep2.

"There's no clear-cut descriptions, but I think this place is more like an open-air spa. Basically, a big outdoor bath, more like a pool than a traditional Japanese hot spring, and everyone wears swimsuits."

My image of this bath had been pretty rustic, maybe because there's several mentions of how far out they are.

I did a quick search for open-air spas on my laptop. Hmm. The results predictably looked like they'd remodeled a hot spring into a luxury heated swimming pool.

"Quite large," Koizumi said, leaning in.

If they'd been somewhere like this, there would've been a huge crowd in the baths, not just the three of them. It would have been pretty lively.

My initial mental image of three lovely ladies enjoying the splendor of autumn in a secluded rural hot spring crumbled away.

Unaware of my disappointment, Koizumi took to his podium once more.

"Let's take a good look at any Episode Two descriptions that seem relevant to the minder's gender.

"First, right here, when the girls emerge from the water, headed for the changing rooms—which are perhaps more like gym locker rooms. 'The minder hung back, following us—at first, but then swooped past us before we reached the building, heading into the changing room first. Probably wanted to make sure to be ready to leave before we were' (P133). Clearly tinged with Tsuruya's opinions."

Haruhi nodded approvingly. "The minder, of course, ran into the men's changing room and finished changing before the girls so he could wait outside the exit of the girl's changing room and prevent them from slipping away."

"Almost certainly, yes. There's no mention of the minder in the changing room, and once they did finish, they 'went outside to find the minder waiting for us' (P133). Speaks volumes to this minder's suffering."

So what do we make of this bit just before that, where it says, 'The minder had a rockin' bod, too. Walking between these two made me feel like a string bean or a stalk of horsetail' (P133).

"Well, the minder's a bodyguard, too. Probably ripped like a martial artist or bodybuilder."

My mental image of the scene shattered so hard that it made me dizzy.

"This one's a close call," Haruhi said, pointing at the page. "See, '...she and her minder were actually quite close. Certainly nothing as distant as mistress and servant' (P135). On first reading, this sounded like a sisterly bond. Subliminally."

"Yes, odds are she wanted to describe them as being close like sisters but decided that would be a bit too far from the truth. And if she specified *siblings*, it might hint that something was up. The best you could do would be *like family*, I suppose."

"But even then, that'd be an invitation to wonder why she didn't just say *like sisters*. I think she was right to pick an expression that skirted the issue altogether."

Clearly, some *intense* proofreading went into this.

"In summary," Koizumi said, smiling like he was in a commercial for bottled spring water, "Tsuruya included a dual-layer trick this time. The gender deception on its own would be difficult to pick out, but the final scenes arose suspicions, and the discovery of the character-swap deception leads us back up the chain of events to the discovery that we have mistakenly assumed the minder's gender. A character presumed to be female was actually male, and where we thought three characters were present, there was actually only two. Discovering both of these deceptions has likely earned us a passing grade."

Was this a workplace evaluation?

"I see," T said. "I acknowledge that you all seem convinced. If you feel you have reached the correct answer, then I throw the matter to Nagato. Have they reached the correct conclusion?"

"...........…"

Nagato said nothing, so it was impossible to tell what she thought, but to my surprise, she looked up from the book, stared at T for two full seconds, and then returned to her role as a book-reading mannequin.

"...Kyam, how should I interpret Nagato's latest demonstration of motor skills?"

T seemed perplexed, but I was no more in the clear. At the very least, Nagato has always been capable of delivering yes or no answers with comprehensible definition, so perhaps she had gained new advanced skills and was now capable of vague answers.

This development clearly concerned Haruhi.

"Yuki, is the answer Koizumi and I proposed incorrect?"

Nagato didn't look up but said, "Not incorrect," in a voice that was barely audible.

"Then it must be right?"

Her head briefly rose and fell. A very Nagato gesture, which was something of a relief.

But...

Argh, how long was this nagging at the back of my mind gonna stick around?

It was like a pill that got stuck in my throat. Something just felt off.

Was that really the resolution of Episode Two?

I felt like there was something else there. For problems like this, I had utter faith in Nagato, so if she said we were right, then we must be right...but damn if it didn't feel like I was rolling around on Tsuruya's palm.

That didn't seem all that bad, but...my inability to pin down the reason was bugging me.

While I was devoting myself to uncharacteristic levels of contemplation, a dish was set on the table before me. I followed the fingers on the edge of the dish up to the maid they belonged to.

"Some sweets to go with your tea?" Asahina asked.

It was *ogura yokan* with a little wooden fork. Any smile Asahina directed at me could be valued in hard currency, so I would drink any amount of tea on that alone, but without losing that smile, she proceeded to distribute *yokan* to everyone. T fixed the reddish-brown gelatinous rectangle with a look you might reserve for an alien's space-travel rations. Maybe she didn't eat a lot of red bean paste back home.

Just as the SOS Brigade+1 was starting this little break…

"You've got mail!"

…the chief's computer announced the arrival of Tsuruya's third missive.

Apparently not learning her lesson, Haruhi read Tsuruya's solution e-mail aloud like she was a program built from the ground up to do nothing but imitate Tsuruya's voice.

"Heyaaaaas! The second story was a *bit* long, so I had to trust my gut on how much time you needed, but did I get it right?

"Yep, you guessed it! We used our drop-in on the village festival to give that minder the slip. Good thing he was the one working that day!

"Obviously, we had swimsuits on at the springs. They're required! Don't worry your pretty little heads about that.

"Was it okay to bail on the gathering? Totally. Everyone there was already connected to our families, and we were only invited to spice things up a bit.

"Putting pretty clothes on and smiling at everyone is easy work, but once is enough for a lifetime. I'm sure you get why we'd wanna run. These events are hella boring, can't recommend going.

"But when we got off the train at our destination, the minder was waiting for us with a big grin. Unreal. Couldn't believe it!

"When the truth came out, we discovered they'd stuck a new kinda of tracker on us that had just hit the market. A nasty little thing that wouldn't wash out, even after our long soak in the spa, and was invisible to the naked eye.

"It's so gnarly. For all I know, there's one on me right now! I'd love to write more about them, but apparently, the things are mega top secret, so I can't! Sorry.

"That sure does explain why security was so slack that day! I thought we'd been super clever, but they were way ahead of us.

Guess we'll have to up our game! Mm, I'm extra motivated now. I'll let you know if it works out. Jus' you wait.

"Anyway, the story I attached this time is the last one! Never fear.

"As you know, I'm off somewhere with my dad, getting hauled all over the map, and this case happened just a little itty bit ago.

"I thought it was sorta neat, so I figured you all should hear about it, but if I started with this, it would all be coming outta nowhere, which is why I also wrote up a couple of travel stories and sent those over first. Consider them, like, prior reading or the opening act.

"Enjoy act three of my travelogue! Ciao!"

* * *

Where am I?

That's sure a dramatic-sounding start, but I have no follow-through.

Let me state up front: All my lines this time will be like the first story and mixed into the narration, so friendly warning not to worry about that.

From this point on, anything in "" is someone other than me, and I guarantee that this time, I won't be using that ploy again.

Anyhoo, I had my arms folded and was staring out the window.

I was in the back seat of a cab. Near sunset.

It was just me and the driver. Not a hired car like last time, just the ordinary kinda taxi you hail outside your hotel.

I was headed to another party venue at some other hotel. Yuck.

There was a reason why I was flying solo. Namely, I felt like it.

If Dad was gonna chip away at my happy school life for these jaunts of his and drag me around to greet people willy-nilly, then I was gonna insist on operating independently as much as was feasible, and he'd agreed to that. Nothing more unpleasant than being paired up with your dad at the hotel *and* the cab.

But I was forced to accept a condition in return, and that's the reason I had my arms folded and was glaring at the window so hard.

Between my clothes and my shoes, I was dressed from head to foot in stuff my dad had picked out, the sort of getup you only ever wear to get an Academy Award.

And I didn't have any Oscars coming my way, just a long, uncomfortable sulk.

I could move around freely as long as I smiled at the party in the designated outfit.

And this time, I had no escape plan.

I'd been informed—well, threatened—that the penalty would be costly. Apparently, they had big news to reveal, and I *had* to be there. I still hadn't located this new tracker, and I was kinda curious what the news was.

The girl's family and mine had been getting real intense about developing super-tiny, micro GPS trackers basically just for the two of us, but this research had led them to some unexpected benefits. One of them serendipity things. Big old windfall.

All kinds of supersmart people had their brains running at full power, just trying to figure out how to make good trackers small enough to foil a couple of kids, and they accidentally figured out some new hypothesis or theory only tangentially related. And since it wasn't what they were supposed to be working on, they just scribbled it down on a Post-it and forgot about it, until another research-type person wandered through and happened upon it. When they realized it fell perfectly in line with their passion project, they raised a huge fuss and got my dad's attention, and he approved the research green light on the spot, and then a bunch of stuff happened, leading all kinds of industries and scientific think tanks and research facilities to get involved in one massive project.

And since this was clearly gonna be huge business for the

foreseeable future, we were throwing an equally huge announcement party.

They'd assembled all the bigwigs and big brains and big accounts and were gonna raise glasses to the success of the project and bring everyone together.

I'd actually been given a lecture on the topic before we came, but I only got, like, maybe 10 percent of it. Something about using genes in lieu of processors and having them calculate whatevers; totally futuristic stuff. What did they call it? DNA computing?

Anyway, what little I understood was still pretty exciting, which was one reason I was showing up like I was supposed to. It was, like, number three on my list.

First would be seeing old friends who showed up at these occasions, and second would be making new friends I'd only run into at events like this.

Getting dolled up in a dress my dad liked sucked, but I did appreciate him providing me opportunities like this. That's how I got to know that girl, after all. Shame I had to miss so much school for it, though.

All this was running through my head while I was staring out that cab window.

Based on the map I'd glanced at earlier, the taxi oughtta be taking me due north. It was a wide road, and the buildings on the side were pretty tall, so I wouldn't exactly call it a picturesque view.

When I tried looking out the other window, the only noticeable difference was the oncoming traffic whizzing past, but at least there were a few gaps between the buildings that let me catch the odd glimpse of the setting sun. Each time this happened, the car interior lit up, and it became pretty bright, so I turned my gaze upward.

The color of the sky right before sunset is real nice, ain't it? Also, the smell of the air right before summer arrives or the smell right after rain hits hot pavement. If they do a revised edition of *The Pillow Book*, they oughtta put that stuff in.

While I was gazing longingly at the receding summer evening, the sun set completely, the night was born, and the cab reached my destination.

This was a gorgeous luxury hotel, several ranks above the one I was staying at. The presentation and networking party were being held in the largest hall they had—I remembered that much, at least.

I paid the driver, got out, and put my party face on.

A bellboy came running over, but I smiled and told him I didn't have any luggage, then asked how to reach the venue, thanked him, and walked as gracefully as I could in that direction. My dad always grumbles that I walk like a kid. Who cares? Lemme walk how I want.

It didn't take me long to get to the venue. There was still plenty of time before the presentation started, but it was already pretty packed. There were round tables placed here and there, and they had started handing out drinks.

I applied my best ornamental smile and waded on in.

First up, I made the rounds by greeting my dad's old business friends, sponsors, and colleagues. People my dad got on with were mostly easy for me to get on with, so this wasn't a problem at all.

Anytime I got introduced to someone new, I kept things affable. Same old routine.

Once that was over, I could start looking for my friends.

"Tsuruya."

One found me first!

"It's been far too long."

The girl rose from her bow, and the smile on her lips was pretty but a bit distant.

She was wearing a chic dress of a subdued hue and making it

look like it was a part of her. I let myself stare. She was so elegant that it was like she added color to the air around her. No comparison with my obvious *I hate wearing this* demeanor. I had the same thought every time.

As I returned the greeting, a server passed by and offered us some grapefruit juice, so I took that and stuck my tongue in it, making sure it was 100 percent fruit juice.

She had a tumbler filled with something fizzy and was swirling it mournfully.

"I'm glad we could meet. It seems like there aren't many people here I can talk to."

Yeah, the regulars at these shindigs aren't exactly our age. This girl and I knew at least one other kid in this predicament, but it looked like she wasn't here tonight. Her family was connected to the project, too, but she must be better at wriggling out of these obligations, I guess. Lucky dog.

While the two of us were catching up, the presentation got underway.

The lights dimmed, and a projector lit up the screen on the stage. Some full-on philharmonic music started booming, and a giant logo filled the screen. Then an epic-sounding narrator began to speak.

The next chunk ran through the project abstract, using images and narration to explain things. The crowd gasped several times. Enough time passed that I finished off a second glass of grapefruit juice.

As the crowd's enthusiasm peaked, the video ended, and the lights came on.

There was a thunderous round of applause, and a thin, older dude took the stage—it was his job to explain stuff. He'd been in the video, listed as the project leader.

For a good long while, he explained things and took questions from the audience, but none of that's got anything to do with my story, so I'll leave it out. The plan was all bioscience jargon, and I wound up feeling like I was listening to a grifter do his thing, which made me laugh.

"The rich gather together, investing their funds in a ploy at getting even richer. Successful projects bring new products to the market and perhaps contribute in some small way to civilization's advancement, but that's simply a side effect of the money made."

This girl was not mincing words tonight.

The man on stage wrapped things up by calling for a toast. The reasons weren't particularly clear, probably just an attempt at mood setting. Glasses were clinking all around us, and they started bringing in carts ladled with food. Another day, another buffet. I hoped some of it was edible.

The volume rose, and a lot of business cards got exchanged.

These gatherings were all about making connections. I'm sure my dad was around here somewhere, but I didn't feel like tracking him down.

I kept hearing bursts of warm laughter from one corner.

I turned to look and saw a man who wasn't quite my dad's age but was too old to call my age.

I felt like I'd been introduced to him somewhere but couldn't recall the name.

The girl noticed me looking.

"Not familiar?" she asked. "He's a distant relative. My paternal grandfather's brother's family, I believe? I've only met him at these types of gatherings, so I assume my father must have invited him tonight."

What's he do?

"He's on the boards of several companies. Far too many titles to remember, but I believe he primarily fancies himself an entrepreneur."

He was swimming in cash, so they brought him in to be a sponsor?

"Very likely."

She did not seem interested.

I kept an absent eye on him and soon realized his card was the source of the laughter.

Each time the girl's relative handed over a business card, he said something that got a huge laugh. He must have a good one-liner that he always used when introducing himself. Whether it was actually funny…

Then someone I actually did know wandered into my field of view. He moved with purpose toward the joking card guy.

He was a young man and had been in the video explaining the project; the captions had said he was a doctor of genetic something.

It didn't seem like the doctor had met the comedian before, so they exchanged cards, laughed, and talked for a minute, and then the doctor turned right around and made a beeline for us.

Out of the corner of my eye, I saw the girl straightening herself up.

"Hi," he said, so I responded in kind. I remembered introducing myself to him once at another party.

He was tall and built like an athlete but easily pulled off that English-brand-name suit. The watch peeking out of his sleeve was totally a casual digital model from the *I just need to know the time* school of thought. He had a face that could mingle freely with the lead cast of a soap and a breezy smile to match. He was a doctor and a genetic researcher, the young hope of the industry, and…he's single.

He remembered me, too, and explained his role in the project with smiles, charm, and even a little wit, subtly emphasizing just how important he actually was. He asked a couple of very specific questions about my high school that seemed like genuine interest, and his replies were impressively apt. Then he turned to the girl next to me, his smile somewhat strained.

"Not having a good time?" he asked. "You've been diligently avoiding looking my way."

She let out a breath like a silent whistle and turned toward him. "I'm fine."

"Sure. I'm a bit wound-up, I admit. Both because I'm able to take part in this project and because I got to meet you."

"You don't say."

"I *do* say."

I must have let it show on my face, because she shot me a glare and then emptied the glass in her hand.

He asked if she wanted a refill or anything to eat, demonstrating consideration, and then swiftly set off. A few seconds later, a few servers carried a round dining table over to us—presumably, at the doctor's request. They refilled both our drinks and left the bottles, at which point, he showed back up, moving like he worked for a five-star restaurant, food piled high on platters in each hand.

He put the platters down and thanked the servers nicely. I dunno how many other drink refills required them to deliver tables, but they bowed professionally and quickly scattered across the room.

The doctor had a glass of mineral water, and he lifted it, cajoling us into a toast. This whole thing was so flawlessly theatrical that I totally played along.

The girl forced herself to look displeased and made a show of raising her glass reluctantly, but she still dinged her carbonated beverage on his glass.

She was being a *hella* obvious tsun before dere, and I just smirked at her.

"Tsuruya, are you remembering better times?" she asked, like she didn't know perfectly well what my grin meant. So unconvincing. Nobody would possibly buy this smirk as nostalgia.

I started to wonder if I was just getting in their way and if maybe I should quietly make myself scarce, so I glanced his way, but the look he shot back said that wouldn't be necessary. I read it as actually preferring I stuck around.

In that case, I was definitely gonna stand right here and enjoy the show.

Best to start by trying to remember what lay between these two.

Well, I knew she had a number of suitors.

And the young doc here was probably a primo candidate.

I didn't have a handle on what her dad was thinking, but I had it figured he was arranging for decent men to coincidentally pop up around her and seeing if she bit. And he wasn't just watching his daughter, but the guys. What did they talk about, how did they respond—I bet every word was gone over with a fine-tooth comb. So voyeuristic.

Which meant Mr. Doctor was *not* on this project by chance.

But she knew all that perfectly well. She knew her parents had the spotlight on him, so she'd stuck to the shade. But each time they met, he slowly pried her heart open—total cliché, right? That's what it looked like from where I stood anyway.

"There's a few things left out of the video I'd love to fill you in on," he said. "The most revolutionary part of this research is…"

Dr. Suitor explained his part of the project clearly, with smart turns of phrase, incorporating comparisons that made it so even a junior high school kid could have understood it. It was like having a really top-notch science article read out loud; the knowledge just poured into your brain. If he were a professor, people would be lining up to get into his classes.

His conversation led us down many side paths, from politics, economics, and sports to the latest viral videos. He was great at holding your interest and did it with just enough humor to get me laughing any number of times.

Meanwhile, she was extremely busy looking away, slowly glancing back at him, and quickly averting her eyes when they met his.

He was talking to both of us equally, but his eyes were almost always on her profile. Like he was pitching words right at the beautiful curve of her ear.

They seemed good together, I guess. Not that I'm any judge.

"What's fascinating is that this whole concept started out as an attempt to maximize conservation of energy in a GPS tracker. But by applying that to the entirely different field of genetic engineering…"

Just as he was getting particularly heated up, someone called his name.

A colleague of his was headed our way.

"There's someone I'd like you to meet. Come say hello."

The colleague turned to us.

"Ladies, I'm sorry, but I'll have to borrow him a minute."

"Go right ahead. No need to get my permission."

"Er, you're sure? Then I'll happily take him!"

The doctor winced and said, "Shouko, see you later."

He walked away. It was a big room, and there were lots of people here. He was soon lost in the crowd.

She let out a little breath that could be read as just about any emotion under the sun and moistened her lips with the long-since-flat contents of her glass.

For a little while, the two of us talked about nothing in particular.

We could fill any amount of time just catching up.

We also munched on the food he'd brought us. As suspected, I didn't care for it.

I told her a few stories from the new school year and got a big laugh out of her on a Mikuru one.

She wanted to go independent as soon as possible, trying not to ride on her parents' coattails, and told me about the shop she was planning on operating.

Stuff like that always made me wonder about my own plans.

Should I take over the family business or not? Part of me wanted to set off on my own on a new journey instead of just follow after my dad. Maybe I should take a day sometime and just stare up at the sky, thinking about my future.

A good fifteen minutes after he'd left us, I noticed she was checking her watch with increased frequency.

Then I heard a little shriek from somewhere. I was sure I had.

But the hum of the crowd around us was loud enough that neither the girl nor anyone else had noticed.

I said I needed to hit the can, then left her there.

I headed toward the voice, and as I left the hall, I found a hotel employee running out of another door, looking quite beside themselves.

This was an antechamber adjacent to the party hall.

I stepped in the open door and found several small tables with a bunch of chairs around them.

Since the main room was standing room only, this area was for people who wanted to sit a spell.

I soon spotted the problem.

Someone was lying on the carpet.

I ran over, and it was him. The young doctor we'd been talking to not fifteen minutes ago.

He was lying faceup with his eyes closed.

There was blood from the back of his head, staining the carpet.

I found more blood on the edge of a nearby table. He'd probably hit his head there. I found it hard to imagine he'd done that voluntarily.

Then I heard a groan. Good, he was alive.

Moving didn't seem like a good idea, so I knelt down next to him. His eyes fluttered open. He wasn't breathing right. I loosened his tie a bit.

You okay? I mean, I can see you aren't, but…

One question on my mind.

Who did this?

He looked up at me. He moved his lips, and a painful breath emerged.

I leaned my ear closer, and the hotel staff came flooding in. The cloakroom lady and the concierge and someone who looked like the owner. They all looked horrified. At the back of the crowd was the staff member who'd gone running off. He had a first aid kit with him.

"Ungh..."

The doctor finally focused his eyes on something—the staff member. Or more accurately, he was looking at the first aid kit. When the staff member moved closer and put the box down, his eyes followed it.

He was trying to say something. What? The answer to my question?

Face screwed up in pain, he nodded slightly. His voice barely a whisper, he said, "Don't swallow..."

Huh? Say that again?"

"...Do not...ingest..."

That's what I thought I heard anyway.

But with that, he passed out.

The rest was a big uproar. Other partygoers started pushing their way in. Someone must have told the girl, and she rushed over, saw her potential fiancé covered in blood, and fainted. It felt like ages before the ambulance crew arrived.

Long story short, he suffered some lacerations from a blow to the back of the head but lived to tell the tale. They did thorough tests to be sure but found no lasting damage to his brain.

Naturally, he hadn't clumsily tripped and hit his head. He'd been grappling with the culprit, been knocked off-balance, and hit his head on the way down.

So this was an assault case.

Feels like a long journey to get us here.

But at last, I can present you all with the problem.

Only one thing I want from you.

Guess the culprit's name.

That's it!

Oh, and just to be clear, the staff member with the first aid kit was just the first on the scene. Not that that's much of a hint.

When I think it's time, I'll send you a better hint. Bye!

* * *

When Haruhi finished, a third silence reigned over the literature club.

The only sound was the rustling as we all read back over Tsuruya's travelogue, Episode Three.

Having learned from Episode Two, we'd printed out copies for everyone in advance. I felt like we didn't really need to have it read out loud, but since we'd done the first two that way, Haruhi seemed to think we should to stick to it, and so we all followed along while listening to her rendition. It felt like being in Japanese class, except when it ended, what greeted us wasn't relief—because Episode Three finally posed the foretold problem. The thing this had all been leading up to.

And I didn't have the slightest clue what the answer could be. I wasn't even sure what Tsuruya wanted to get out of all this. Was there a fatal flaw in my reading comprehension skills?

But I clearly wasn't the only one confused. Haruhi and Koizumi had both adopted contemplative poses, staring at nothing. Even Nagato had put her book down and was staring at the Ep3 booklet.

T had been grumbling about her Japanese reading skills from the get-go, and she'd ignored her booklet entirely, having spent her time fully concentrating on listening to Haruhi's rendition. Next to her, Asahina had her eyes locked on one point of the page, not moving a muscle.

The club member least likely to read a mystery had locked onto a sentence that I'd clearly read without batting an eye. Had there been something that obviously out of place?

"Shouko?" Haruhi whispered.

"A dying message...or...," Koizumi muttered.

Seemed like everyone was stuck on different things.

Since the meeting chairman and our chief were both sinking into a sea of thought, nobody was taking charge. Gratingly, the only other person not mulling over something specific was T.

"Aren't you in the mystery club? Don't you people solve mysteries for fun?"

"Sometimes," T said. She pulled the printout closer and started writing on it with a ballpoint pen. "But I'm not in charge of whodunits. It's outside my wheelhouse. I've never once solved one. I'm more the type to *just* read."

A reading specialist?

"And this is a problem for the SOS Brigade! As an outsider, all I can do is sit on the sidelines cheering everyone on."

I looked closer at what she was writing and discovered she was adding *furigana* to all the kanji in Ep3. Muttering vocab under her breath. Occasionally...

"Kyam, what's *kozaiku* mean?"

Like, when you describe a woodworker who's good with their hands.

"A ploy. An unpolished scheme that will soon be discovered," Nagato corrected, not looking up.

T nodded to herself. "And this Chinese idiom–looking thing you pronounced *fuukoumeibi*? What does that string of kanji mean?"

The name of a famously pretty dancer in Luoyang during the Western Han dynasty. The *Zizhi Tongjian* contains an account of her dazzling beauty.

"'Picturesque.' It's a term of praise, used to describe particularly spectacular landscapes," Nagato said.

"And *hyoutan kara koma* is…?"

A gourd so big that you can fit forty shogi pieces in it. People in the Edo era used to carry them around like that so they could play shogi anytime. It evolved to be a term meaning "let's play a round."

"A horse from a gourd. A windfall. An example of an unexpected phenomenon. *Koma* here means 'horse,' not 'piece.'"

While Nagato and I were teaching T some advanced Japanese, Koizumi looked up, selecting one of his vast repertoire of faint smiles and directing it at us.

Well? You solve the thing?

"No."

So that smile was his way of rebuking us for goofing off when there was a mystery to solve.

"As far as whodunits go, it's a bit unusual," he said, pointing at the last page. "It doesn't ask us to identify the culprit, merely their name. Curious."

How are those different?

"Perhaps in ordinary writings, they would be equivalent. But given the problem posed here, we must assume otherwise."

Why?

"'Why?'" Haruhi repeated, swiveling her chair in our direction. "Because the culprit is patently obvious!"

Then who is it?

"Think for yourself sometimes! Your grades will never improve copying off other people's answer sheets."

I wasn't planning on majoring in detectivology.

"You say that," Koizumi said, "but surely you have some idea?"

"Yeah, sure," I admitted. I flipped through the printout. "This dude Tsuruya called the card comedian. The girl's father's grandfather's brother's heir or whatever."

"Why do you think that?"

Because the only real characters in this thing are the charming doc and the card comedian. And since the former is the victim, that means the latter must be the culprit. By process of elimination.

"Reverse engineering a solution from a metafiction perspective is generally considered an illegitimate approach..."

Don't look at me. When did the SOS Brigade do anything the proper way? Our whole MO is defying reason. We're both in this mess together!

"You have a point there. And the challenge Tsuruya sent us is hardly your standard mystery, is it?"

He glanced toward Haruhi there.

"Kyon's right," she said. "The culprit is obvious, so clearly not the problem. That's why we're told to figure out the name instead. Very Tsuruya. I like these logical leaps of hers."

She started tapping the desk with her pencil.

"Mikuru, any tea left? All this reading aloud's left me parched."

"Oh, of course!"

Asahina had been staring at one line in Ep3 this whole time, but Haruhi's voice snapped her out of it.

"Just a moment!"

Slippers pattering, the SOS Brigade's maid went back to her real job.

I glanced at Nagato, too, and she'd abandoned the printout and resumed her original reading stance.

"............"

This was Nagato, so it was entirely possible she already knew the answer, but if she did, she showed no signs of it. Was this because she knew we didn't want to have it blurted out or just... how she always was?

Once again, Koizumi took the wheel.

"Let's take a look at any passages that might provide a hint of the culprit's name."

"Yeah. Starting with the most obvious one," Haruhi said, clearly on board.

"By that, you mean the dying message?"

"He's not dead, so that term ain't right, but whatever. Sure."

"*Fainting message* just doesn't have the same ring to it."

Nobody cares. Let's move on.

"Well," Koizumi said, flipping through the pages, "just before passing out, the doctor says a few words to Tsuruya. We must assume these are a clue to the culprit's identity."

"It's certainly the most obvious one."

Haruhi picked up her mug, remembered it was empty, and put it back down. Asahina hustled over to the chief's desk with the teapot and filled it with warm tea.

"Thanks," Haruhi said and drank half the mug in one gulp. "The doctor says two very similar things. 'Don't swallow' and 'Do not ingest.' I bet if we fiddle with those a bit, it'll get us the card comedian's name."

How would you convert those phrases into any sort of name?

"Figuring that out is the key to the problem posed," Koizumi said. He was placing check marks on his copy of Ep3. "First, it is highly likely that the card comedian and 'the girl'—Shouko—have the same family name. Are we in agreement there?"

Since they were connected via paternal grandfather, that seemed reasonable.

"If we can work out Shouko's family name, then we'd automatically know the card comedian's. Anything in this that provides a hint to what her other name might be?" Haruhi turned her gaze toward the other two episodes.

"Not that I recall," said Koizumi. "I'd even say it's the other way around—figuring out the card comedian's name would lead us to Shouko's full name. Perhaps that's the point."

"After all this time being a nameless girl, I gotta think there's a reason her name suddenly pops up here," Haruhi said.

"Exactly," Koizumi nodded. "In all three episodes, this 'Shouko' is the only time any names are specified. Episode One was almost entirely just the girl and Tsuruya, but Episode Two had the minder with them for most of it, so it's actually rather surprising that nobody ever used a name."

Because using a name might have blown the gender deception?

"A family name would hardly be an issue."

"Hang on," Haruhi said, raising her right hand and putting her left to her brow like she was checking for a fever. "That's not it at all. If she's gonna use the name *Shouko* at all, it would make equal sense for it to show up in the first two episodes. So turn that around—why was it only revealed in Episode Three? That's super bothering me."

Common sense dictates the name *Shouko* must be a clue to the card culprit's name.

"Well, yeah, but…" She didn't look satisfied.

What happened to your usual snap decisions, wild hunches, and logical leaps?

"Don't be silly. I always think things through."

If you mean that, I am officially frightened.

"Another mystery is why *Shouko* is written in katakana," Koizumi said, getting things back on track. "Would the kanji be some kind of a giveaway?"

May I make a prediction?

"Go ahead."

Tsuruya ends Episode Three with a promise. "When I think it's time, I'll send you a better hint" (P182). Doesn't that imply it's impossible to solve without any hints?

"That's certainly a possibility," Koizumi said, stroking his chin. "How much time before Tsuruya sends us the next hint? That length will be an indicator of just how high her opinion of us is."

If she sends us the hint anytime soon, that'll mean she knew we gave up quick.

"I bet the first hint'll be the kanji for Shouko. Just guessing."

She said that, but Haruhi's guesses were pretty much always right.

"Then let us assume we'll need a hint to ascertain the kanji there and attempt to work out the card man's name from another angle. Tsuruya describes him in some detail, so one can assume this business card of his also hides a clue."

That card would definitely have his full name on it, so if we could get a look at his card, we'd know everything.

"Tsuruya writes rather a lot about him exchanging cards. Like, she 'soon realized his card was the source of the laughter' (P176). Or 'each time the girl's relative handed over a business card, he said something that got a huge laugh' (P176). 'He must have a good one-liner that he always used when introducing himself' (P176). This suggests there's something about the name on the card that becomes a quick joke with the addition of a word or two spoken aloud."

Getting constantly teased about a funny name sounded exhausting.

Anyone know any names that could be turned into jokes when introducing yourself?

"At the moment, I have no idea. The only thing I can say for sure is that the family name alone would not be the source of humor."

"If that was all it took," Haruhi chimed in, "then Shouko could be using that same joke. And Tsuruya would have known about it by now. But Tsuruya said she 'couldn't recall the name' (P175), and it sounds like she's not really sure what sort of joke this might be. So we can deduce the joker's card joke involved both his names."

Now I understood even less. Could really use that hint right about now.

Haruhi propped both elbows on the desk and put her cheeks on her palms.

"The funny name and the doctor's dying messages, 'Don't

swallow' and 'Do not ingest,' have gotta be related. Tsuruya asked, 'Who did this?' (P181), and these two lines are his answer, so we have to assume they indicate the culprit's name. But since the victim was fading in and out, his mind likely went in an odd direction and produced this inscrutable response."

"Yes, in the famous words of Drury Lane, 'the human mind is capable of even more amazing things than that, in the instant before death.' Dying takes us close to God, so the leaps made while delivering a dying message know no bounds! Although, in this case, he merely drifted into unconsciousness."

Was I the only one who thought that quote sounded like a desperate rationalization?

"Since he was just fainting, he definitely didn't get all that close to God, then. It's kinda half-assed, as far as dying messages go."

This was an extremely disrespectful conversation.

"There is one other critical scene in this passage," Koizumi said, raising an index finger to his brow. "Directly after delivering this message, note the doctor's gaze. 'Or more accurately, he was looking at the first aid kit. When the staff member moved closer and put the box down, his eyes followed it' (P181). This makes it clear the first aid kit is a key item."

So then…the card comedian's name:

1. Is odd enough to provoke laughter.
2. Potentially the name of something known for being undrinkable.
3. And might be found in a first aid kit.

"An excellent summation."

That was definitely the brightest smile he'd had all day.

"Now we must all let the wings of our imagination fly free and hope we can reach the correct answer if the missing piece comes our way."

Optimistic. Might as well start by researching what's in those first aid kits.

But just as I was reaching for my laptop…

"You've got mail!"

…the hint we'd all been waiting for arrived. Flawless timing.

"That was fast! I figured she'd keep us stewing a while longer."

Haruhi took a noisy sip of her tea as she opened the e-mail. Once again, she read it aloud.

Unlike the previous e-mails, this one had no attachments and didn't beat around the bush. It consisted entirely of the following four lines:

> Hint 1: *You can use dictionaries or the Internet to look it up.*
> Hint 2: *It isn't the name of anything in the first aid kit.*
> Hint 3: *Her family traditionally put the kanji* nao *or 'esteem' in their names.*
> Hint 4: *You can use katakana for part of the culprit's name.*

Just to be thorough, we printed this out and made sure everyone had a copy. Two of these hints seemed specifically directed at me.

"I thought she'd be doling them out one at a time, but she sent a bunch."

"Perhaps being mindful of how long we're allowed to remain on school grounds. If we mulled these over one by one, we'd run out of time. Either way, we do have to work down the list, so perhaps she just couldn't be bothered sending so many e-mails."

Once our two main thinkers had exchanged views, Koizumi got the ball rolling.

"Let us begin by stating all information gleaned from these clues."

"Shouko's name is definitely written like *Naoko*, with the family's favorite kanji read as *shou* instead. The *ko* might be the character for 'lake' or 'fox' instead of 'child,' but that's irrelevant, since what we need is the culprit's name."

"The tricky bit here is the reading of this 'esteem' kanji. The girl gets the *on*-reading, which gives us *Shouko*, but there's no guarantee the card guy's the same. Even if his name is written with the kanji for 'esteem' and 'one,' it could be read either as *Naokazu* or *Shouichi*. And that would change the joke."

Maybe his joke was simply about how to read it? Or it could be wordplay that only required the kanji. Business cards usually have *just* kanji on them.

"Good point," Koizumi said.

He rose to his feet, dragged the whiteboard out of the corner, and wrote the kanji for "esteem" in the center, and the two readings, *shou* and *nao*, on either side.

"That said, hint four tells us part of the name could be written in katakana instead, so we can deduce the joke is less about the kanji themselves than the reading. And in Episode Three, it says, 'Each time the girl's relative handed over a business card, he said something that got a huge laugh' (P176). Based on this, just seeing the name alone is insufficient; he needs to take a specific action to complete the gag."

A joke involving a word with *nao* or *shou* in it, and a phrase short enough to be expressed in a name?

Maybe if I did a search for it, I'd get something.

"Hint number one." Haruhi grabbed a mouse. "But does that mean we're free to look as much as we like because we won't find squat? I'm also puzzled by her bringing up dictionaries."

Perhaps this was time for Nagato's stockpile of weird dictionaries to shine.

"That's the thing, Kyon," Haruhi snapped. "Why a dictionary, and not an encyclopedia?"

Those two words had different kanji but were both read *jiten*, so I'd need a dictionary to remind me of the difference.

Koizumi helpfully wrote both words on the board.

"Generally speaking, encyclopedias are multivolume sets with entries explaining things in great depth, while dictionaries, whether mono- or bilingual, give definitions and examples of usages. Encyclopedias are more specialized, but students like ourselves more commonly reference dictionaries."

So understanding the card joke didn't require the advanced level of detail present in a specialized encyclopedia?

"I bet you can get it with common knowledge, but it's also just tricky enough that Tsuruya thinks we might need a dictionary to figure it out."

Whose intelligence level was Tsuruya basing that assumption on?

I glanced at Nagato, but she was in default impassive-reading mode. Still wasn't sure if she'd solved everything and was simply staying out of it or if this was an indication that there wasn't enough information to bother thinking it through.

Outsider T was still analyzing Tsuruya's writing on a textual level and had roped Asahina in as her kanji instructor.

An adorable maid working as a home tutor for a blond exchange student was a painting that would look great on any wall. The fact that all she was actually doing was telling her how to read kanji just made it cuter.

"Each of the four hints contains something of value," Koizumi said, adding more words to the board. "The second clue, 'It isn't the name of anything in the first aid kit,' is the only negative phrase, but perhaps the most significant of all."

He wrote *first aid kit* and put an *X* on it.

"So what *is* in a first aid kit?"

Medicine, bandages, Band-Aids. That level of first aid kit could be found anywhere, but if we really wanted to know the exact contents, we'd have to phone the hotel.

"We can't and don't need to," Haruhi said, swirling her mouse around her pad. "What's key here isn't the contents of the kit but the kit itself. The victim is a doctor, so why was he so oddly fixated on a first aid kit as his consciousness faded? This must be a vital clue to the culprit's name."

"And this doctor was not just a doctor, but a researcher. If we examine this from a medical perspective, perhaps we can glean something more from the significance of this first aid kit."

I was not a doctor, or a medical student. Not even a prospective one.

"Nor am I."

Koizumi erased the X-ed out *first aid kit* and wrote the words again.

"I feel completely ignoring the contents would be premature."

The phrase you used for *premature* has *shousou* in it, and that includes our kanji of the day. Any chance it could be read *naohaya* here?

"None," Haruhi said, dismissively. "Yeah, this 'It isn't the name of anything in the first aid kit' doesn't mean it isn't something in the kit at all. It's probably a word connected to something that is."

"If it's not a brand name, then perhaps it's the generic name everyone uses? Like aspirin?"

"I think we can rule out ingredient names. Aspirin and acetaminophen both broadly qualify as the names of things in a first aid kit."

"Even if not the specific names of those items?"

Then Koizumi got a flash of inspiration.

"What if it's not a noun?"

"That's it!" Haruhi dropped the mouse and locked her fingers behind her head, glaring at the ceiling. "But I have no idea what that leaves us with, specifically."

I did a quick image search for first aid kits.

They were mostly square wooden boxes with crosses on the top. I think we even had one at home. The contents were just standard over-the-counter drugs, bandages, gauze, compresses, and ointments.

"Kyon, do some free association on first aid kits!"

I dunno about that, but looking at these had reminded me of one thing.

"Oh? What?"

"This was when I was younger than my sister is now."

I was a curious kid and was rummaging around in the first aid kit. The bottles of medicine were particularly interesting. I was checking each out in turn. One of them was a brown bottle with a liquid inside. It was pretty old, and the label too worn to read. I figured the fastest way to figure out what it was would be to open the lid, bring it up to my nose, and take a sniff.

"And what happened?"

Agony. I was writhing all over the floor.

"What was in it?"

Ammonia. I think it was for beestings or something, but I've yet to encounter another odor anywhere near that strong. Just remembering it makes the back of my nose hurt.

"Later, I'd find out the way to check the smell of bottled medicine was to place your hand over the opening and tip it."

Sepia-toned memories came flooding up.

"I also learned the importance of warning labels. If I'd known it was ammonia and known what ammonia was, I'd never have tried to smell it."

Koizumi was rubbing his eyes just imagining it.

"Ammonia is used as a form of smelling salts. You see it sometimes in Western…mystery…"

He trailed off midsentence, so I looked up to find him frozen to the spot, mouth still open. His eyes unfocused, like he was looking at a hologram I couldn't see. And this pseudopetrification effect had spread to Haruhi, as well.

Her jaw was hanging wide-open, and her eyes were every bit as wide.

After a minute, she blinked slowly.

"Er, huh? But then…," she rasped. "So that's why 'Don't swallow'? Not because you can't drink it, just…literally. 'It isn't the name of anything in the first aid kit' means…this?"

"I believe so." Koizumi nodded. "If the doctor's dying message relates to the first aid kit, not to the contents or the medicine, but the words written there…"

Haruhi and Koizumi moved like they were twins, both reading Episode Three from the top. They stopped on the same page, looked up, and spoke in unison.

""Aha!""

"Dammit," I said.

What have you two figured out? Is it that weird that the first aid kit back home had ammonia in it?

"Kyon," Haruhi said, with a smile that—creepily—could only be described as meek. "Your exploits were a portent of disaster. I want to travel back in time to officially thank little Kyon. Do you even realize how important what you just said is?"

I averted my eyes from her smile and got smacked with another.

"The importance of warning labels," Koizumi explained. "Your words! That is the key to unraveling the dying message."

"Not all the medicine in a first aid kit is consumable! There's medicine for beestings and ointments for itches. And what do you think is written on those labels?"

Don't swallow or *Do not ingest*?

"I dunno if they slap that on every medicine around. And they're probably a bit less direct about it. I mean, not that many people would be tempted to swallow ointments. But there's definitely something like that on bottles of ammonia."

So the doctor's mind went to the first aid kit, to medicine in it, to the warning label, and then to connecting the writing on that warning label to the culprit's name, and after saying that warning aloud, he passed out? What the hell? That doesn't even make sense.

"It's not just a warning. Naturally, it's also the culprit's name."

"That's what's on the culprit's business card! Although, naturally, not word-for-word the same as the doctor's dying message."

Don T'Swallow, or *Du Notin Gest*?

Where was this dude from?

Haruhi and Koizumi glanced at each other, their smiles matching.

"That's where the dictionaries and Internet come in."

"The key is that Tsuruya said, 'That's what I thought I heard anyway' (P181)."

Just as this mystery was feeling increasingly pointless…

"You've got mail!"

The instant she clicked on it, Haruhi's smile got even brighter.

She read the one-sentence e-mail in Tsuruya's voice.

Hint 5:   *Where am I?*

Does that mean…where Tsuruya is currently staying?

According to the e-mail, she was with her dad, running all over the place, and if 'this case happened just a little itty bit ago' (P170) was referring to this dying-message case, she probably wasn't back home yet.

Was figuring out her travel itinerary our next problem?

"It is, but it's also a hint."

Koizumi opened the A4 printout of Episode Three to the second page.

"Where is Tsuruya's location in Episode Three? One scene gives us a clue to that—and only that one. Look again at the pages describing her cab ride. She describes the view outside the taxi window."

I focused my optical nerves on the relevant passage.

All I could find on the view outside the window was that she said, 'It was a wide road, and the buildings on the side were pretty tall, so I wouldn't exactly call it a picturesque view' (P172). But that could be anywhere. How could we narrow that down?

While I was glaring at the printout, Haruhi started clicking her tongue and waggling a finger.

"No need to name the exact location. You can go bigger than that."

She dropped her finger to the page.

"The key here is the direction the taxi is headed, the location of the sun, and the direction of oncoming traffic."

This was getting complicated. Koizumi, take over.

"It's extremely simple," he said, with the confidence of the well-informed. "Tsuruya actually describes the scenery quite well. Suggesting its significance. If you reread it with that in mind, oh my! There's several elements that don't jibe with our common sense."

He wasn't making it any less complicated. But T and Asahina were still studying together, and Nagato was reading, so I had nowhere else to turn. I had a brief moment where I wished Yasumi was here, but I soon drove that horrifying idea from my mind.

Oblivious to my inner turmoil…

"First, note the direction of Tsuruya's gaze. She is looking out the window at the nonpicturesque scenery. Then she says, 'When I tried looking out the other window, the only noticeable difference was the oncoming traffic whizzing past' (P172) and 'there were a few gaps between the buildings that let me catch the odd glimpse of the setting sun. Each time this happened, the car interior lit up' (P172)."

Koizumi went back to the whiteboard and drew a malformed rectangle that I assume was intended to be the car. He then drew two circles on either side.

"'The taxi oughtta be taking me due north' (P172), so…"

He drew an arrow pointing up.

"The sun sets in the west, so when that light was falling on her face, we can assume she was facing left."

If you were headed north, then the only way to look at the sunset would be to turn left.

"And that's where she saw something entirely outside the realm of our typical experiences."

Leaving a bit of a gap, he drew a sunlike circle to the left of the rectangle and then drew two vertical lines, one on each side of the car—indicating the road, I think.

Here, he turned to me.

"Picture it in your mind. You are in a car. You turn to your left. What do you see?"

I pictured myself getting on a bus, sitting down, and looking left.

"Houses, vacant lots, stores…etc."

If there was a passing lane, then cars driving alongside us.

"Wait…cars?"

Even I got it now.

"Oh. Oncoming traffic."

"Precisely!"

Koizumi drew a third vertical line to the left of the line he'd drawn on the car's left side.

"Tsuruya was in a moving taxi, facing left, but she saw 'oncoming traffic whizzing past' (P172). As you know full well, traffic in

Japan flows on the left, so we are only familiar with oncoming traffic on our right. Which means…"

He drew a new rectangle between the lines left of the rectangle and four circles and put a down arrow next to it.

"Tsuruya was in a country where the traffic is on the right. This doctor-assault incident did *not* take place in Japan."

"Get it now?" Haruhi said, rummaging in her bag. "This is why the first hint said 'dictionary' and not 'encyclopedia.' Here."

She handed me an English-Japanese dictionary.

It took me a good thirty seconds to parse the meaning of that, and then I turned the proffered tome down and woke up my laptop.

Haruhi didn't seem particularly put out. Mouth like a sleeping cat, she put the dictionary back in her bag,

"Okay," I said. That was all I could say. "I get that Episode Three takes place abroad. But what does that mean?"

"It casts suspicion on the language the doctor spoke."

Koizumi scribbled *Mr. Dr.* on the board.

"Nowhere does it specify this man is Japanese. Now that we know the setting is international, odds are he is from that locale instead. Meanwhile, she says, 'While I was gazing longingly at the receding summer evening' (P173), so we can surmise the seasons match Japan's, and this takes place in the northern hemisphere."

"The name of country doesn't matter, so no point thinking about it," Haruhi jumped in. "Let's just assume it's America. That assumption won't cause any issues. And that would mean the doctor was speaking English."

How do we know that?

"That's the only way the dying message makes sense."

Really?

"Really. Everything he said before passing out? 'Don't swallow' and 'Do not ingest?' He actually said that in English!"

Koizumi followed the same line of thought, adding, "He whispered a dying message in Tsuruya's ear in English, and she translated that into Japanese for us. Hence her statement, 'That's what I thought I heard anyway' (P181). Betraying her uncertainty! Anyone who regularly reads works in translation knows what a difference the translator's interpretation can make. Even the choice of characters' first-person pronouns—"

I held up a hand, cutting him off.

So we knew where the sleight of hand had taken place. But we didn't know what kind of magic had been performed. I still didn't see anything pointing to the culprit's name.

Haruhi and Koizumi smiled in sync, like they'd rehearsed it.

"We actually lack sufficient clues to pinpoint what language he spoke. However, we have all been learning English for several years now, and with no clues to the contrary, that seems the most obvious assumption. It is the foreign language we are most familiar with."

I thought you said reverse engineering was illegitimate?

"It is occasionally important to bend the rules. Rather than be stymied by calcified ideals, it is far more profitable to keep one's perspective fluid."

Sure, like, generally. But what about this long conversation the doctor had with Shouko and Tsuruya?

"Naturally, all in English. It's certainly possible that the doctor was bilingual and spoke to them entirely in Japanese, but even if that's true, it doesn't matter here."

I guess I wouldn't be surprised to find out Tsuruya could speak several languages at a native level.

"Practically speaking, as long as we can confirm the doctor's dying message was in English, the rest ceases to matter," Koizumi concluded.

Cool. We'll go with that, then. Can you just tell me the answer already? The problem Tsuruya posed for us says we've gotta "guess the culprit's name." You both look like you've figured it out, but you never know; this might be one of those *you both have different answers* things.

"Kyon, that's a painful possibility," Haruhi said, delighted. "Right, then I'll give you a hint. Let me see…"

She tilted her head a couple of degrees sideways, like Nagato did on occasion, and thought for a few seconds.

"Ishikawa Prefecture," she said. "Well, Koizumi? A little free association."

"An excellent hint," Koizumi said, blithely. "Allow me to provide half the answer. The card comedian's given name is Takenao. See?"

Haruhi's look made it clear she agreed. If I'd held a bar code reader up to her face, it would have told me, *I leave the rest to you, Koizumi.*

"The *nao* part is the kanji for 'esteem' again, but the *take*… Well, the character for 'military' is always a safe bet, but we can't really say that for sure. Tsuruya's third hint comes into play here; *take* could even be written in katakana."

That's enough preamble. What do you think that whiteboard's for? And that dry-erase marker in your hand? If you remember how to use them, get on with it.

"You are but one step away from the answer! Are you sure you don't want to work it out for yourself?"

If you and Haruhi beat Tsuruya's challenge, then that's a victory for the SOS Brigade. You can take the credit.

"If this were a mystery novel, this would be the perfect moment for a Challenge to the Reader…"

Who cares?

"Just tell me the culprit's name."

"Very well," Koizumi said, looking slightly disappointed. He turned his back and started writing. "I can't be one-hundred-percent sure, but I believe these are the right characters."

You couldn't possibly call his handwriting good, but there it was. The card comedian's name.

Notobe Takenao.

Not too sure of the family name, I read it out loud in Japanese name order.

But no sooner had the words left my mouth than someone broke up laughing.

I looked and found T with her hand over her mouth, face buried in her shoulder, shaking with laughter. I thought she'd been focusing on Asahina's Japanese lesson, but apparently, she'd been keeping one ear on us as well. And I guess she did come from an English-speaking country.

So how was this a hilarious gag? If you had to be good at listening comprehension to get it, I didn't think I'd get much use out of it myself.

"So we said the doctor's dying message was 'Don't swallow,' but that was translated into Japanese, right?" I said, pressing further. "But in English, what he actually said was…'Notobe Takenao'? How do you get 'Don't swallow' from that? Is this a game of telephone?"

The room had divided into two camps. The only people not smirking were me, Asahina (blinking furiously), and Nagato (reading). Okay, that was half of us. Guess I didn't need to count.

"I'll explain later, but the culprit's card joke required an additional phrase. And we have to remember that the victim was a doctor looking directly at a first aid kit."

Koizumi swung the marker like a conductor's baton.

"In light of that, what was the exact wording of the doctor's dying message before Tsuruya's translation? If we know that, then it all becomes clear."

Koizumi began writing something horizontally.

"I believe what he said was…"

He turned around, popping the cap back on, and took a step sideways, revealing the English phrase beyond.

Not to be taken

"Depending on the situation, this phrase could mean many things, but assuming the medicine in the first aid kit was produced for an English-speaking market, something like a bottle of ammonia would have a warning label that might well read, *Not to be taken orally.*"

He popped the cap back off (that didn't last long) and scribbled a few kanji below.

"If we translate that back into Japanese…"

Some very angular kanji there, but legible enough.

Fukuyou Kinshi

Okay, so *orally* meant "swallowing." And since you shouldn't do that…Tsuruya had gone with *nomu na* or "don't swallow." The thought process behind the translation was clear enough.

"Perhaps she thought those kanji would be too much of a hint. If you search for them, the first hit you get will give you the phrase *not to be taken*. You'll soon see why."

Right. Sure.

And we go from *Not to Be Taken*…to *Notobe Takenao*.

All this buildup for a pun? And a bad one. *Notobe*, fine. But getting *Taken* from *Takenao* would take some *willful* sabotage even in the wildest game of telephone.

"Thus, the extra step," Koizumi said, flashing his pearly

whites. "Remember the joke he used when handing out his business card. That card, naturally, had his name on it. And he was handing these cards out at a party in a country we're assuming was America. He would, logically, be meeting very few Japanese speakers, so would the cards be in Japanese? Hardly seems likely. Japanese businessmen working abroad either have a separate set of cards in Romaji or two-sided cards with both languages on them. So his card…"

He proceeded to write the man's name out again. Instead of kanji, he used the English alphabet. I expected the order to change, but Koizumi kept it as *Notobe Takenao*.

"I believe he kept the name in the Japanese order. It's common to reverse the names on English-language business cards, but there's a growing movement to dispense with that practice. Mr. Takenao is either part of that movement or simply realized he could use his name to get a laugh out of new acquaintances if he kept it in this order. His motives matter little."

Associate Professor Koizumi's lecture did not end there.

"When he exchanged cards, I believe he covered the last two letters—*ao*—with his finger, talked around the missing *t*, and told everyone his name formed an English sentence with an actual meaning to it. Not a claim many can make, and a joke about how he was 'not to be taken,'—lightly or orally—would be an effective way of getting his name remembered after a single encounter. Especially if he was speaking to doctors."

Not-to-be Taken-ao.

Perhaps the doctor had remembered it broken up like that. And when he was on the verge of passing out and trying to say the man's name, he happened to spot a first aid kit, and it came out as a more regular English phrase instead.

Had Tsuruya figured out what he meant on the spot? Yeah, there was no way she didn't know this comedian's card joke. Yet she'd pretended otherwise, written the whole thing up as a Challenge, and sent it our way. With the first two episodes thrown in for good measure.

How generous of her. I was almost touched. What had driven Tsuruya to do this? Should we just accept it all in the spirit of fun?

Something was bugging me. Something unsettling that I couldn't quite put a finger on.

Haruhi seemed thoroughly satisfied with a job well done.

"We don't need to consider the motive, right?"

"I'd say motives are an issue of the inner workings of the human heart and impossible to uncover through deduction alone. We can, of course, speculate... For example, perhaps the card comedian was also in the running for Shouko's hand, and this is the result of a broken heart, a common enough reason for assault cases like this. Or perhaps the doctor was secretly an agent for a criminal syndicate, and the card joker was trying to purge that influence from his relative's life. We can imagine all sorts of things. And for precisely that reason, attempting to pick a motive is inherently futile. Nor did Tsuruya expect that of us."

"Good point. It's been hundreds of years, but we still don't know what motivated Akechi Mitsuhide to take out Oda Nobunaga at Honno-ji. Wondering what someone was thinking at the time does us no good. I mean, people mostly act on impulse. And all of us come up with reasons for our actions after the fact. I'm a proponent of the theory that the whole Honno-ji event was just a fit of madness. Mitsuhide just happened to be in a traitory mood that day! Normally, he'd never have done it, but he happened to realize he was in a position to pull it off and acted before he could stop to think."

While Haruhi and Koizumi were debating motives, I remembered something. Before Tsuruya's e-mail arrived, Koizumi, T, and Nagato had been having a debate about the concept of fairness in a mystery.

On that basis, could we say Tsuruya's problem was fair?

"It certainly isn't the most generous problem, but if you work out that it's set abroad, you've got a good chance at solving it."

"Knowing there was a narrative trick involved helped a lot," Haruhi added.

"The trap Tsuruya hid in Episode Three made it seem like they were speaking Japanese, when actually, they were speaking English. A deception applied to both the setting and the language used. But we were expecting it. Between Episode One's age trick and Episode Two's gender trick, we were all assuming there would be something like that here. In other words, the first two episodes were the biggest hints to solving Episode Three."

So they weren't just any random old stories, then. And we'd gotten to know Tsuruya herself better. How she was just as entertaining as a kid and would likely still be like this ten years from now—a weirdly comforting thought.

Still…

…this feeling swirling inside me… It wasn't that I didn't trust Tsuruya or anything. I just had a vague suspicion that we were still being fooled somewhere. It was like her smirking face was floating in the air just above me. And I couldn't figure out where it was coming from, which only made the itch worse. I was just sure we were missing something.

"I hate to sound picky, but I have one more question."

At this, Koizumi put the marker down, turning toward me. "Which is?"

"Did this *actually* happen?"

"Oh!" he said, eyes widening. "What makes you say that?"

"The timing's a bit too perfect. On several levels."

Tsuruya being overseas on family business and at a party for the launch of a new project, sure. But did cases involving people with extremely specific name gimmicks actually happen?

"Perhaps because one did, she decided it was worth informing us about it. And…" Koizumi gave Haruhi a glance that only I could see. "Things that appear extremely unlikely do seem to occur on occasion. And it's an established fact that there is a substantial discrepancy between our ideas of what is probable and the actual odds of them occurring. The birthday paradox and the Monty Hall problem are perfect examples."

I'll have to look those up later.

"So that means her actual name is Shouko Notobe?" Haruhi said, scowling at the computer screen and pointlessly swirling the mouse around. "Tsuruya's answer e-mail's a bit late, huh?"

Yeah, I was thinking the same thing.

So far, she'd sent those out right as we finished, but with Ep3, she was taking her sweet time.

"Think of the time difference. I dunno where she is, exactly, but it's probably the middle of the night. She might have dozed off!"

Still…

"Perhaps Tsuruya believes it will take us longer to reach the answer. In which case, we should be patting ourselves on the back."

Or maybe we hadn't hit 100 percent yet? What if we let ourselves get stuck at 70 percent?

"Don't be stupid, Kyon," Haruhi scoffed. "Even Tsuruya can't monitor the clubroom in real time. How would she know what we know?"

Her timing so far had been downright uncanny, but…now that you mention it, that's a fair point. Tsuruya might be a bundle of energy you could easily label *hyper*, but she wasn't clairvoyant and couldn't possibly know just how far our deductions had taken us. Still, she'd sent those first two answer e-mails with such perfect timing that it sure seemed like she knew the moment we'd solved them. I mean, logically speaking, I knew she couldn't possibly have known that, but…

Crap, I was stuck in a thought loop.

I shook my head, trying to free myself, and spotted something extremely unusual.

"……………"

Nagato had her eyes fixed on me. An unusually piercing gaze.

What? Why was she trying to bore a hole in me with her eyes?

But then she looked away, her eyes locking on something else.

I turned my head, following her look.

She was looking at T. All she could see from her position was the back of T's blond head.

Nagato swiveled her emotionless face back to me once more.

"?"

All I had were question marks.

What was she trying to tell me?

I stared at Nagato's wordless anomaly for a full five seconds.

"…………"

And Nagato did something genuinely astonishing.

She rose to her feet like there were strings attached, dragged her folding chair over to the main table, sat down again, and…

"…………"

…stared directly at T's face.

I was not the only person gaping. Haruhi, Koizumi, and Asahina all looked like they were touring the Louvre and the Winged Victory of Samothrace had suddenly started dancing.

T looked up from her forest of *furigana* and said, "Is there something on my face, Nagato?"

She sounded confused. Like Nagato's glare was physically repelling her, she leaned way back and held a hand up to hide her face, palm facing us.

Having observed this action, Nagato looked at me again.

Clearly telling me to work it out.

Work what out?

What was T's hand hiding?

Wait...

If our reasoning *was* actually reaching Tsuruya...

A torrent of facts rushed through my mind.

Time lag. Young Tsuruya. The previously nameless girl. Shouko Notobe. The first two episodes were the biggest hint. The case took place overseas. English. Uncannily timed e-mails. The last e-mail not arriving. The one outsider in our midst. The exchange student who'd joined our class that spring. T.

I could almost hear the pieces click in place.

"...Oh," I said. That's what Nagato meant. I was pretty sure I had it. "So that's what's going on, T?"

"What do you mean, Kyam?"

I stood up and walked over to her.

T put her hands up in surrender, looking down.

I took a deep breath and yelled "Hah!" right at her head.

Loud enough that Asahina squeaked and levitated several centimeters above her chair.

I think I was allowed that much.

Haruhi and Koizumi looked at me like I'd blown a gasket, and I said, "We don't need any more e-mails, Tsuruya."

Speaking directly to the hairpin attached to T's bangs.

A moment later, an unfamiliar ringtone echoed through the room.

T pulled her phone out, put it on speaker, and laid it on the table.

"Heya, Kyon! You got me good!" Tsuruya's voice rang out. She seemed to be enjoying herself. "I did *not* see you being the first to work it out!"

Well, it was more than half Nagato, but I wasn't gonna mention that.

Haruhi and Koizumi were staring at the phone so wide-eyed that you'd think they were related. After a minute—still perfectly in sync—they both put a hand to their head and said, "Ohhh."

Haruhi pursed her lips. "That explains it! I shoulda known. It was T all along!"

"Huh? Huh?" Asahina alone was still looking around the room, confused.

"How far are you?" Tsuruya asked.

"The girl in the first two episodes isn't Shouko. It was T."

When I looked at T, she was managing to smile with only half her mouth.

"And her hairpin is actually an eavesdropping device. That's basically it."

"That term sounds so underhanded! Can't we call it a high-spec directional-mic-plus-radio transmitter?"

Fine, whatever. How's it work?

T unclipped her hairpin and handed it to me.

I took it without really thinking, but no matter how I looked at it, it was just a flimsy piece of metal. I couldn't figure out where a mic, transmitter, or battery would go. Only Nagato could possibly have detected it. Can't underestimate the human race's scientific advancements.

As I examined it, T explained, "The microminiature pinhole mic collects sound, sending it to my phone, which then transmits it to Tsuruya's phone. It's the latest creation of the labs that are a joint undertaking between our two families. I don't know the full specs, but…"

If they could make micro GPS trackers, this would be a cakewalk.

Tsuruya's voice pulled my attention away from the phone. "What gave the game away?" she asked.

"Your timing, for one. It was just a bit too perfect."

And also…T being here.

She didn't exactly swing by every day. Even when she did, she usually didn't stay long.

But today of all days, she and Koizumi got super into their mystery talk, and just as that was wrapping up, Tsuruya's e-mail arrived. And with a *solve the case* challenge, almost like Tsuruya knew we had a mystery-research-club member in our midst.

No matter what the statistical likelihood was, I felt confident that was too good to be true.

And then the flawless gaps between the answer e-mails. So perfectly timed that we could only assume someone was relaying our conversations to Tsuruya. If we actually did have an informant in our midst, that explained everything. And there was little chance that informant would be a member of the SOS Brigade.

I did wonder if someone had planted a bug in the room in advance, but even Tsuruya wouldn't go that far, and even if she did, Nagato would know—so I ruled that out.

Without even using the process of elimination, Tsuruya's coconspirator had to be the girl from another club who didn't usually spend this much time here.

"Perhaps I was a bit too blatant."

"Or," Haruhi said, "was the timing of the e-mails meant to be a hint? That you could hear us?"

"Maaaybe."

Tsuruya was generous like that.

"More importantly, how'd you know the girl from the first two stories is the same person as this girl you're all calling T?"

"Something's been bugging me since I heard Episode Two," I said, pulling over the printout. "The Tsuruya lines in quotes."

"Yeah, that'd do it." Tsuruya's laugh crackled over the phone's speaker.

"We knew Episode Three was set abroad, so what if Episode Two was, too? And that thought cleared up my concern."

It had been like dominoes falling.

"If you know that, then yes." Koizumi spread out the pages. "Tsuruya says six lines that sound like the minder."

"You look like you've stepped out of an impressionist's painting, miss."

"Oh, miss! This is most, most improper!"

"If your father saw you like this, whatever would he say?"

"A year is enough time to adjust any plans. But what your father will make of this, I could not begin to say."

"Any further stops you'd like to make, miss?"

"Then we shall proceed as planned."

While Koizumi was doing his exposition thing, I settled back in my folding chair. I'd managed to land a solid blow and felt content at last.

With a brief nod to me, Koizumi smiled faintly and said, "Tsuruya, I assumed the reason these lines were spoken so politely and out of character was because the way you actually talk to the girl was different from your narration. That you'd been speaking like this all along."

"I thought you were just goofing around," Haruhi jumped in. "Imitating the minder's way of speaking to make fun of him."

"But neither explanation was true."

Koizumi glanced at me, looking suitably impressed.

"These lines were all spoken in a foreign language. In other words, all the dialogue in Episode Two was translated into Japanese."

"Yup! We were speaking English."

Koizumi turned to T. "Does Tsuruya's English sound that polite to your ears? The way it's translated in Episode Two?"

The loss of the hairpin had left her bangs swinging free, so T brushed those back and said, "Mm, she uses proper grammar and by-the-book idioms. Although, she tends to stress the vowels a bit, which undermines that effect."

"Mwa-ha-ha, yeah, I ain't exactly at a native level yet. Working on it!"

On the other hand, T's English got translated as pretty standard Japanese. It was her native language, so of course she spoke normally. When T actually spoke Japanese, she sounded a bit more distinctive, with some unorthodox vocabulary choices. And Tsuruya had even translated her English with a different first-person pronoun, perhaps to capture that different vibe.

"If we know the setting is foreign, it follows that this applies to many characters, too."

"I'll just say it was somewhere in Europe," Tsuruya said.

"Episode Two does say, '...others were just dressed like medieval European country girls' (P136) and 'Definitely just like a lady dressed as a medieval European village girl' (P138), so perhaps we should have taken that more literally."

"Yup."

The kind of European country that grew grapes and had outdoor spas. My vague, meager imagination could only come up with a mix of France and Germany.

Koizumi looked down at T's phone.

"Then it follows that Episode One was also set overseas. Likely somewhere farther north than Japan."

"I was wondering about that bit at the start," Haruhi said. "Where it goes, 'Maybe it was different at night, but the sun was still doing its thang' (P108). Weird to have a party like that in the early evening, right? Wouldn't you just have a dinner instead? But if the nights are super short, that would explain it."

"And at the end, where Tsuruya says 'lying still in the darkness like this got me good' (P116) and falls asleep while hiding under the bed. Was this because you were jet-lagged?"

"Maybe I was! It happened a while ago, so I don't really remember."

You could picture Tsuruya's expression from her voice alone.

"But that's not enough to tell you who the girl is, right?"

"The key to unraveling that mystery lies in Episode Three alone," Koizumi said, as if he'd been waiting for the question. "If 'the girl' in all three stories was the same, there was no need for Shouko's name to appear only in the third."

"Meaning?"

"If the girl in the first two episodes was Shouko, why hide her name? In fact, if you were being thorough about hiding the international setting, including a Japanese name at the start would be highly effective."

He picked up the stack of paper.

"The fact that the girl was the same in the first two episodes is revealed in the e-mail accompanying Ep2. 'Me and the girl from the previous story have been running into each other now and then ever since. Once again, we'd both been dragged along by our dads... This one's a hot-spring episode! We hit up the baths together' (P126). Which proves it!"

"Mm-hmm."

"From there, to the first girl's identity..." Koizumi ran his finger across the page. "At the start of Ep3, it says, 'This girl and I knew at least one other kid in this predicament, but it looked like she wasn't here tonight. Her family was connected to the project, too, but she must be better at wriggling out of these obligations, I guess' (P174). This is clearly directly referencing the previous girl."

Haruhi looked at T. "It's a bit roundabout, but Tsuruya does tell us 'she' isn't there. 'Cause you're here."

Why aren't you there? Isn't this family business?

T thumped her chest with pride.

"I'm an exchange student! I've traveled to distant lands to further my studies! Students should devote themselves to their educations. I can hardly be expected to play hooky just to go to some boring old party."

Come to think of it, this girl was every bit as rich as Tsuruya. She didn't really seem like it. Maybe it was the way she talked. Tsuruya was likely a bad influence.

"Let's list up the steps that allow us to identify you."

Koizumi grabbed the dry-erase marker again and resumed his torrid affair with the whiteboard.

He scribbled the following lines.

- *Episodes One and Two are set overseas.*
- *The girl in Episodes One and Two is not Shouko.*
- *The girl in Episodes One and Two is (most likely) foreign.*
- *The girl and Tsuruya are close.*
- *T was transmitting literature-club discussions to Tsuruya.*
- *Therefore, T and Tsuruya are close.*
- *T is an exchange student—a foreigner.*
- *Thus, T is (most likely) "the girl."*

"Just 'likely,' huh?" I said, frowning at the parentheticals.

Koizumi answered with a smile, then added, "However, she is the only native English speaker from abroad whom any of us know personally."

Second time today. I thought you said reverse engineering solutions from a metafiction perspective was illegitimate?

"When the given problem includes metatextual elements, and those of us tasked with solving it are required to consider the contents of the text and information gleaned from an outside perspective, we can logically conclude it is the only legitimate means of deduction."

Ease off on the jargon. I can't keep up.

"You're the one who realized it first. Did you not follow this logical progression?"

Hmm, more like...you know. Nagato was weirdly interested in T's hairpin, and there'd been something bugging me about

Ep2's dialogue, so, like, it all suddenly connected up in my mind, and I'd already said a bunch of things about how good Tsuruya's timing was on her e-mails, so the rest just came together. If Nagato wasn't here, I wouldn't have figured it out. I'd merely borrowed her cosmic powers, which was definitely not playing fair. Couldn't say that in front of Haruhi or T, though.

Koizumi seemed aware of this wrinkle. He glanced once at Nagato, then said, "Remember the discussion we were having before Tsuruya's e-mail arrived—specifically, about the devices authors use to specify a range of suspects, eliminating the possibility of a culprit from outside the scope of the work. The Challenge to the Reader serves that purpose adroitly."

That conversation felt like it took place a *long* time ago.

"The question hidden within the three episodes is: Who is 'the girl'? Tsuruya is not so ungenerous or mean-spirited as to expand the number of potential suspects to the billions of people alive on this planet. If she were, she would not lay so many clues within the stories or send us a list of five additional hints. It was always going to be someone we could name—someone we knew."

He turned to the interloper from the mystery club, who was sitting on the guest folding chair.

"Tsuruya sent the answer to us in person. Narrowing the field to one. The only doubt remaining was whether we noticed the question existed in the first place."

T smiled elegantly. "Honestly," she said, "I was pretty nervous about it."

"The answer was before us the whole time. I must admit, I'm impressed by the irony of that misdirection."

"Hide what you're looking for in plain sight!" Tsuruya said.

"Your favorite purloined-letter plan." Haruhi nodded.

"Tsuruya's Challenge specified that we deduce the Episode Three culprit's name from the dying message, but behind that question lay a secret one—who was 'the girl' in the first two episodes? If we had let that pass unnoticed, would she have remained silent, or...?"

"Oh, I would've told ya." Tsuruya snorted.

The reason no e-mail arrived after we wrapped up was because she was waiting for us to notice.

Koizumi smiled, playing with the marker cap.

"To what degree were you involved, T?" Haruhi said, turning to our classmate. "Did you know everything she was gonna e-mail? You're the girl in the first two stories, but I bet you knew the third story, too. And you knew the trick the whole time!"

T looked around for help.

"..........."

Nagato had seemingly lost interest and had returned to her paperback. T seemed impressed.

"You haven't read me my Miranda," she said.

Well, this ain't America. You can reserve the right to remain silent all you like, but you've gotta pay for your own lawyer.

"Go on, tell 'em," Tsuruya chimed in.

T sighed, brushing the hair off her ear.

"Pictures paint a thousand words."

She scooped up her phone, tapped the screen a few times, and then held the pillbox-sized screen up to me.

"Seven years ago, one of many snapshots taken at a certain party."

In a room with a gaudy chandelier, two little girls were standing cheek to cheek, posing for a selfie. Little Tsuruya in a fancy dress and T's innocent smile definitely made for a compelling image, like two mischievous fairies who'd just crossed over into our world and formed a new idol act.

Haruhi, Asahina, and Koizumi all came over to look, too.

"Hey! Kyon! Move," Haruhi said, straining her neck, mug in one hand. She rapped the side of my head lightly and forced her way in. "Oh, how cute! Neither of you changed that much. You just got bigger."

"Oh! Wow! So! Cute!" Asahina sounded like she was in rapture. I wasn't sure why it came out in such a singsong voice.

"Proof you've known each other some time," Koizumi said, looming over my shoulder like a haunt.

"I want a copy of that!" Asahina said, clasping her hands.

T nodded right away. "Just gimme your ID! I'll send it over. You don't mind, right, Tsuruya?"

"Not at all."

Haruhi went back to the chief's chair.

"So you know Shouko, then, T?"

"Let me answer your earlier question instead. I did have prior knowledge of the events of Episode Three."

The reason she hadn't tried to guess the culprit (or their name anyway) despite being in the mystery club was that she was actually helping pull this whole thing off. Better to stay silent than say too much and blow your cover.

"That's true, but I'm also at a total loss when it comes to narrative tricks relying on Japanese grammar," T said, sounding weirdly proud of it. "I couldn't explain those even if I wanted to."

She turned to Haruhi.

"I do know Shouko. Tsuruya introduced us ages back. One of those Asian beauties who look younger than they actually are. She's actually graduating college next year."

"She's older than Tsuruya? I guess...in hindsight, that comes across."

"She's in her twenties!" Tsuruya chimed in from afar.

"The three of us occupy similar positions in our families. Inevitably, we end up face-to-face anytime we all get dragged out on the road, which naturally led to us bonding," T explained. "And while I'm blabbing, this Mr. Doctor from the story is actually my brother."

By this point, I was well past having even the slightest clue how I should be reacting.

"He and Shouko have been intimate for several years. I have several brothers, but he's got seniority."

So he's the eldest?

"I guess we should lay it all out there," Tsuruya said. "Shouko's distant relative with the business cards? You were right about the kanji. *Take* is written with the same character as 'military.' I dunno if their ancestors were warriors or nobility or what, but they've kept that 'esteem' kanji thing going. As for his motive... Well, I ain't gotta explain that, do I?"

"No," Haruhi said, sipping at the last of her tea. "If the motive was unusual, I'm interested, but...you make it sound like it wasn't."

"Nope. Just your typical drunken tiff over matters of the heart."

Still assault. If they'd brought in the law, I imagine it would become a touchy subject for everyone.

"Was your brother okay?" Haruhi asked.

"Totally fine, all healed up," T said, grinning. "I hear he's so absorbed in his research that he's totally neglecting Shouko, though. There may well be a crisis brewing that determines if she's gonna be my future sister or not."

"Don't worry about *them*!" Tsuruya laughed. Then her tone grew grim. "Okay, I've gotta move. Once I hang up, I'll be out of touch for a bit. Anything else you wanna talk about? Other than souvenir requests. I mean, I'll take those, too, but..."

Was there anything left to say? A pretty open question. We'd just wrapped up the mystery, so I couldn't think of any other questions.

Same went for Haruhi and Koizumi. They were both blinking in surprise.

When nobody spoke up, Tsuruya said, "Then I'm hanging up! I'll return bearing gifts, so look forward to it! Buh-bye!"

She hung up rather quick. Maybe she was on a train or an airplane.

"I'll get some fresh tea started."

The thoughtful maid grabbed a tray and started her rounds.

Haruhi folded her arms and leaned back in her chair, seemingly mulling over Tsuruya's last words. Koizumi was busy combining all three episodes into one booklet with binder clips. Nagato was, as per her wont, reading.

"Um," Asahina said, hesitantly raising a hand. She was gathering up the mugs and disposing of any cold leftovers. She gave T an awkward glance, then made up her mind to press on. "Why is everyone only using your initial?"

"Oh, that?" T said. This time, her smile was distributed evenly across both sides of her mouth. "This is a name bestowed upon me by my friends in class."

"It's technically not her initial," I said, feeling more explanation was required. "T, let Asahina know what your real name is."

The visitor from the mystery club took a deep breath.

"Ottilie Adrastea Hohenstaufen-Baumgartner. A pleasure to meet you."

She rattled that name off like it was nothing, handing her empty guest mug to Asahina.

Who the hell was this girl? That was too many names for any one person. It sounded like a name of a character from the imaginary history of a heroic/galactic space opera set in the distant future. It was downright weird that she didn't have a *von* in there somewhere.

"I actually do," she admitted. "I have to use it in formal settings, but if I'm honest, it causes nothing but trouble, and my family's name is impossible enough to remember, so I always leave it out. If that makes sense."

"Huh...," Asahina said, at a loss for any other response. "So where does the *T* come from? The middle part of *Ottilie*?"

A number of nickname candidates had been proposed, but the girls in class had gradually chopped it down to the katakana *ti* (like Asahina said), and just as that was gaining steam, Taniguchi happened to be in charge of the class records for the day and included the line, *The exchange student's nickname has settled on as T.*

Both *ti* and T sounded the same, but T herself said, *"This is the finest nickname I have ever received. I approve."* Having stuck her flag in the alphabet camp, she insisted on shaking Taniguchi's hand, and my dumb friend agreed to it, sweating profusely and with the most awkward smile I'd ever seen.

T twirled a strand of hair around her finger.

"I hear Japanese names are more than just sounds and contain inherent meanings. Like *Haru* is 'a spring day,' or *Koizumi* is 'an ancient spring.' It's fascinating. *Nagato* is 'a long gate,' right? But my name doesn't have any meaning that could be translated into Japanese. It's not like I actively dislike my name, but it makes me sound like a character from some old tragedy, which...is somewhat concerning."

Koizumi bade farewell to the whiteboard and sat down, asking, "So when did you fall in love with mysteries? What got you started on English-language orthodox novels in particular? I'd love to know whose work you read first."

"It's difficult to be that specific. I've been an avid reader ever since I can remember. Likely my brother's influence."

Guess she was the adoring-little-sister type.

"The doctor?" Haruhi asked.

"Oh, no," T said, wincing. "The youngest of my older brothers—my twin."

And she was a twin. Quit adding such unique character traits. This was already giving me heartburn. You could only burden a single character with so much.

T glared at me. "You are very rude, Kyam. My traits are all totally normal stuff."

Sure, compared with time travelers, aliens, espers, and Haruhi Suzumiya...

"Hmm, a twin brother?" Haruhi said, eyes gleaming. "I'd love to see him! Is he in Japan?"

"Our faces are very similar, so I'm not sure you'd get much out of it."

Only die-hard narcissists enjoyed staring at themselves in a mirror.

Haruhi stared the blond girl in the face, genuinely interested in her for the first time all day. "Your twin brother didn't show up once in all three of Tsuruya's stories. He wasn't with you?"

"Oh..." T shifted uncomfortably, then she parted her lips. "He's, uh, how do I put this...? Not fit for polite society. Incapable of reading a room? Rude? Arrogant? Bohemian? Ugh, I can't think of the right word in Japanese."

This just seemed to be making Haruhi all the more curious, but not me. I definitely didn't need any more inscrutable characters joining the fray. Fortunately...

"I'm not even sure where he is now. Entirely possible none of my family does. My father appears unconcerned, so I'm sure he's safe. He'll probably show up in time for Christmas."

Haruhi made a noise that veered awfully close to a snort.

T made a face and recrossed her long legs. "When we were very young, he used to read books out loud. And I listened to them. Many of them were mysteries. That had a profound influence on me, and it became a permanent hobby."

By this point, Asahina had recovered all the mugs and had them arranged next to her. She was slowly pouring water from the kettle into the teapot, a stopwatch in her free hand.

Watching this, I asked, "What about Tsuruya? If you're at North High, that's because she helped arrange it, right? Is she...?"

I trailed off, unsure what I was trying to ask. Eventually, I settled for "What is she to you?"

T straightened up, being very direct.

"Tsuruya is my mentor."

In what way?

"In many things but primarily Japanese. She's been a huge help there."

Are you sure Master Tsuruya didn't teach you weird Japanese for kicks?

T looked offended. "'Weird' how? I am painfully aware that I don't speak it as well as natives like yourself, but Tsuruya said it comes across as quite charming and I'd have nothing to worry about."

That was one way to describe it. Tsuruya's own Japanese was no less eccentric, so if she studied under the master of Tsuruya-ese, then it was only natural that her own language would end up becoming rather distinctive.

"What do you mean, 'distinctive'?" T asked, looking surprised.

I gave her a long look and decided she was genuinely curious.

I'd have to have a long think about how to phrase this.

"I'm been told the Japanese have a tendency to be rather…*mouton de Panurge*, and as a result, being a little different from everyone else would be seen as amusing. But you've got me concerned now." She did look worried. "Let's get down to brass tacks. How, exactly, is my Japanese weird?"

Maybe T thought her Japanese sounded just like a regular teenager. But odds were she was just trying to say, *Huh? What? Weird how?*

If I interpreted it that way, it explained why her demeanor, expressions, and gestures all seemed a little strange to me.

"It's not weird at all," Haruhi said, hovering somewhere between reassuring and dismissive. "I totally think you're amusing. Don't worry, you don't need to change a thing." Every muscle on her face conspired to form a smile. "The way you speak might well turn out to be a powerful asset in your arsenal. It helps complete the moe package! You've heard people use the term *gap appeal*, right? People love it when a character's speech patterns don't match their appearance! According to my research anyway."

This sounded like the least reliable research ever.

Like a border collie leading a lost sheep, Haruhi declared, "I believe Tsuruya taught you Japanese specifically so that you would be different from others, the kind of friend who stands out in the crowd. She did a great job. The way you speak swiftly earned the approval of everyone in class, regardless of gender."

In our classroom, T was always all smiles, steady and constant no matter whom she was talking to. She had no fear and possessed a boundless curiosity—I'd never seen her without someone to talk to. She was a social animal. Like nothing could be more delightful than talking to other people.

There was no trace of the sullen little girl Tsuruya met in Episode One, sitting alone in a corner. Maybe she still acted like that at home, but I'd be willing to bet all the change I had in my pocket (except the five-hundred-yen coin) that Tsuruya's personality modification program had played a big part in that transformation.

"My gratitude, Haru," T said, bowing her head. "Those words have renewed my confidence. I shall continue to call Tsuruya my mentor and polish my language skills with her patronage."

Her smile was so warm, I could swear it raised the temperature in the room by one and a half degrees.

Haruhi's smile rose up in sync.

"I wholeheartedly approve of that oath. And now that everyone's happy, I have one more thing to ask. You mind?"

"Of course not, Haru," T said, cheerily. "Go right ahead."

"We thought we'd figured out all the tricks in the three episodes you and Tsuruya prepared, but there's actually more, right?"

T's smile turned to stone.

"Wh-why do you say that? I have no clue— *I'm sure I don't have the foggiest.*"

T lapsed into English, her face a mask. Only her lips moved, and when her eyes did shift evasively, you could almost hear a creak escape.

"Kyam, why is it so hot in your lair? Is this the legendary Japanese summer heat I've been warned about?"

She grabbed the collar of her sailor outfit and fanned herself with it. Meanwhile, Haruhi rested her chin on her hands, grilling her.

"I knew it!" she said. "Something was bugging me! Like it was caught in my throat."

"Aha," Koizumi said. It had been a while since he'd spoken. "Just before Tsuruya hung up, she asked an odd question. To my ears, it sounded like *Is that all?* In which case, I must agree with you."

Perhaps sensing it would soon be needed, he turned his gaze to the whiteboard. Seriously, don't.

Haruhi stroked her lips with her fingers.

"I'm gonna figure out what's bugging me," she announced. "T, don't say anything. I'm sure it'll pop out any second…"

She fixed the air above her with a glare.

"I feel like there was a vital hook in something *somebody* said…," Koizumi said, staring at the same spot and striking a thinking pose.

Suspect T shrank herself down in a chair, her gaze locked on her phone like it would come to her rescue. Nagato's attention never once left her book.

The meaningless background sounds of the sports teams and wind ensemble seeped softly through the walls of the literature club room.

The whole club+1 was here, but the moment all of us fell silent, the vibe quickly became uncomfortable. Haruhi was usually the most boisterous, but she and her biggest yes-man (Koizumi) were both lost in thought, and the resulting spectacle was like encountering an endangered species in the wild, a momentary glimpse of our chief embodying the concept of a sound dampener.

The one outsider, T, spoke not a word. Nagato was being even quieter than her. The only sound the room generated was the pleasant clatter of Asahina making tea.

And in time, that clatter resulted in actual tea.

As Asahina happily made the rounds with her tray of mugs, she said, "I blended several kinds of leaves together. I've tried a lot of different things, but it usually doesn't work out well. This is my one success!"

I peered into the mug and saw a dark-brown liquid steaming away. I think this is what the word *fragrant* was designed for. It smelled familiar but strange, like Japanese tea, like Chinese tea—I didn't have the words for it, but it definitely smelled good.

I quickly took a sip. Out of the corner of my eye, I saw Haruhi absently do the same thing.

I'm not sure which of us got there first.

"!"

"?!"

Both Haruhi and I threw our heads back and attempted to swallow the liquid in our mouths as quickly as humanly possible, but it was hot, so it didn't go down right, and we spent a good ten seconds struggling before managing to get it all lodged in our bellies.

Seeing us both gasping away, Koizumi quietly took his hand off his mug.

"Huh?" Asahina said. "Is something wrong with it?"

Wrong? I'd never tasted anything so bitter in my life.

"It's strong," Haruhi said. "Ludicrously strong. What in God's name did you put in it?"

"I-it's that bad?!" Asahina gasped.

"Mikuru, write this blend down. We'll make it the loser's punishment for future games."

Let's at least call it an emergency wake-up medicine. This was the result of Asahina's hard work. It was possible we'd get used to it and acquire a taste for this stringent harshness.

"Huh…? Um…"

Asahina picked up her mug with both hands and took a sip like a squirrel nibbling on an unfamiliar nut found in a distant corner of the forest.

"Eep!" she said, clapping a hand over her mouth, eyes wide. Then she wailed, "I'm so sorry! I forgot to add the sugar!" and started handing out sugar-sticks and spoons to everyone.

Sticking a spoon in one of these traditional mugs was an odd sight, but after stirring for a minute, Asahina's shocking original tea blend was—surprisingly—quite pleasant.

That chaotic vortex of bitterness, harshness, and acridity was somehow entirely pulled into a harmonious whole merely by the addition of a little sweetness.

"Oh, it *is* good," Haruhi said, staring at her mug in shock.

"Whew," Asahina said, patting her chest. She then stirred some sugar into Nagato's tea, since Nagato was clearly not about to let go of that mystery novel anytime soon.

I had a feeling Nagato would have consumed it without noticing a problem, but watching this little interplay between the time traveler and the humanoid interface©Data Overmind warmed the heart.

T was acting like she'd been brought in for interrogation, all hunched over with her hands on her knees. I had no clue what she was trying so hard to hide.

Having accidentally tricked Haruhi and me into poison-testing the tea, Koizumi calmly finished stirring in the sugar and took a sip.

"Was it like strong black coffee before adding the sugar?" he asked.

Don't act like a food critic if you haven't tried the brew from before.

I bet it was like chocolate liquor before they add any sugar—not that I'd tried that myself, but I think I'd read something about them using cacao drinks as a tonic in ancient South America.

"From the Age of Exploration," Koizumi said. "Not an era modern sensibilities can approve of wholeheartedly, but the foodstuffs and produce found on the American continent that were brought back to Europe enriched the world's cuisine, and for that, I am glad."

"Tomatoes, too," Haruhi said. "And chili pepper, potatoes, corn... I can't even imagine what Italians ate before tomatoes were imported to Europe."

Taking a break from the Tsuruya problem, she spent a moment pondering medieval Italian cuisine, but as she lifted her mug... her hands froze.

"Sugar...tomatoes..."

Haruhi set the mug down, staring into Asahina's original blend.

"Not *didn't* add it... *Couldn't*," she muttered, cryptically. "Kyon! Imagine pizza without tomato, chili pepper, potatoes, or corn."

The pizza shops' menus would be much shorter.

"It wouldn't even count as pizza! It's missing several vital ingredients."

What's your point? We can do a deep dive on the history of pizza some other time.

Koizumi seemed to have caught her drift.

"A vital component is missing... If that was a story, we would consider it incomplete. Yes?"

"Exactly, Koizumi."

Can't believe you got it from that. Well done, Professor of Haruhi-ology.

"So?" I said. "What's incomplete?"

"Naturally," Haruhi said, resuming that grin of hers. "Tsuruya's problem and the third episode."

I looked at T. She was playing with the sugar-stick and made up her mind to actually add it to the guest mug.

"Why did Tsuruya send us a mystery game in the first place?"

We're going that far back?

"Not just because Tsuruya is a die-hard mischief-maker?"

Haruhi waggled her fingers dismissively at this suggestion.

"When did you find out Tsuruya was like that? We certainly get that impression from reading these three episodes, but the actual time we've spent with her gave no indication she was so dedicated to mischief, she'd go concocting an elaborate game like this. She was always just a fun, easygoing, cheery upperclassman."

Now that you mention it… Given the time difference, sending all these e-mails from America or wherever was definitely a lot of effort.

Who would do that without a good reason?

So what *was* her reason?

Haruhi turned the blade of her smile on our cowering guest.

"Perhaps we should ask T."

Her voice grew uncharacteristically gentle.

"Tell us, T. How much of these episodes are made-up?"

T spent a long moment stirring her Asahina blend with a spoon, eyes scanning the table, but having determined there was no spoon rest available, she let go. There was the soft sound of metal tapping against pottery.

"I have no idea why you've reached that conclusion," she said, meeting Haruhi's eyes with grace and a faint smile. "And I'd like to know where we went wrong."

So did I. What's going on, Haruhi?

"For one thing, why is T here?" Haruhi took a sip of her sugared blend. "I had T pegged as Tsuruya's plant and coconspirator. I figured that's why she had to be in the room on the day Tsuruya sent these e-mails. And since you found the bug, Kyon, that went from suspicion to confirmed fact. With me so far?"

No arguments here.

Haruhi gave me a satisfied nod. "Second—you said it yourself, Kyon. The timing issue."

The e-mails certainly arrived with uncanny timing, and that was why I thought there must be a bug somewhere.

"Before that, even," Haruhi said, picking up her copy of Episode Three. "Your first take on this story. Remember?"

What was it again?

"You said the following:

> "'Tsuruya being overseas on family business and at a party for the launch of a new project, sure. But did cases involving people with extremely specific name gimmicks actually happen?'

"Ring a bell?"

Can't believe you remember that. Also, don't try to imitate me. It's creepy. Also, Koizumi, I'm sure you snapped your fingers as a sign of agreement, but it's super smug, so don't ever do it again.

"But sure, I did say that. What of it?"

"That's the answer, isn't it? It just so happened that Tsuruya left Japan a few days ago. It just so happened that she encountered a mystery at a party overseas. It just so happened that Tsuruya knew both the victim and the culprit. It just so happened that the victim said something to her that sounded like a dying message. It just so happened that the culprit's name lent itself to a narrative trick. How many coincidences are we gonna rack up here?"

That was certainly the most uses of *just so happened* I'd ever heard in a single paragraph. Far too many. Any more, and we'd have to retire the phrase for good.

"I admit, it's one coincidence too many," I said. Not that I'm trying to be T's lawyer here. "It may well be true that three coincidences equals a conspiracy, but that doesn't *prove* anything. Do you have any more tangible evidence that these stories are fictitious?"

"I have several pieces of corroborating evidence." Haruhi waved a hand at the pile of printouts on the table. Guess she was the prosecutor here. "Figuring out the third episode was set overseas allowed us to uncover the language deception, which in turn allowed us to narrow down the actual wording of the dying message. That led us to speculate that the first two episodes were also international and gave birth to the notion that the girl in those two stories was actually T, not Shouko."

All true.

"Pretty dang unnatural, right? Just as Episode Three had that thing about oncoming traffic, there ought to have been hints in the first two episodes that this was not Japan. She could easily have added those. It's actively weird that none cropped up."

Were there really none?

"I mentioned one. But how high the sun was in Episode One doesn't really tell us if they're in summer in a high-latitude country or just at a longitude where the sun sets on the late side."

Maybe she figured one hint they were abroad was enough.

"If you're making a deduction game, you have to be thorough," T insisted.

Haruhi shot her a look.

"Speaking of unnatural," Koizumi said, breaking his silence, "the sights described in Episode Two certainly qualify. Are any real harvest festivals that outlandish?"

"And if we're doubting the reality of things," Haruhi said, "one character really stands out."

Her eyes met T's.

"Does Shouko even exist?"

T almost answered, then stopped herself. Clearly deciding she was better off hearing Haruhi out first.

"The entirety of Episode Three is suspect," our chief continued. "The crime took place in a reception room adjacent to the party venue. Given the size of the party, I imagine this was not a small room. And there were a lot of people attending the event. Yet somehow, the doctor and the card comedian were alone together? Seems unlikely."

"As is the fact that Tsuruya was the only person who heard the scream and went running," Koizumi added.

So…what? First, a string of coincidences, now a list of unlikely events?

"There's a simple explanation for this list of coincidences and improbable turns," Haruhi said with an extra-strength grin. "All three stories Tsuruya sent us were completely made-up."

Eventually, I was the one who broke the grip of the ensuing silence.

"Okay, so what does that mean? Tsuruya and T teamed up to send us a trio of original compositions? A three-part novel with multiple narrative tricks embedded and a final request to guess the culprit's name?"

"Not quite right," Haruhi said, miming a pistol with her hand and aiming it at T. "Remember what club T actually belongs to. If someone's gonna trap us in a mystery game, is Tsuruya really the most likely candidate?"

I could think of any number of organizations that stood against the SOS Brigade. But Nagato's foes, Koizumi's opposition, and Asahina's enemies also seemed like they'd be unable to get to Tsuruya. The student council certainly stood no chance.

"Oh. The mystery research club?"

Haruhi shot me an approving grin, like a math teacher to a student who'd just written a particularly elegant proof on the board.

"Yup," she said. "Same place that snuck a tall tale about the anatomical model into the reference data on the seven wonders. T, who exactly thought up that spooky mystery?"

"The club boss, of course," T said, throwing her hands up in surrender. "Haru, they whipped that up on the spot the moment they heard you were interested in the idea of seven wonders."

"And they were the secret director behind the dying message this time, too?"

T put her hands down but didn't deny a thing. She took a sip of Asahina tea.

"All this time, I thought Tsuruya was behind this, and T was her accomplice! But it was the other way around! T was one of the ringleaders. It was the mystery research club that talked Tsuruya into helping their ruse. While pretending it was all her doing!"

"That explains it." Koizumi nodded. "I thought the deductions involved were a little far-fetched. This mystery game is incomplete!"

"Well, if you've figured that out, no use hiding it," T said, setting her mug down for another banzai. "I think there's something you're supposed to doff at times like this, but I'm afraid I don't have one. I'll have to bring a hat with me next time."

She dropped one hand but kept the other raised.

"I do have a few corrections, if I may?"

"Go on, T. Best if we're on the same page."

"First up, Episode One is completely true. The picture I showed you earlier was taken then. Next, Episode Two is *mostly* true. There are a few embellishments mixed in. The festival we went to is actually pretty famous, so if we wrote it as is, it might have given away which country we were in. That's how it ended up being a little on the weird side."

T looked up, meeting Haruhi's gaze.

"And just to be clear, Shouko really exists. So does my brother, and Takenao Nottobe. But as you correctly surmised, no assault took place. The two of them have known each other as long as Tsuruya and I have. The story itself might give you a bad impression of Takenao, but I'd like to make it very clear the real one isn't like that. He doesn't even use his business cards for a dumb joke or do any stand-up comedy routines about his name. Well, maybe if someone notices it and outright asks."

"Okay," said Koizumi. "So the fictional parts of Episode Three are…at least some of the conversation Shouko and Tsuruya have, everything about Takenao's behavior, and everything after Tsuruya hears a scream. Correct?"

"I think that's right," T said. "And before you ask, the planning and development were all done by the president. Tsuruya and myself supplied ideas, but it was the mystery research club that put everything together. The boss personally came up with the outline for Episode Three, and then Tsuruya did a rewrite on it. Tsuruya wrote Episode Two, then the boss did a few edits. And we got permission from Shouko and Takenao to use their names."

Who in the hell was this president? I didn't need any more people bringing complications into my life.

"Well, I enjoyed it," Haruhi said, heedless of my concerns. "But you were aware you were handing us something pretty far from polished? Why have us take a run at something unfinished?"

"This story is an embellished version of actual events. We're thinking about using it as part of an attraction at the next culture festival. Assuming Tsuruya is available to help. The way you solved it and the flaws you pointed out have shown us several ways to improve on it. On behalf of the entire mystery club, I thank you for your assistance."

So we were basically play-testing their mystery room. Crafty.

"It was Tsuruya's suggestion that we try it on you, but this is partly your fault, Kyam."

I had not been expecting this attack.

"Kyam, we based this whole concept on the I-novel you wrote for your club magazine. The president said we were honor bound to let you have the first shot at it."

I just felt used.

"But just between you and me, the two of us were definitely hoping to pull the wool over your eyes."

I could picture the smirks on their faces.

"Haru, lemme ask, what would you say is the biggest problem?"

"That'd be you. In other words, the identity of 'the girl,'" Haruhi said, not hesitating at all. "An attraction that can't be solved unless you're sitting right there fails whether it's finished or not. You've gotta fix that!"

"The actual wording of the challenge provides no way to ascertain 'the girl' in the first two episodes isn't Shouko, but someone else entirely. We spent a lot of time thinking about how to work clues and hints into the text proper. After all, we wanted to hide the fact that she was me as much as possible. Thanks to you, I think we've seen the light at the end of the tunnel."

T flipped the booklet over, writing something in English.

"I imagined Haru, Koizumi, or Nagato would find their way to the answer there. That said, Nagato! Why did you suspect something was up with my hairpin?"

"I was wondering that myself!" Haruhi said, vaulting out of her seat. She headed my way, hand out, palm up. The hairpin had been in my possession since T surrendered it to me, but I handed it off, and Haruhi inspected it carefully. "Where's the mic switch?"

"I flipped it off before handing it to Kyam."

I couldn't even tell there was a switch.

Haruhi held it up to the light.

237

"How'd you figure it out, Yuki? What gave it away?"

".............."

Nagato slowly looked up, spent a moment with her head tilted, seemingly searching for the right words, and then said, "Hunch."

This was clearly a lie, but she was already back to her book.

And for some reason, both Haruhi and T bought it.

"Well done, Nagato! You are a modern *Hitokotonushi*."

T was out here comparing Nagato to the god on Mount Katsuragi, but like, how did she even know about that god? I guess the kanji did mean "master of the monosyllable," so maybe it was just a coincidence?

"If it was a hunch, then say no more," Haruhi said, very on-brand. "By the way, Mikuru, is it actually true Tsuruya's out of school for family business?"

Startled, Asahina looked up from the postcard she was taping to the tea caddy. (It read *Sugar MANDATORY*)

"Oh yes," she said. "She said she'd be out a few days and asked if she could see my notes when she got back."

I doubted even Tsuruya would play hooky for several days to just to pull a fast one on us... Probably.

"Do you know where she is, T?"

"I can confirm it's definitely family business," T said cheerily. Seemingly glad she didn't have to lie anymore. "We actually timed this whole plan around her schedule. The other way around would have been a bit much."

Haruhi humphed at this. "Well, now I'm the one with a hunch," she said.

She grabbed Episode Three and pointed to the first page.

"I bet this is a hint! The first line of the narration!"

Koizumi and I leaned in to see. It said...

Where am I?

"T, call Tsuruya for us."

Wasn't she going somewhere?

"If I'm right, she'll pick up."

T let out what sounded like a sigh but tapped on her phone's screen.

Before the third ring even happened— "Heya! Faster than I thought! You work out a question for me, then?"

Tsuruya's voice sounded a little muffled, like she had to keep her voice down. She was probably riding on or in something.

Haruhi put T's phone to her ear, listened in silence for a moment, then grinned and put the phone back down. Hands on her hips, she said, "Where *are* you, Tsuruya?"

"Ha! Ha-ha. Oh, you're already that far, huh? Did Lie blab?"

Ottilie, Ti, Lie. This girl had a lotta names.

"I did not! Haru guessed."

"Oh! Then say no more."

Koizumi and I glanced at each other. Haruhi and Tsuruya seemed to be communicating, but all I was getting out of it was these two were on the same wavelength.

I opened my mouth to butt my oar in, but before I could…

…there was a noise like someone popping a balloon, the clubroom door slammed open, and a voice like a banshee screamed "Booyah!" in my ears.

"Eep!" Asahina shrieked, lifting a good five centimeters off her seat.

"…………" Even the ever immobile Nagato actually turned and looked.

"Mikuru! I'm back, baby!" the banshee said.

Tsuruya was standing there with a paper bag in each hand.

She'd brought us *soba boro* cookies.

T quickly got Tsuruya caught up to speed.

"I was planning on making you think I was abroad and then popping out to surprise you!" Tsuruya said, settling down on a

guest chair. She popped one of her own cookies into her mouth. "But you worked that part out, too?! Man, you can't fool the SOS Brigade. I give up!"

"Where'd you e-mail from?" Haruhi asked.

"Home. We got back today, and I've just been lying around the house."

Asahina got out the mug with a circled *tsuru* kanji written in permanent marker and handed it to her.

"Couldn't afford to miss any of the wiretap feed," she said, like a hardened criminal. "But I had what you're calling 'episodes' written out in advance, so all I had to do was bang out the bodies of the e-mails."

She flashed a smile my way.

"And just as I was putting my uniform on to head on over here, *someone* decided to blow out my headphones. I mean, maybe I deserved it, but…"

She took a slurp of the properly sugared blend of tea.

"This trip didn't require a passport, which made it perfect for springing the mystery story on all of you. We'd have preferred to give it a few more drafts first, but heyo."

"I know the president looked a bit unhappy," T said, nibbling at one of the *boro*. "Nevertheless, he was rightfully concerned that if we missed this opportunity, we'd never get another. Also, these Japanese cookies are rather delish."

Haruhi took a bite of the *yokan* she'd been ignoring, then reached for the souvenir cookies.

"You and the mystery club tight?" she asked while closely examining Tsuruya.

Tsuruya made a face, not sure how to answer. "Lie told me their plan, and it sounded like a blast and a half, so I hopped on board. And I'd been wanting to try writing up some stories from my life. Which was pretty tough in practice! I compared notes with that president while I was working on 'em, but it still took way longer than I thought."

"As a result, we learned a lot about T's background," Haruhi said, grinning at our classmate. "And the Notobe clan! I haven't met any of them, but I feel like I already know Shouko."

The two non-Brigaders glanced at each other, grinning. Must be an inside thing only people who knew both Shouko and Haruhi would get. Which didn't include me.

Since the initial flurry seemed to have subsided, I had a question.

"Okay, Tsuruya, how long were you on standby outside the door?"

"Wut? I did no such thing."

She was a third-year student. King of the school.

"I was just in the hall on my way here when Haru-nyan called. So I just kept going and slammed my way in!"

But once again, your timing was uncanny. It was like an act of god that Haruhi had called you right at that moment, but... Okay, we'll chalk that one up as a coincidence.

"But how'd you know I was close by?" Tsuruya asked.

"Hunch," Haruhi declared. Her confidence as boundless as it was baseless. Her way of thinking had never once been constrained by the concept of logic.

"Then say no more," Tsuruya said. We kept coming back to that one. "Not surprised it was Nagato who picked up on the mic. Can't fool you!"

The hairpin made its way back to Tsuruya.

How did that flimsy bit of metal manage to pick up all our voices? I really wanted to know how that worked.

Tsuruya closed one eye.

"I could tell you, but you'd have to sign an NDA."

I had made a rule of not signing things I didn't understand. You never could tell what might lead to you finding yourself in the French Foreign Legion.

That got a big laugh from her, and she flicked the hairpin into the air.

"Kyon, even with Yukikko's help, I can't believe you figured this one out. I was sure no one would notice!"

It was kinda obvious. She never wears a doohickey, then today of all days, she wears one, and it isn't even holding her hair back? You gotta wonder what's up. I dunno the names for all the stuff girls put in their hair and can't exactly hold forth on the finer points of fashion. That's the only reason I didn't say anything.

T brushed the cookie crumbs off her skirt.

"I should have started wearing it a few days back to compensate. Only reason I didn't..."

Because that was the intent, right?

T's beatific smile was all the answer I needed.

After that, the conversation circled around Tsuruya.

Where she'd been, what she'd been up to, requests to share more travel stories in person, not as essays. Haruhi, T, Asahina, and Nagato all listening to her, absorbed in their girl talk, and as I watched from the outside, someone came over to me.

Koizumi gave me a meaningful glance, and I caught his drift, swallowed the last of my tea, and stood up.

"Gotta hit the can."

"I'll join you."

In the hall outside the room, he shot me that damn faint smile of his.

"That hairpin," he said. "I feel like I've come face-to-face with a Chekhov's gun."

A what? Was this like Pavlov's dog? No, wait. I might have heard of this one. Tell me more about this gun.

"A playwright from the days of the Russian Empire, Anton Chekhov, once said, 'If in the first act you have hung a pistol on the wall, then in the following one it should be fired.' In other words, an item of significance should not merely be part of the decor; if that item is not part of the story, it should never appear in the first place. An important dramatic principle. Put more simply, *don't use foreshadowing without following up on it*. It's become a core aphorism vis-à-vis plot construction."

A principle that had yet to have the slightest bearing on my life, then.

"In the case of her hairpin, she was wearing an accessory she's never worn before—the sort of minute change in routine that Chekhov euphemistically referred to as a gun. Foreshadowing you only picked up on because you see her every day in class."

It seemed a little too obvious, but they'd clearly wanted it pulling double duty as a bug and a hint. These people were definitely keeping an eye on their consumer-satisfaction index.

"Also," Koizumi continued, "Chekhov might be most famous for his plays and fiction, but among his many works were some orthodox mysteries. A comedic short story called 'The Safety Match,' despite being written over a century ago, reads like a satire of modern mysteries, proving the passage of time has not fundamentally altered our sensibilities, or perhaps that the debates the mystery genre spurs are destined to repeat themselves like the Buddhist cycle of death and—"

Sorry, but I don't have a euglena's flagellum of interest in the finer points of Russian literature, so save this topic for T and Nagato.

By this time, we'd reached the men's room. But I didn't actually have to go or have any real business in this dimly lit corner of the school building, so for lack of anything better to do, I washed my hands and checked myself in the mirror.

Still, this concept where every item had to serve a purpose was like writer's bondage. There had to be some useless things around to add visual interest, surely.

Alarm bells started ringing in the corner of my mind.

A hairpin that looked like a simple piece of metal but was

actually a directional mic. A bit of tech that was hard to believe modern science was capable of making. Show that to anyone not aware of the background, and they'd think you were lying to them. At best, they'd say:

It's like an OOPArt!

Reminded me of the fake-treasure-map mess Haruhi got us mixed up in back in February.

That day, I'd told Tsuruya where to dig, and she'd obtained a device. I'd seen a photo of it.

It was a metal rod about ten centimeters long. An alloy of titanium and cesium, which made no sense for an object supposedly buried there for three hundred years.

...I couldn't escape the feeling that we'd need that artifact eventually.

Was that a harbinger?

"No, can't be," I muttered, talking to myself. I could tell Koizumi was giving me a look. But he soon realized I was still thinking and left me to it.

Tsuruya was a lot, but she wasn't a superpowered wonder girl. Unlike Nagato, Asahina, and Koizumi, there was nothing about her beyond the ken of any mere mortals. The fact that she was still not a permanent member of the club proved it. Even if she had any supernatural powers, Haruhi's unconscious power would long ago have assigned her to the SOS Brigade's roster—or ensured she was a founding member.

The fact that this had not happened proved she was actually normal.

Tsuruya was involved with the club but kept her distance; whether that decision was based on raw instinct or some level of conscious understanding, I couldn't tell, but I liked her where she was.

She was the one upperclassman I could count on in a pinch. Except when it came to alien/future/esper-based sci-fi gadgetry.

Why not? Well, she might be as proactive as Haruhi, and her family might have the structural power of Koizumi's agency, but she wasn't like them—she was a normal person residing in the realm of common sense. Ordinary high schoolers could hardly be expected to deal with Data Overminds, Kuyoh Suoh, or hostile time travelers.

So I couldn't count on her for that kind of stuff.

I'd just have to handle those things myself. The mystery metal rod Tsuruya was holding on to was definitely a thing *I'd* have to deal with in due time.

But that notion was tugging at the back of my mind, like a mild premonition.

I had no such powers, so it was definitely just gut instinct, probably not worth taking seriously, but...

"Then again, you didn't accompany me here to discuss Russian firearms, did you?" I said, drying my hands with my handkerchief.

"When did you realize the truth?" Koizumi asked, doing the same.

What truth?

"I had it pegged at midway through Episode Two."

He put his handkerchief in his pocket.

"You make an excellent Watson," he said. "You ask perfect questions with perfect timing."

Timing was clearly gonna be the word of the day.

"Every question you asked was extremely apt."

I just said what I felt.

"Are you sure you don't have the whole thing solved?"

You think way too highly of me. My hunches aren't as accurate as Haruhi's, and if I had figured everything out, I ain't a good enough actor to pretend I hadn't.

"I'll take your word for it."

That's easier than expected.

"There's a category of orthodox mysteries in which the Watson character reaches the truth before the actual detective."

Orthodox mysteries basically have no rules, huh? I was starting to wonder if this *orthodox* word actually had any meaning at all.

"What about you?" I asked.

I was pretty sure there were no spies within the SOS Brigade. Koizumi was the only one even remotely likely. He'd certainly been known to provide safe events to keep Haruhi from doing anything too crazy—while she was focused on those diversions, there was no chance of her bending reality.

"I mean, you getting deep into that conversation with T is what gave her the excuse to stick around."

His smile never wavered.

"It seemed more like they were hoping I'd provide solutions in a pinch. At the very least, with the dying message—given the right hint, it was highly probable that Nagato or myself would be able to ascertain Takenao Notobe's name."

We started walking back to the room, shoulder to shoulder.

"Anthony Berkeley wrote a novel of that title, you see. In Japanese, it's known as *Fukuyou Kinshi*, but the original English title was *Not to Be Taken*. Which is why it comes up on a web search. That's why I said, 'You'll soon see why.'"

He looked momentarily downcast.

"We were all playing the same game, but I was on easy mode. Or it felt like I was, at any rate."

If Koizumi had been in on it, I'm sure Tsuruya or T would have blabbed that by now, so I'll take his word for it this time.

"But one thing that's been on my mind…"

Go ahead.

"When we finished Episode One, Suzumiya jumped right to a conclusion. I was concerned that her idea would be the truth, or used as a trick in later episodes."

Oh yeah, the thing about the Ep1 narrator not being Tsuruya, and the girl being Tsuruya instead? And then she'd suggested neither one of them was Tsuruya.

"Both ideas proved wrong."

Yeah, it was a random shot in the dark before we had any clues to work with.

"Do you really think that?" Koizumi's eyes were fixed somewhere in the vicinity of my temples. "If it were anyone else, you'd have a point. But this is Suzumiya."

Fair. I guess I at least get why it's bugging you.

"If Haruhi's intuition had turned out to be on the money, that would have been because she warped reality to get the truth she wanted."

"We would also have to consider the possibility that she'd unconsciously given herself precognitive powers."

Those both sounded bad.

"But neither one happened."

Did Haruhi's first impression being wrong mean her powers were fading? Or common sense was winning? Or was this outcome what she'd subconsciously wanted?

"Given Suzumiya's innate extrasensory abilities, the off-the-cuff deductions after reading the first episode could easily have led right to the truth."

We were taking our time walking back.

"She wouldn't even have needed to 'guess.' Her random burst of intuition would have *become* the truth. The answer the mystery club prepared would have been rewritten in that instant, becoming the sole truth, the only truth that had ever been."

We had to wrap this discussion up before we reached the clubroom. I shifted down another gear.

"But as you said, none of that occurred. Her intuition flew far from the mark, and the answer was not adjusted to match."

In which case...hooray, right? Why the long face?

"If this means Suzumiya's reality-altering powers are diminishing, then I agree." He stroked his chin. "But what if that's not the case? What if Suzumiya unconsciously chose to reach the answer without reality alteration?"

Where's the problem with that?

"Even a whim counts as a conscious act. If her unconscious desires overcame her conscious ones, overrode them, and altered the outcome Suzumiya actually desired, that means her unconscious energy is now more powerful than her conscious equivalent."

She's always doing all kinds of crap unconsciously. The closed space being a prime example.

"If her conscious and unconscious minds are opposed, the latter winning out is a big problem. I hope I am unduly concerned, but if this trend continues, her powers—which were never exactly manageable to begin with—will become impossible to control at all."

Unconsciousness beats conscious. So...you mean, she might unleash her ludicrous power, and even she won't be able to stop it?

"In simple terms, yes."

But nobody, ourselves included, could tell if Haruhi had interfered with the outcome of the mystery game.

"True. The late Queen problem only occurs because the detective exists solely within the story itself. They are incapable of perceiving anything outside the bounds of it. Nor should they be. The detective is neither the author nor the reader and thus has no means of knowing anything except what is described within the story itself."

Just like how we couldn't figure out the heliocentric theory while we believed the world was flat? Nah, that's a stretch.

"When a character shares a name with the author—and this is not exclusive to Ellery Queen—the character and author are not the same. After all, you can't have a character who knows everything and controls events like an omnipotent god."

One reason ancient Greek lyric poetry could impress while also being no fun at all.

"However, Suzumiya can do just that. She is capable of interacting with and influencing the reality in which we exist. We—aliens and time travelers and espers—only exist due to the manifestation of her powers. The SOS Brigade members were selected at random and coincidentally included three such supernatural beings. What are the odds?"

If we're ever in trouble, I'll have to make her buy a lottery ticket.

"I believe the odds of her winning will remain within the standard parameters. I think I've said this before, but she's been consistently sensible when it comes to everyday activities like that."

He laughed like this sidebar had been a great joke.

"Imagine Suzumiya as the detective in a whodunit. She is within the story yet has the power to arbitrarily rewrite said story. What happens then? The story progression is determined not by the author or the reader but by the intuition of a character within it."

You might as well get a book where the ending and identity of the culprit changed every time. Sounded like a plus to me. You could enjoy a single book any number of times.

"I would imagine not."

Why are you so sure?

"Because Suzumiya's alteration abilities would affect the world outside the story. Even assuming the culprit was different on the first and second reads, the reader themselves would not notice the difference. If the second truth becomes reality, then their memories of the previous truth would be altered to match. Rereading the book would simply result in you perceiving it to have the same contents it always did."

I'm not big on having my memories messed with.

"The phenomenon alters everything, so it isn't specifically

altering anyone's memories in particular. After all..." Koizumi paused for a beat. "Suzumiya is doing all this unconsciously."

Can't complain when you put it that way. I know as long as it doesn't go out of control, that's far better than her doing anything intentionally. But if Haruhi was what Koizumi said, then it was like having someone in the story who didn't know she was an omnipotent god.

In that light, then yeah, like Koizumi said, it was kinda scary.

"Eh, it'll probably work out okay."

As long as Haruhi was preoccupied with other things, then she wouldn't feel the urge to muck with the world, even unconsciously. Might as well keep the harmless events coming. Like this one or the seven-wonders thing.

The literature-club door was in sight. I could hear four girls chattering away inside.

There was something I should ask.

"What's up with that Tachibana girl?"

Seemed like he saw that coming.

"She and her group are tired of playing at secret societies. Chasing after Sasaki clearly won't get them anywhere. Only potential issue is..."

Kuyoh Suoh?

"Yes. But as far as she's concerned, I must insist on staying out of it. That is for you and Nagato to handle."

And T's just normal.

"I believe so."

Well, good.

As we stepped back in the club, Tsuruya and T were getting to their feet.

Off to report the results to the mystery club's senior crew.

"I offer my deepest gratitude for your help today," T said, bowing low. "I have once again confirmed the pleasure of knowing each of you. You're all every bit as wonderful as Tsuruya made you sound. *Thank you, my friends.*"

She then made a big show of shaking my hand and Koizumi's. We were gonna see each other again in class the next day, but the situation left me with no choice, so I shook her hand back. As she finished up with Koizumi, she said, "We'll have to discuss our favorite Father Brown short stories next." I guess there were priests writing mystery novels now.

Meanwhile, Tsuruya gave me a hearty slap on the back.

"Yo! Today was a blast and a half! I was grinning the whole time! We gotta do this again," she said as she waved at us on her way out.

"Absolutely!" Haruhi said, leaning back in her chair.

"Bye!" Asahina said, clutching her teapot.

I looked around the room, feeling like I was searching for the mistake—and then realized Nagato was out of place.

"........."

Her book was closed. She wasn't reading *anything*. Her short-haired head was staring fixedly at Tsuruya's back. It didn't take long before the two visitors were completely out of sight, but Nagato's gaze betrayed a strength of will far beyond anything I had ever sensed from her before.

Tsuruya and T vanished like the two angels on the Thoth tarot card for The Sun, and the clubroom was once again filled with silence and the sounds of athletes practicing.

Koizumi sat down next to me, diligently bundling the three episodes together and reading them again from the top.

Feeling like our chief was being weirdly quiet, I looked her way, and she seemed sort of out of it, staring at nothing, calmly sipping the dregs of her tea.

It was like a scene from an art movie, a shot of someone savoring the warmth of daily life with an eerie sort of calm.

Placid Haruhi was rather unnerving. Maybe that just meant she had me thoroughly trained.

While I was wrestling with that notion, our eyes met.

She furrowed her brows, and she glared at me a moment, then glanced away, focusing on her computer screen.

Not sure what to do with my hands, I pointlessly stared at the bottom of my mug, and our club maid came over to me.

"Would you like another cup?"

I looked up at her glorious, smiling visage, saw the teapot in her hands, and said I'd be delighted. And while I was at it, I asked another question.

"Asahina, when you were reading Episode Three, you were staring at one spot like you were trying to put a hole in the page. What was bugging you?"

She was a third-year now but still never felt like she was any older than me.

Pouring tea into my mug, she replied, "Oh, that? I, uh, got hung up on the phrase *DNA computing*."

"Can I ask why?"

She just smiled at me. We stared at each other for a while, then I hung my head.

Does that mean it's classified?

I asked that question with a glance, and the eternally in-training maid just broadened her smile, putting a finger to her lips. Then her apron skirts fluttered as she shuffled back toward the kettle, like the human embodiment of a tea-making fairy.

DNA computing. I didn't know how that worked or even have foggiest idea of the basic concept, but did they go inside your body? I remembered something Asahina the Elder had said.

It exists within our minds in an abstract form.

My mind took a leap.

I'd only realized we were being bugged because Nagato moved her chair to look directly at T's face.

What if she wasn't looking at the hairpin but at T herself?

What if there was a listening system embedded inside T's body? If the hairpin was merely a dummy, and the actual bug was inside her...

"No way."

That was clearly too out there. I dunno how futuristic the tech would have to be to make that possible.

Still...

...what about location trackers?

In the answer e-mail for second episode, she'd said, "For all I know, there's one on me right now!" No matter how carefully she washed herself, it stayed put. An unknown GPS tracker invisible to the naked eye.

What if these miniscule micromachines really were implanted inside Tsuruya's and T's bodies?

And Nagato had been staring at T, and Tsuruya in turn, with spooky intensity not just because she'd noticed this but because she was destroying, disabling, or eliminating them? It was eminently possible that a wave of panic was spreading through the Tsuruya and the Whatevergartner staff right about now.

There was only one reason why Nagato would do that; they'd provided her with an entertaining mystery game, and she was simply returning the favor. For as little as she'd participated, she must have enjoyed it in her own way. Or known the answer from the start and elected to remain an observer.

But all this was just in my mind. Pure speculation.

I glanced at Nagato's profile. No expression on her face, attention fully on her own book, not moving a muscle.

But for a fleeting second, I could have sworn the corners of her lips were tracing a gentle upward curve, one so subtle that it was beyond my ability to confirm with my eyes.

I took a sip of tea and savored the sensation of the hot liquid as it cooled off in my mouth. I turned my gaze to the window. The green leaves of the cherry trees were waving in the breeze from the mountains.

Summer was almost here.

AFTERWORD

It's been far too long. I've got to start things off by apologizing for making you endure an agonizing wait between volumes. I'm so sorry. I can't apologize enough. I honestly can't even think of any excuses; this is purely the result of chronic laziness and my stupid, stupid brain. For everyone going "I wasn't exactly *waiting*" but who still picked up this volume, thank you.

This is not the first time I've been at a loss as to how to handle the afterword. I never have much to say about my own work and prefer to spend as much time as possible talking about unrelated things, but it's not like I lead a particularly interesting life and definitely don't have a stock of anecdotes to share with you—in fact, I'm pretty confident I could tell you my life story in less than fifteen minutes.

My stance on afterwords was explained by the Hong Kong mystery novelist Chan Ho-Kei (best known for *The Borrowed*) far better than I could ever manage, so allow me to quote him here. After explaining that he never intended to write one at all, he said:

> I believe that once a work has been "birthed" by its
> writer, the text takes on its own life, and readers are

free to see and receive whatever they want from it, each person embarking on a unique journey. Rather than having the author go on at length about what is or isn't there, why not allow the reader to experience it in person?

But after saying all that, he then proceeds to give a pretty detailed breakdown of his own work and what led to him writing it, likely because the work in question is a clear attempt to capture the tumultuous history of its setting.

Meanwhile, *The Intuition of Haruhi Suzumiya* contains three stories of very different lengths, but absolutely no important societal themes or even any particularly complex portraits of the human experience. "Random Numbers" in particular is something I came up with in the bath, while thinking about how RSA codes work. But coming up with ideas or solutions to the so-called shower thoughts is apparently pretty common, and you see a lot of stories along those lines. There are many theories about why baths stimulate your mind. But I think the key is that beyond early childhood, most of us wash ourselves without the need for conscious participation. Nobody's sitting there thinking, *After I'm done with my left arm, I'll move on to the right, then my back, chest, down to my stomach and my legs, and then I'll have to dump the hot water from the washbowl all over myself.* I imagine most of us do everything from getting undressed to getting out on auto-pilot. As an aside, my body has been programmed to the point where I automatically go straight to the fridge after getting out of the bath. This is also why we occasionally snap out of it and wonder if we've washed our hair yet. But since we aren't consciously controlling our bodies but turning our minds off and letting our bodies fend for themselves, our brains might well mistake this state of affairs for something more alarming. They panic and shoot signals down our neurons, giving our unconscious minds a real workout, and the result is that whatever thoughts were stagnating in our conscious minds get resolved, the answers lobbed in from out of nowhere with a *heads-up!* I think the same phenomenon is why taking a walk—itself an action requiring little to no thought—is said to be equally effective when you've got a lot on the mind. Maybe I should write a paper on it, but if the phenomenon has already been named and analyzed, sorry.

"Seven Wonders Overtime" started with a question from my editor. "Does Haruhi's school have seven wonders?" And that led to "What seven wonders would Haruhi come up with?" and what would the other characters think about that, and when I ran that simulation through my mind, this story popped out. But I wonder how many schools actually have seven wonders? Unrelated, but when you're having trouble sleeping, I recommend generating random characters and running them through slapdash plots, and before you know it, you'll be sound asleep.

"Tsuruya's Challenge" is a bunch of stuff I've always wanted to do all tied up in a single story. Lots of self-quotes and stuff about how Tsuruya talks. I hope all three stories bring a look of joy to your face, whether that be a smile, a smirk, or a grin.

I'd like to express my deepest thanks to everyone involved in producing, distributing, selling, and reading this volume. May we meet again.

A FINAL NOTE

Words fail me when it comes to what happened at Kyoto Animation on July 18, 2019. I feel like I could write forever and it would never be enough, and that this is something beyond the capacity of mere words. So there's not much that I can write here. What I can talk about are the little memories stored in the corners of my mind. So many Kyoto Animation staff members helped animate this series. I can't thank them enough for what they did. I only met a few in person and spoke to even fewer, but there are a number of moments that remain seared into my mind even after all this time.

So the following are my personal recollections.

If I remember right, I first visited Kyoto Animation early in 2005. One of the first people I met was Yoshiji Kigami. He introduced himself by saying, *"Kigami, written as* tree *and* above.*"* Clear, easily remembered—and I've never forgotten it. But I'm afraid I was unaware of who he was at the time. It was much later that I learned he was one of the world's top animators. But even I could tell the rest of the staff had the utmost faith in him.

The character designer and chief animation director for *The Melancholy of Haruhi Suzumiya* anime was Shouko Ikeda, and I remember her being in those meetings very early on. She gave me a warm smile and then asked very pointed questions like, *"How does Haruhi smile?"* Off the cuff, I said, *"Like a half-moon on its side yawning open,"* and then figuring it would communicate the idea better, I drew a few pictures on a piece of paper. If you're curious what that answer led to, check the key visuals Ikeda drew.

Naomi Ishida was the color designer, and I remember her from a visit to the studio with Noizi Ito. The two of them were looking at an image of Haruhi on a monitor, getting really nitty-gritty about the specifics of the coloring. I especially remember when they got to Haruhi's shoes. Ishida had a mouse in one hand and asked Noizi, *"How's this?"* *"A little darker."* *"Like this?"* *"That's it."* To my eyes, the two colors were basically the same, but to the two of them, they were worlds apart. The craftsmanship was astounding.

I first spoke to Futoshi Nishiya (chief animation director of the second season and *The Disappearance of Haruhi Suzumiya*) while visiting a hospital to do location scouting for the movie. At the time, there was concern about a new strain of influenza, so when a bunch of us rolled in wearing masks and carrying cameras, the patients gave us some very strange looks. I was sitting on a bench in a waiting room, and Nishiya came over to me, looking very serious. I wondered if something had happened, but he said, *"I may have made the characters too cute. What do you think?"* I could see it being a problem if they weren't cute, but how could "too cute" ever be an issue? I said I couldn't see the slightest smidgen of an issue, but he was clearly still thinking about it. I couldn't help admiring his perfectionism.

Yasuhiro Takemoto was the director of the second season and *The Disappearance of Haruhi Suzumiya*, but all my memories are from the nigh weekly script meetings we had for the first season. I remember more about the idle chatter than the actual scripts. We talked about all kinds of stuff, from the World Rally

Championship to Wimbledon to old *Famicom* RPGs. I wouldn't necessarily call myself the most social person in the world, so I suspect this was his way of keeping me engaged. In hindsight, I really appreciate that consideration. The last time I met him was several years ago, at a Kadokawa thank-you party, and as we parted ways, we said the lines everyone takes for granted: *"We'll have to go drinking together sometime."* The fact that we'll never make that happen leaves me with nothing but grief.

I wrote this to the best extent of my memory, as accurately as I could, but perhaps some of these memories are faulty. I hope you'll excuse that.

Finally, there are two things I feel should be said.

I won't forget you.

I won't forget what you did.

If you agree with these statements, read the subject as plural. Feel free to rewrite them as you please.

My memories are tiny things. Other people have far more memories than I do. Those memories belong to them.

I intend to treasure the modest memories that remain with me.

Thank you so much.

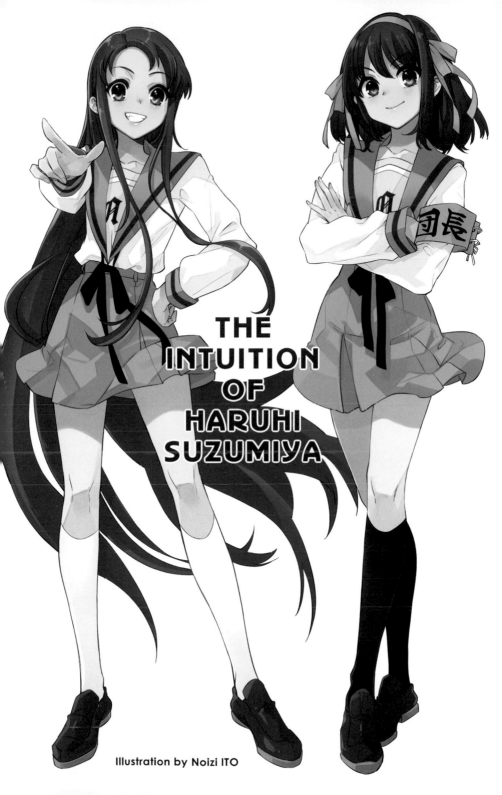

THE
INTUITION
OF
HARUHI
SUZUMIYA

Illustration by Noizi ITO

Date

Of all the things she could have sent us, Tsuruya had gone with a Challenge to the SOS Brigade.

Date　　　　　　　／　　　　　／

skrit

THE
INTUITION
OF
HARUHI
SUZUMIYA

NAGARU
TANIGAWA
&
NOIZI ITO
START!